P9-CBQ-903

Virgin River

Virgin River

A Barnaby Skye Novel

RICHARD S. WHEELER

A TOM DOHERTY ASSOCIATES BOOK
NEW YORK

This is a work of fiction. All of the characters, organizations, and events portrayed in this novel are either products of the author's imagination or are used fictitiously.

VIRGIN RIVER: A BARNABY SKYE NOVEL

Copyright © 2008 by Richard S. Wheeler

A Forge Book
Published by Tom Doherty Associates, LLC
175 Fifth Avenue
New York, NY 10010

www.tor-forge.com

Forge® is a registered trademark of Tom Doherty Associates, LLC.

Library of Congress Cataloging-in-Publication Data

Wheeler, Richard S.
    Virgin River : a Barnaby Skye novel / Richard S. Wheeler.—1st hardcover ed.
        p. cm.
    ISBN-13: 978-0-7653-0709-5
    ISBN-10: 0-7653-0709-X
    1. Skye, Barnaby (Fictitious character)—Fiction.   2. Wagon trains—Fiction.
3. Tuberculosis—Patients—Fiction.   4. Indian women—Fiction.   I. Title.
PS3573.H4345V57 2008
813'.54—dc22

                                                                                    2007041947

First Edition: March 2008

Printed in the United States of America

0 9 8 7 6 5 4 3 2 1

For my gifted friends Michael and Kathleen Gear

Author's Note

This is a work of fiction. But it is drawn from actual circumstances in southern Utah, in 1857.

Virgin River

one

S moke hung in the air, and Barnaby Skye took it for a sign. Somewhere on this day of birth the mountaintops were burning. Freshets of chill air brought the scent to him, though he knew of no fire and the season was very late.

The Shoshone women had driven him off but he didn't mind. The birthing of a child was women's mystery and women's honor. They would not even let Mary endure her travail in Skye's own small lodge. Too small, they said. A woman needed space to bring a child into the world.

Skye's older wife, Victoria, of the Absaroka people, was with them. There was naught a man could do but wait, or walk restlessly, for the women didn't want him close to the place of Mary's ordeal for fear he would cast a dark spell over it.

Mary's labor had started in the night, and before dawn the women had taken Mary away from him and into a lodge prepared by Chief Washakie's women. And after that, no one came to him with news. The men left him alone with the dawn; the women pursued their mysteries.

Mary's people, the eastern Shoshones, were camped this gusty October on the Popo Agie River where it tumbled out of the Wind River Mountains, a place thick with elk and yellow grass and firewood and gossiping winds. It was a good place for a baby to be born.

Barnaby Skye went to greet the dawn, which was coloring the eastern horizon. He climbed a hillock and lifted his arms to the heavens and welcomed the newborn sun. It was something he had learned from the Indians, maybe a little like morning prayers in the Anglican world he had been torn from so long ago when he was a boy in London. Sometimes he thought that religions were not so far apart. Let the theologians worry about it. His own religion had come down to reverence for all the mysteries.

Jawbone, his ugly blue roan colt, found him there, the pair of them temporary outcasts until this birthing time passed. Jawbone lowered his ugly head and pushed it into Skye's belly, and Skye pushed back. It was a morning communion. Skye thought that the pair of them had more bone than brains in their skulls. It was a question which of them had the ugliest snout. Skye's vast and pulpy nose erupted between his eyes, tumbled downslope in a widening hogback, and dominated everything below, while Jawbone's massive jaw dwarfed the head above it, giving him a demented look.

Skye wondered what it would be like to raise this child; it was late in his life to be having children. He didn't wish for a boy-child or a girl, for that was the road to disappointment. Instead, he prayed that he might welcome and nourish whoever and whatever became the flesh of his flesh.

He could barely manage the terror of fatherhood. Was he going to provide a safe haven for the girl, a dowry? Could he offer the boy an inheritance, a schooling, a chance to prosper?

He could give the child none of those things. He was an empty-purse man of the wilderness, living with his two wives' tribes, making a thin and erratic living guiding Yanks in their endless westering. Who was Skye but an outcast, a bit of human flotsam?

He lifted the battered top hat that had been with him most of the years of his exile from England, and settled it over his roughly shorn graying hair. The rest of him was adorned in soft golden leathers, quilled and beaded by his wives, but the top hat was England; the top hat separated him from chiefs and Yanks and Spaniards. The top hat told the world he was Mister Skye, a man who had made the western reaches of North America his home ever since he jumped ship at Fort Vancouver. He had come to cherish his life in the New World, but sometimes the pangs of loss caught him as he remembered his mother and father and sister snug in London's bosom. He wondered if they lived. He wondered if this child being born would ever see those English grandparents or aunt or maybe unknown cousins. He wondered whose nation this child would claim, if any, for Skye was a man without a country.

The strengthening sun caught the snow-tipped peaks south and west of him, each peak blazing as if a silver coin had been embedded at its peak to dazzle the eye. Was there ever a range so noble as the Wind River Mountains? Some infinitude above, the dark-timbered slopes gave way to gray rock and ice fields with mysterious footprints caught in glacial hollows and beaded totems hanging from timberline sentinels. Now the waking sun probed the canyons and valleys, casting vast blue shadows where night still lay. But the day was beginning, the day when Skye's life would grow by one and a newcomer would fill his lodge.

Jawbone whuffed, and Skye turned to see Victoria toil up the path above the Shoshone village. Her people were Crows and she was known to them as Many Quill Woman. He had married her long ago when he was a trapper and given her a name fitting a queen of England. She looked cross, but she often did when she was her gayest.

"Dammit, Skye, what are you doing up here? You have a child."

He caught her hands. "A child? And Mary is all right?"

"A man-child, and she is weary. It went hard, and she is worn."

"A boy! A son! Is she resting?"

Victoria slid arms about him and they embraced. He felt the churn of her feelings, for she had always wanted a child, but no child had ever come to them. Now he felt the joy permeating her; it might be Mary's birth-child, but Victoria would be no less a mother.

"Am I permitted?" he said at last.

"They sent me for you."

"Is there anything, any custom, I should know about?"

"Hell no, Skye. But you could pay the town crier to announce it."

"I will do it!"

They descended into the silent village, where life was stirring and wood smoke layered the air. The generous birthing lodge stood apart, across a small brookside meadow. Victoria led Skye there. He felt increasing alarm but could not fathom why. He discovered beads of moisture on his brow, and couldn't imagine how it had rained on a clear day.

She paused, smiled, and scratched on the lodge door, this ritual politeness an affirmation of the sanctuary within.

"Come," said a voice Skye did not know. There were

grandmothers here, and medicine keepers, and midwives. Skye suspected that most of the women in the Shoshone village had a role in every birthing.

He doffed his hat and entered into the dim light, the only illumination from the smoke hole, and found Mary lying on softest robes, bare-breasted, the little thing at her brown nipple, her thighs covered with a soft blue and white Hudson's Bay blanket.

Skye hadn't the faintest idea what to do. He knelt. Mary gazed up at him, her face worn, the flesh of her eyes dark, her hair damp. Yet she smiled. He turned to the little one, small as a mouse, its flesh copper in the dimness, its sparse hair jet. He could not see the eyes. It was swaddled in a soft doeskin receiving blanket. His little arms lay upon her breast.

"My son," he said. "I have a son." Then, "Are you all right?"

She nodded. He thought she was so weary that even a nod was a reached-for exertion.

He found Mary's hand and pressed it in his own. It was damp and limp. Truly, this woman had suffered and was worn down to nothing. Around the lodge, other women knelt or sat, mute and observant. He feared he was not doing what was required. He feared they disapproved.

"Have you a name for this boy?" he asked Mary.

"Yes," she said. "A name that came to me, a mystery. And have you a name for him?"

"Me? A name?" Skye was momentarily taken aback. Was he to give a name to this infant?

"A name from your people, a name from my people," Mary said.

The infant stirred. He looked like a wrinkled gnome. Skye wondered if this misshapen little thing could be a man. Could ever be anything but some stunted little wretch.

A name! Why hadn't he thought of a name? Never was a male so unready for fatherhood as Barnaby Skye. Junior? God forbid. No, there was a name, his father's name, his father who would never see this grandson, yet whose name the child would bear. Skye's father had been a London import and export merchant, buying tea and silk from the Indies, and his name was Dirk Skye. The child would be Dirk. It was a name little known to the Yanks, a name not even common in London, but Barnaby Skye, son of Dirk, suddenly felt the hunger to honor his father.

"Dirk," he muttered. "Dirk?"

"Dirk? What does it mean?"

"Ah, it's a short sword carried by British naval officers. But that . . . I think there might be other . . ."

"A short sword. That is a good meaning," she whispered. "Dirk, Dirk."

She gazed at the suckling infant, fashioning this odd name and blessing him with it.

"And have you chosen a name?" he asked.

"The name was given to me," she said.

He waited, not inquiring in what manner this name was given. Had some shaman given it? Had someone in her family named this infant?

"My people call the Star That Never Moves the Star of the North. This boy will be the Star of the North in my tongue. North Star. For the North Star is always there and all the people of the earth know where they are because of the star that never moves."

"North Star? His Shoshone name is North Star?"

She nodded and closed her eyes. Plainly, she needed rest. This firstborn had come into the world amid pain.

"Sleep then, Mary. I will go tell the world that we have a

fine son, and this is a moment of joy for all the people, and for you and me and Victoria."

With one last glance at the little suckling thing on his younger wife's bosom, he retreated into the soft autumnal morning and found the village crier.

two

With the arrival of a son everything changed. Something new was burning in Skye's bosom. He wanted to give this boy every chance to make his life whatever he wanted it to be. Skye knew, in his very marrow, that soon the tribes he lived among would be facing a strange new life, probably as farmers or ranchers, and that this flesh of his flesh would need to find a path of his own, a path that might not be the path of his parents.

This son of Barnaby Skye would learn to read and write and do his numbers. This boy would master a vocation. This lad would be schooled in a college. This youth would have every advantage that life had stolen from Skye long before, when a press gang on the cobbled streets of East London had plucked him at age thirteen from his family and stuffed him aboard one of His Majesty's warships where he was a powder monkey and a surgeon's assistant when he wasn't in the ship's brig for insubordination.

This boy would know comforts and a home with a roof. This boy would not be condemned to a desperate life as an exile. This boy . . . this Dirk, this North Star, the Star That Never Moves . . . this firstborn son who arrived so late in Skye's life, would carry Skye's blood and vision into the future.

So this birth clawed at Skye. He needed money. He didn't know how long the roving life of the tribes would last, but he knew that each spring, thousands of wagons rolled west from the frontier settlements, Yankees plunging into the new lands across the continent, heading for gold out in California or rich, moist farmland in Oregon where a man scarcely needed to scratch the soil to bring up a bumper crop of anything a man chose to raise.

They were coming. They would forever alter the life he had known. He wondered how much Mary and Victoria fathomed all that. Victoria, at least, had been East with him once and had seen a world she had scarcely imagined and it had darkened her. She clung fiercely to the old and hallowed ways of her people and studied the Yankees coldly.

He knew the West. He couldn't stop the Yankees but he could be a guide, and maybe keep peace between Indians and whites. He could earn good money, and maybe do some good for his wives' people.

The next May, when the baby was strong and prospering, he took Mary and Victoria and Dirk to Fort Laramie, there to await the great annual migration, and there to offer his services to those Yanks plunging into the unknown West. Mary was reluctant to leave her village close to the mighty Wind River Mountains. Washakie's people had been generous with her, and North Star rode in a handsome cradleboard, quilled with bright images that would bring him luck and fortune. He was a placid boy, and Mary was a strong mother who shouldered the board or held it across her lap as Skye and his wives migrated eastward, their world compressed by snow-topped mountains, while tender shoots of new grass carpeted the valleys.

They traveled alone, a man and two women on horseback, along with three packhorses and an Appaloosa pony that pulled a travois with the lodge cover anchored to it. Skye wasn't really expecting trouble, but he rode with his old Hawken across his lap. Now he had a son to protect as well as his wives.

They tarried now and then, never according to a schedule or white-man's clock, sometimes to permit Mary to clean away the urine-soaked moss in the cradleboard and pack fresh moss around the little boy's bottom. The nights remained chill and sometimes mean, but the land reveled in the warmth of the new summer, and erupted in pasqueflowers and wood lilies and gentian, and evening stars, lady's slipper, columbine, cinquefoil, and pestemon, pink and yellow and white and purple and blue, which embroidered wide slopes and made the whole world a receiving blanket for his boy.

They descended arid stepped canyons until they reached the mighty North Platte, where the well-worn trail would take them straight into Fort Laramie. But no one was traveling it this early, and they let their ponies fatten on the tender spring grasses at every wayside. Even Jawbone, whose energies outran his appetite, steadily put on weight, which only made him all the uglier.

One day they ran into a blue-bloused patrol from the fort, and Skye visited with the commanding lieutenant, a man he knew slightly.

"We're hearing there'll be record numbers passing through," the lieutenant said. "Some have already checked through Fort Kearney."

"That's good news for me. I'm a guide," Skye said.

"You're Skye. Hardly an officer in the corps doesn't know you by reputation. It's that hat, Skye."

"Mister Skye, sir."

"That too. You're the man to get your clients where they're going."

"I've been lucky, sir," Skye said.

"There's trouble brewing this year, Mister Skye. If Mister Buchanan gives the word, the army's marching for Great Salt Lake City. He's fed up with the Saints. They're, what's the word? In breach of law. They're cooking up some insurrection. That's the word coming out of the telegraph wires. A little homegrown rebellion. Polygamy and all that."

"How might that affect me?" Skye asked.

"There'll be a lot of California trains passing through Utah Territory, sir. And there may be trouble. The Saints are not in a peaceful mood."

"I'll watch out for it, then, Lieutenant. But I'd be more concerned about keeping oxen away from loco weed, or making sure water's good."

The cavalryman eyed Skye speculatively. "This year may be different," he said. "It's been my pleasure."

He raised an arm. The troopers spurred their mounts and trotted upriver in the benign spring sun, a platoon of bluebellies who eyed Victoria and Mary with hooded thoughts.

Skye didn't much care for the Yankee cavalry and had an Indian's wariness of them. And yet he lived with them, and they left each other alone. He watched them trot west, the hooves of their well-shod mounts leaving prints in the soft spring soil.

Already some Yank wagon trains were at Fort Kearney. It wouldn't be long, then, unless rain mired them. And there would be ample hire for Skye. The westering Yanks wanted experienced men to lead them. He usually needed only one fee to see him through the year, but this year he wanted two or three hires if he could get them. He had a son to think about. He wanted to put money aside with Colonel Bullock, the sutler at the post, who kept Skye's accounts. This year, Skye intended to work until the snows stopped him. This year he would begin to build whatever was needed to educate his boy. This year . . .

"Why do they all wear the same color?" Victoria asked.

"Why does each tribe have its own way of making moccasins?" Skye replied.

It was the response of a man without a country. He remembered his days and months and years in the Royal Navy, where there was a uniform of sorts, but a seaman could virtually create his own uniform out of what was at hand, including ship's sailcloth. Only the officers were dressed like copycats.

The uniforms made a cohort, a small nation of brothers aboard the warships floating slowly over the lonely seas. But here he was, traversing a two-rut artery across a wild continent, belonging to no cohort other than his own family.

They rode through increasingly rough country as the North Platte sliced through pine-darkened slopes, and finally raised Fort Laramie in the middle of a cloudy spring afternoon. It lay sleepily in a vise of piney hills, not yet disturbed by the deluge of settlers heading west. Smoke drifted from a few chimneys. Outbuildings spread from the original fortified adobe post. Skye and his family paused. This was the only presence of Yank power for hundreds of miles, and manned by only a handful of troops, many of them raw recruits, some of them straight off immigrant ships.

Victoria had never liked being there, and now she gazed stonily, her lips compressed. But Mary, filled with wonder, studied the fort eagerly.

He steered his family toward the sutler's store, operated by his old friend Colonel Bullock. There, Skye outfitted each year, and there, the retired Colonel Bullock, the Virginian who operated the store, acted as Skye's agent, steering travelers who needed guiding or protection to Skye. There, Bullock kept accounts for Skye, advanced him goods when he couldn't afford them, kept Skye afloat in an uncertain and perilous world.

Skye loved the place, not only because of the colonel's warmth and hospitality, but because it contained everything a border man might need. There were unbleached cotton sacks of sugar and flour, cases and crates of hardtack and sweets, well-greased rifles and revolvers, shelves groaning with bullets, lead, molds, powder, caps, flints, knives, blankets, kettles, beads, awls, dyes, molasses, and of course crockery jugs of Kentucky's finest.

Victoria loved the store if not the rest of the post, and would soon be digging through fragrant bolts of calico or gingham or flannel, looking for a few yards of this or that, along with needles and thread, buttons and bows. This year, with Mary along, Skye knew he would be buying whole bolts of cloth—if he could.

He slid off Jawbone at the hitch rail but did not tie him. The horse could not abide being tied to anything and would tear everything apart. The women slipped off their mares and tied them, along with the pack animals. On the sutler's broad veranda were hewn-log chairs, and on these sprawled several strangers, hawkish Yanks with a squint etched permanently in their weathered flesh.

"Good afternoon, gents," Skye said.

They nodded but did not reply. He felt their gaze on him and his wives as he plunged into the cool and shadowed store, with its burlap sacks and crammed shelves and casks and barrels. He made his way to the office cubicle at the rear, lit by a real-glass window, and there found the trim graying Virginian at his ledgers.

"Mistah Skye!" Bullock roared, bounding to his feet.

The handshake was as firm and warm as any on earth.

"Colonel, this is my new wife, Mary, of Chief Washakie's people . . . and here . . ." Skye gently lifted the cradleboard from Mary's shoulders.

"A pleasure, madam. You've made a noble match. And greetings to you, Victoria. Yoah family's expanding by leaps and bounds. My land, Mistah Skye, you've whelped a child!"

"We have a boy. Among Mary's people he is North Star, or the Star That Never Moves. And among the English, he's Dirk."

"Dirk? As in dagger?"

"As in my father's name."

"And what will he be to a displaced Virginian late in federal service, suh?"

"He will be the inspiration that will fatten your accounts, Colonel. For I mean to give him a schooling. And schools cost money, and money is what I will be grubbing from now on."

"A fine fat child," Bullock said. "Those are your eyes, and your unmistakable beak. That beak will stamp any child of yours, Mistah Skye. It's the envy of every man who's ever met you. I don't own the half of that beak. That and your two gorgeous ladies. And those bold cheekbones and the child's warm flesh are those of your lovely lady. And I imagine the hair will be too, dark and silky, unlike your unruly mop!"

Mary smiled shyly.

Skye laughed, a giant ripple of pleasure bellying up from his middle.

"A family, Skye! Now I'll have you in debt the rest of your miserable life! A family costs pounds and shillings, dollars and cents! You'll have to work for a living. Work and grub like a farmer. And how's that offensive colt you've brought along?"

"Jawbone's nigh onto an adult now, and getting more and more ornery. If you'll observe, he's not capable of being tied. He also kicks anyone but us, and will let no other mortal approach him."

"Skye, he's very like you, then. But I imagine Jawbone kicks with greater accuracy."

They laughed.

"So, then. You're looking for business again, when the rush begins, eh?"

"Not just one this time. I'll take employment until the parade quits for the year, Colonel. A newborn son does that."

Bullock sighed. "It won't be so easy anymore, Mistah Skye. This year, you face competition. A lot of competition. This year seems to be different in ways I intend to discuss with you as soon as the opportunity arises."

three

olonel Bullock was a man who measured everything he said, and now he was plainly selecting his
words carefully. Mister Skye knew that the sutler
was also being tactful.

"Some outstanding trailsmen have shown up here, Mistah Skye. They mean to take over the guide business hereabouts. They believe it'll be a lucrative enterprise. I would
expect, sah, that they'll be very competitive." The colonel
dabbed at his gray Vandyke, as if he didn't like to own the
words that had filtered through it.

"Who are they?" Skye asked.

"Their head man is Millard Manville. A most pleasant
gentleman. I always think highly of anyone with freckles.
He's been twice to southern California, and once to Oregon,
and says he made all three trips without significant loss to the
wagon company and complete satisfaction all around. He
was twice a captain clear from Independence, and once was
elected midway along, when one wagon train rejected the
man leading them."

"And the others?"

"They all claim to be experienced men, Mistah Skye. Eight in all, I hear, and they've been over the trails and are ready to take others. One's been twice to Sutter's Fort, once over the Sierras in winter. A miraculous trip, I'm told."

"I see. And why are they here looking for work? Independence is the place where guides hire out."

"I don't rightly know. It's a riddle. Perhaps it's something you can discover. Sometimes calamity afflicts a wagon train, and its members elect someone else . . ."

The colonel was delicately posing something that Skye would look into. Just who were these guides and how successful had they been? The leader of a wagon train not only had to know wagons and teams, the land, the watering holes, the natives, the safe places and dangerous ones; he had to get along with people and help them through trouble. He needed to win the trust of his company. He needed to solve dilemmas and smooth crises. A successful captain was hard to find and his services brought him a fine wage.

"I think we'll manage," Skye said. "For a quarter of a century I've roamed the American West, and that will serve me well, I imagine."

Bullock slowly shook his head. "Normally it would, Mistah Skye."

That set off some alarms in Skye's head. He would introduce himself to these rivals and form his own judgment. The discreet sutler would reveal little more.

"Well, Colonel, let's see about my credit."

"It's credit you're depending on, my friend, for at the moment you are, let's see, a bit in arrears."

That was bad. Much of Skye's next employment would be consumed paying off debt. And that debt would increase this day because he was in need of powder, lead, tea, sugar, needles, thread, an awl, and sundry other items.

"Ladies," said the colonel to Skye's women, "you just select what's needed, and I'll put it on the books."

"I'll clean out your whole damned store," Victoria said.

The sutler laughed. He always enjoyed Victoria's salty language, which she had picked up from the trappers. The women drifted down dusky aisles filled with treasures brought a vast distance by ox power. For Skye's family, the sutler's store was a magical place.

"Now you've got two and a half to support," the colonel said. "Which means your expenses will rise by five." His bright eyes burned cheerfully. It was as close as Colonel Bullock ever got to a joke.

"Colonel, these guides. They're going to be trouble for me?"

"I'd say they'll give you a hard time, sah. But count on me. There's always people rolling through here who want something more than a wagon captain. They want someone who can take 'em where no one's walked before. Someone who's been over the western horizon and come back to tell about it. That's you, sah. I'll send you word of any prospects, but you'd be smart to hang around my front porch when the wagons roll in, because that's where this gaggle of guides is going to be."

"I may have to do it."

"And there's the other thing. You've a name for yourself. Wherever seasoned border men gather, they talk about Mister Skye. When a man's name's spoken with respect, you can count on business. When travelers in St. Louis or Independence or St. Joseph ask for a man to get them through, your name comes up. You're right there, with the Sublettes and Jim Bridger and Broken Hand Fitzpatrick, right there with men whose name is carved on the farthest tree of the farthest wild, sir, and that alone ought to bring you all the business a man could want."

Skye never knew how to handle comments like that, talk about his reputation, as if he had one, as if he were some sort of legend rather than a lost man struggling to stay afloat in a wild land. He lifted his battered silk top hat and smiled and settled it again on those unruly graying locks.

"Never heard of him," Skye said.

"Ah, and Mistah Skye, this year they're not allowing grazing on the military reservation. Grass and hay are short. You'll have to subsist your stock somewhere upstream. Anything downstream will be chewed down to the roots by the wagon trains."

"Up the Platte?"

The colonel paused. "I hear that's where these new fellows are camping. It's on the trail, and that gives 'em a better chance at doing business."

That's where Skye himself had camped in previous seasons.

"The Laramie River, then," he said. "I don't know that I want my wives and my boy camped next to those gents."

"A wise choice, sah."

"How many trains are coming? Any word?"

"More than ever, I hear. This is getting to be a mighty business. Americans are always pulling up their roots and heading west. Next thing you know, the republic will have states on the Atlantic and Pacific, and territories in the middle. That is, if there's not a war between North and South, which is what I think will befall us one of these times." The Virginian stared out the window. "It's not something I look forward to."

Skye left the shopping to his women and drifted to the spacious veranda, where a variety of rough-looking men sat placidly on benches, under a roof, and watched troopers drill on the nearby parade ground.

Skye stood at the door, absorbing these gents. They were tough customers, all right. Some wore Colt Navy revolvers, the current sidearm of choice, at their hips. Most were bearded, and gazed at the world from beneath grimy broad-brimmed slouch hats, well bleached by sun and banded with sweat stain. The odd thought struck him that they didn't look much like captains of wagon trains, though he couldn't say what a captain should look like.

They noticed him now, and some smiled. He sensed no hostility among them, but rather a lively curiosity that matched his own.

"I reckon you're the squaw man we've been hearing about," said one, rising. He was a big fellow with an open, cheerful face, freckles, and good humor exuding from him. He extended a big, freckled paw. "Millard Manville here."

"Barnaby Skye, sir."

"Ah! so it's you. All we hear is Skye, Skye, Skye. You've a reputation that humbles us, Skye."

"Ah, it's Mister Skye, sir. It's a preference of mine."

"Mister Skye, is it? Very well, if you claim Mister, then you're Mister."

"And you, Mister Manville?"

"Mister's the last way to address me. Call me Millard, call me Old Soak, call me Old Goat, call me Sonofabitch. But if you call me Mister, I'll reckon you're jabbering at someone else."

"Well, I'll call people what they prefer."

"By God, Skye, you nail a man down fast. Now, we've

been sitting here admiring that horse. We none of us have ever seen a horse like that."

"That's Jawbone, and he's not known for being handsome."

"Not known for handsome! Mister Skye, that horse is a grand champion of ugly."

"I wouldn't dispute it, Mister Manville."

"Mister is it? We've got to retrain you, that's all there is to it. Now that horse. It stand there untied, and when a body approaches, it clacks its teeth and gets fit to take a piece out of the nearest hide."

"He won't tie, Millard. And you'd be well advised to stand clear, always."

"He kicks, does he?"

"No, sir, he kills."

"Kills! Maybe he's a candidate for a bullet, then. An outlaw like that."

"No, he's been trained to do what I ask of him."

"Dangerous horses should be shot."

"Anyone who harms him will be paid in kind," Skye said so slowly and distinctly that the words carried across that porch.

Manville stared sharply at Skye, but said nothing. The moment's fun had drained away.

"I imagine I'd better see how my women are doing, before they buy out the store," Skye said.

"Now, hold on a moment," Manville said. "I've organized a guide outfit here, and there's no reason for us to compete. You're the man I've heard about for years, the man whose name crosses lips everywhere."

Skye thought he would at least listen.

"I've got eight men now, and more on their way, and

31

before the season's high, we'll have twenty men offering guide services. Good seasoned men. Lots of those wagon people, they figure they can get to Laramie all right, but then it gets tricky. They know it and they want help. So this year, we'll have some help to offer."

"And you want to include me?"

"Why, Skye, you'd be our star attraction. Fifty percent of the proceeds of your guiding, all yours, and we get you the clients."

"That's it? That's the deal?"

"Oh, there'd be a few conditions, sir. You'd have to leave your squaws behind. We don't want the dusky princesses with us, and most white people would take offense, you with a pair of native ladies. Some white women, they'd take alarm. Some white men, well, for the good of your ladies, sir, you'd want them in some safe place where you can squirrel them away until you return."

"Sorry, my wives and I are together, and together we move people through dangerous country. When you hire Mister Skye, you get me, my Crow wife Victoria, and my Shoshone wife Mary, and our new boy. I'm afraid not, Mister Manville."

"I don't suppose it'd help if I asked you to think it over, Mister Skye."

"No, sir. There are some things I take for sacred, and you've touched one."

four

ards of cream and brown calico, scarlet ribbons, mother-of-pearl combs, needles and thread, an awl, two paring knives, a one-gallon copper kettle, a four-point tan and blue blanket, brass tacks, a string of jingle bells, cake sugar, molasses, two balls of lavender soap. The women were aglow. Skye added a red can of Dupont powder and a bar of silvery galena, caps, patches, a ramrod to replace his damaged one, a ball mold, a half pound of coffee beans, Earl Grey tea, a sack of oats, and a gray crockery quart of Tennessee sour mash, hardly enough for a whistle-wetting.

It added a hundred and seven dollars to his debt and barely covered his needs.

"Just sign here, my friend," Bullock said. Skye dipped the nib into the inkwell and scrawled his signature on the ledger page, an acknowledgment of more indentured servitude. He was worried. And yet every spring, about this time, he negotiated with westbound travelers and came out on top. He ought not to worry, but this time he did. There were rivals sitting out there on that veranda.

These treasures he loaded into the panniers on his slack-jawed pack mule under the observant gaze of those gents on the porch. No word was spoken, but he sensed his every act was being studied, and probably found wanting. The Yanks had horse-loading rituals and conventions he barely grasped. They swore by the diamond hitch to load up a pack animal. He preferred the reliable canvas compartments, and now he carefully balanced the load on each animal so the packs would ride easily.

"Mister Skye, I reckon you might be heading up the Laramie crick, but you'll be disappointed," said Manville. "My herders are camped there and subsisting thirty-some mules over several square miles. Not much feed, I'm afraid. We have mules, a team of ox, and horses all feeding west of Fort Laramie. And we have a dozen more men coming, all with their own stock."

"And you're on the Platte also?"

"I'm afraid we are, sir. Truth to tell, we've spread over every inch of pasture anywhere close to the post. In fact, I have a crew upriver cutting whatever native hay they can manage. They wouldn't take kindly to a latecomer trying to horn in. I'm afraid it wouldn't be pleasant for you."

Skye absorbed that bleakly.

Manville was smiling. When did this cheerful man not smile? At a funeral? No, Skye thought, Manville would smile at his own mother's funeral.

"I'd like you to meet my wives, Millard. This is Mary, and the child in the cradleboard is my son, North Star. And this is Victoria, my mate of many years."

The smiling Manville offered a freckled hand to each. "Lovely, lovely, dusky princesses," he murmured.

"Well, sonofabitch," said Victoria.

"Ah! You have a choice assortment, Mister Skye!"

Mary smiled, these niceties sailing past her.

"I should like to meet these gentlemen," Skye said, nodding toward the sprawled Yanks lounging on benches.

"Why, it would be my privilege."

Manville circled widely around Jawbone, who clacked his yellow teeth, and Skye followed.

They were all assessing him. And they all looked hard and fit and able. Skye met, in turn, Willard Maple, Joshua Barns, Jimbo Trimble, a man known simply as The Cork, who looked a little like he'd thrown the cork away, and another wiry fellow, younger than the others, who announced himself as Jed, no last name.

"We've more floating around, Mister Skye, all veterans of the trails," Manville said.

Oddly, Skye had heard of The Cork. A year or two earlier the man had driven off, with gunfire, a group of Omaha Indians seeking a toll for crossing their lands, wounding two and stirring up some trouble that required army intervention and a goodwill payment to the Omahas. The others were unknown to him. They were neither friendly nor unpleasant, and their gazes settled on his wives in ways Skye didn't like. No one ventured any conversation; nods sufficed. This outfit was keeping to itself.

"Pleased to meet you, gents. Maybe we'll cross paths on the trail," Skye said, trusting in civility.

They nodded.

Skye knew something intuitively. His intuition about men like these rarely failed him. The reason they were here, and not in Independence, was that they had sour reputations as wagon train captains. Reputations floated around Independence like commodities. Captains of good reputation won a good wage. Most of these gents, Skye suspected, had been voted out of office en route for various weaknesses, ranging from recklessness, to lax discipline, to excessive discipline, to endangering the party, to malice. Some were drunks. Others got into trouble with irate husbands or fathers.

Once in a while a good man got busted by bad or slack people in a wagon train; more often there was plenty of reason to pitch out someone while en route, and elect a substitute. Here, far from the rumor mills of Independence, they had a good chance of employment. Back there, their reputations would defeat them. Manville had simply rounded up the rejects and brought them here, his guide-shop opening for business just ahead of the rush. Skye took one last look. He swiftly absorbed whatever there was to know, and for a man as aware as Skye, there was plenty to know in the cut of a man's clothes, the condition of his hands, the armaments at his waist, and the look in his eye. Most would make decent enough wagon captains. A few might well be serious troublemakers. One, Trimble, was probably trouble waiting to happen.

"Well, good day, gents. I believe I'll have word with Colonel Bullock," he said. He left his women to look after his animals and slipped into the shadowed interior of the post store. He wanted to learn a few things more.

"I suspected you might want an additional word with me, Mistah Skye, now that you've looked over the litter," the colonel said.

"It appears they've locked up every possible campsite near the post," Skye said. "And feed is short."

"They have. Transients are allowed one night here. You may as well pitch your lodge and let me look into it."

"I thought of heading downriver."

"That would get you nowhere. The post is subsisting its

36

stock downriver at the moment, in essence snatching the grass before the wagon trains roll in. But let me talk to Colonel Brewerton. I have in mind, Mister Skye, a few army maneuvers."

"Such as?"

"Hiring on, sir. Stable man, laundress, cook, you name it. It'll depend on the post budget."

"Shall I wait?"

"Come with me."

They were swiftly ushered into the commanding officer's offices, where Skye found himself shaking hands with a natty, dark-haired colonel with great bags under his eyes and a waxed mustache.

"I'll get right to the chase, Colonel," said the post sutler. "Forgive me for consuming your valued time. Our old and esteemed friend, Mistah Skye, is a bit inconvenienced this year by those locusts and lizards swarming all over my porch. They've pretty well commandeered the river bottoms and every blade of grass westward, and mean to keep others off it. It occurred to me, Colonel, that the post might have a few coins in its cash box for, oh, a stable man, or a laundress or two, or a cook, or, let me see, a bar man in the officers club room, or maybe even a haycutter, or maybe a translator or vocalist or mandolin player or master of the harmonica. Employment that would let this great scout and guide erect his lodge and see his five horses subsisted until he finds employment with the migrants."

"Mandolin? Harmonica?" Skye started to object, but Bullock's bland smile silenced him.

Brewerton shook his head. "The army, Colonel, is on low rations, and there's not a cent in the budget for any of it."

"Ah, a pity. I don't suppose the officers want a mixologist

for the club house, a man with dandy stories to tell, stories of war and peace, wild men and civilized, volcanoes and glaciers and Hottentots and two-headed wolves. He can pour a little amber liquid as well as the next fellow, and only sample every other drink. It would all come out of the officers' own little pot of gold, of course."

Brewerton sighed, stared out a real glass window at a company of troops doing a carbine drill on the parade, and then turned toward the sutler.

"It's the horses," he said. "I can't give a mouthful of army feed to Mister Skye's horses. And from what I've heard of Jawbone, I'm not sure he should be on the grounds."

Skye's hopes sank.

"But let me think on it, Colonel."

The sutler saluted out of ancient habit, and he and Skye retreated.

"Camp downriver, Mistah Skye, and come back tomorrow. I'll wager that Brewerton, a legend in the army for squeezing the regulations until they bend, might conjure up something. And besides, he owes me a few favors."

This season would surely be different, Skye thought. But with a client or two, he'd be far and away.

He collected Jawbone and the ladies untied the lead lines of the rest of the ponies, and he led them downriver.

"Where the hell are we going?" Victoria asked.

"We're pretty much shut out of our usual camp this year. So we'll head this way for the time being."

"It'll be eaten down to nothing when the wagons come."

"Yes, but the colonel's working on it."

Mary looked worried. "I did not like those men," she said.

"It's almost impossible to like a Yank," Skye replied. "But now and then there's a civilized one."

"My people think they are savages, Mister Skye," Mary said.

Victoria cackled.

They drifted downriver, past the ferry across the North Platte, past the ruins of an old trading post, along worn paths that had seen a heavy traffic and would see more in a few days. At least there was tender green grass for the moment.

He paused in a valley where ridges offered jack pine firewood and protection from the wind. And there would be grass enough for the nags.

"Let's put up the lodge, ladies, picket the horses, and celebrate."

"Celebrate?"

"If you don't want any, I'll finish it off myself."

"You damn well better share," she said. "I've been waiting a whole year."

They laughed, and their joy was caught up on the spring breezes.

five

$\mathcal{E}$ verything would be just fine.

"Mistah Skye," said Bullock the next morning. "Our friend Brewerton has worked his usual wonders. You're on as a stableman and your ladies are on as laundresses. The only thing is, no cash wage. They'll subsist your horses and feed you. Set up your lodge near the stables, my friend, and make a show of shoveling manure, and see to corralling some wagon trade for yourself."

"That's bloody kind of the colonel," Skye said.

"Don't thank him; he'd rather not have you hovering about headquarters. He says he's honored to do a favor for a man like you, and perhaps he'll call on you when the need arises."

"Well, then, send him my regards."

Skye lifted his venerable top hat and settled it again. Out of sheer age it fit his head perfectly. The ladies were again wandering through the store, conjuring ways to empty Bullock's shelves.

The usual loungers were out on the veranda, enjoying the fine spring day.

He found Victoria examining fowling pieces, lifting one and another up and dry-firing them.

"We're on," he said. "The post commander's anointed me a stable man, which means I get to fork a lot of manure, and you're laundresses, rub-a-dub-dub. We and our mounts will be subsisted."

"Talk English, dammit."

"They'll feed us. We can camp on the post. Maybe I'll pitch some hay or scrape up some horse apples now and then. Maybe you'll scrub a blue shirt or two. Meanwhile, we're right here, and we can look for clients."

"Me scrub a shirt? Blue-bellies are dirty and they smell."

"Then you can improve their grooming."

She squinted. "There's nothing any woman can do to improve savages," she said, her brown eyes bright with wicked joy. "All right, I'll wash shirts, then, but not long johns. I don't do long johns."

Skye laughed. "I'll shovel whatever I have to shovel," he said.

Out at the hitch rail, their rivals had gathered around Skye's menagerie, and in particular Jawbone.

"Skye, old boy, if that's a horse, then I'm a kangaroo," said the one called Jimbo.

Skye detected the edge. This was not just joshing, which was fine with him. They were itching for an incident.

"He's my medicine horse," Skye said.

"Medicine, ho, ho," Jimbo retorted.

Skye plucked up Jawbone's single braided rein, which was connected to a woven hackamore, and led his party into the yard, the packhorses and the travois pony carrying the small lodge ambling along past scruffy barracks, headquarters, a guardroom, a mess hall and kitchen, latrines, a warehouse, and out to a stable area. Skye selected a slight rise that would drain away rain, and nodded. In very little time their lodge rose almost in the shadow of the post, and the women settled in. Mary beamed, released the infant from the cradleboard, and let him lie on a soft robe within the lodge.

Skye led the unburdened horses to the stable sergeant.

"Expecting you," the sergeant said. "The colonel said to leave that one alone, but stable the rest."

"That's Jawbone, and yes, he's dangerous. He's also the best friend a man could want out in country where a man needs a friend."

"Wish I had a few nags like that," the sergeant said. "We'll feed 'em up, Mister Skye, and welcome to the post."

"My ladies will wash a shirt or some britches, but no union suits," Skye said. "It's part of the deal."

"Smart women," the sergeant replied. "I might give my duds a rinse."

This was a fine spring day, with playful zephyrs, moist and redolent of upland snow, sliding across the parade ground, tickling the grass, and delighting all living things. Any day now the first of the migrants would arrive, probably sorry they started west so early and got themselves mired in mud.

They just wouldn't learn. The early migrants exhausted their stock trying to drag wagons through gum and clay, but at least their oxen got all the grass they could eat. The first ones were the foolhardy ones, and Skye hoped they would not end up as his clients.

That lasted about an hour. Skye spotted Millard Manville, flanked by his flunkies, striding toward the lodge at the stables. There was still a smile pasted on the man's handsome freckled face, but it probably would vanish at the first opportunity

"Skye, why are you here?"

Skye chose his words carefully. "Employment, sir."

"Employment! You aren't even a citizen. What sort of employment?"

"Perhaps you'd like to talk to the stable sergeant, Mister Manville."

"Employment! A Brit who's a deserter from the Royal Navy and a pair of red sluts!"

"You will want to apologize to my wives, sir."

"Apologize? What for?"

"You will apologize to my wives at once."

The blow caught Skye entirely off guard. The fist to his gut rocked him, stole air from him, and toppled him, sending his hat flying in the breeze. He hit the ground hard.

Skye couldn't breathe. He sucked air but his lungs wouldn't work. Above him, Manville laughed. Skye saw Victoria dodge into their lodge and emerge with her bow strung and an arrow nocked.

"So much for English pansies," the handsome Yank said, enjoying himself. "I'll have a word with Brewerton. What was he thinking, hiring a British deserter and a pair of savage sluts?"

Skye finally recovered his breath, stood slowly, and studied this group: Manville, their leader, and five of his "guides," who seemed more and more like simple toughs, a species of highwaymen planning to exploit the traffic flowing through Fort Laramie some day soon, charge them a fat guiding fee or else . . .

Jimbo nodded toward Victoria. Manville turned, finding the arrow aimed at his chest.

"Put it down, little lady."

"Get out or you die," she said.

"Put it down!"

"Try me."

She stood her ground. Two of the guides started after her.

"One more step and you die," she said. The arrow never wavered.

Manville snapped an order. His men halted. "We'll talk to Brewerton. We'll talk to the whole damned United States Army. You'd better pack up your tent, Skye. You're on your way out, as fast as you can run. Get off this United States post. Let me tell you something: you hang around here, that outlaw horse dies. You keep on hanging around here, you'll hang from the nearest tree, and that brat will have his brains bashed out. And as for the squaws . . ."

Skye saw how this would play out. The Yanks hung together. He smiled suddenly. "It's Mister Skye, sir."

He clamped his top hat on his head and watched the Yanks troop toward the post headquarters. His gut hurt and he wondered how long it would be until he would be breathing without pain. Defeated this time. He hadn't seen it coming. That was something to remember. That's how he was: he needed only one lesson to learn what needed learning.

The women didn't wait. They dropped the lodge and loaded it. Skye collected his ponies and headed for the sutler's store.

He found Bullock shelving a new load of gingham.

"It appears, sir, that I will be moving on."

Bullock listened, squinting and angry.

"Not much a sutler can do, sah, but I have my ways. Let me know where you'll be. I'll fetch a client to you; count on it. There's no point in you hanging around here, getting Jawbone executed and maybe you and your ladies as well. You're not a citizen. The army won't help you, no sah, not at all."

"That hollow, two miles north of here," Skye said.

"A good choice. When I've found a client, I'll send word."

The hollow was a hidden valley in the black hills, usually watered with a seep during the spring but dry most of the year. It would do for a place to stay out of sight of the Yank cartel. If Manville's men knew Skye was still around they would come hunting. Skye knew he could count on it.

He didn't like it, but neither did it bother him. He had survived a quarter of a century in utter wilderness by staying out of harm's way. It was a law of the wild: one didn't confront a hostile war party. One didn't confront a giant grizzly. In the face of overwhelming force, you dodged, you hid, you survived to live another day. It did not offend his manhood to make himself invisible now. He didn't need to be brave, and he didn't need to have others think of him as a brave man. He knew who he was, and what he could do if he had to.

He hadn't waited for Brewerton to retract the invitation. Even if the commandant had thrown all the resources of the post into protecting Skye, it wouldn't have lessened the danger to Jawbone and Skye's family. Skye mused on how an infant son changed things. Now he had an heir to protect and nurture, along with two wives.

He took his family away from Fort Laramie while Manville smiled at them. The Platte was swollen with spring runoff and flooding the marshy areas along its banks. They took the post ferry to the north bank and rode into the hills, in deep quiet. Soon they were following a game trail through jack pine forest. In half an hour or so they would top a ridge and drop into a grassy valley, and there make camp. It was only a short ride from Fort Laramie and the hubbub that would soon engulf the post. They would be close, but invisible.

"How are we gonna pay Bullock if we've got no one to guide?" Victoria asked, out of the blue.

"We'll get someone. Bullock will send word."

"A squaw man and two Indian women," Victoria said tartly.

"That's the way they think," Skye said.

"Maybe we should start on some buffalo robes," she said.

Scraping and tanning buffalo robes to trade was the only other option. But it would take over a hundred hides to pay their debt. It really was no option at all.

six

Now would come the difficult part, but Hiram Peacock was not born to avoid trouble. He had written of his plans to the commanding officer at Fort Laramie many months ago and had gotten no response. But he hadn't really expected any. The mails were uncertain, especially when sent to the ends of the earth.

The hubbub at Fort Laramie was exactly what he had been told to expect this time of year, when scores of wagons, each bearing a family or more, were rolling west. All this had been vividly described to him by Nathaniel Wyeth, a New Englander like himself, who had walked these very paths and knew everything there was to know about traversing the unexplored and unknown continent.

Peacock needed to find that odd duck, Mister Skye, and find him fast before his services were contracted by someone else. No one but Skye could fill the bill, or so he had heard not only from Wyeth back there in Massachusetts, but also from various contacts in Independence. Skye it had to be, though if Skye was not available, one of the veteran fur-trade men—a

Sublette, or Fitzpatrick, or maybe Bridger—might suffice. Peacock had perishable cargo and could not afford delay, nor could he afford any mismanagement.

Of course they had warned him not to judge Skye at face value. Peacock would, they said, meet a barrel-shaped man with a huge nose and squinty blue eyes, wearing a battered silk top hat and trail-stained buckskins. The top hat would be ventilated by two or three bullet holes. Skye would have a profane Crow Indian wife and a truly monstrous gray horse. There would still be some London in his voice. But he was the best man, the man who had survived for decades in a land where men perished daily. He had always delivered, getting his clients wherever they were going.

Peacock's wagons were parked as close as he could get to the post sutler's store, where, he was informed, all transactions of this sort would be sealed. In his party were ten persons in addition to himself and his hired man, mostly youths, every one of them gravely ill. They had consumption, that terrible lung disease that slowly strangled them and put them in their graves. He himself was healthy enough for the moment, but only for the moment. His wife, Emma, had perished of that very ailment, and now was gone forever from his benign gaze. "I'm gone now, Mister Peacock," she had whispered hoarsely a year earlier, and breathed her last.

He had with him one healthy man, Enoch Bright, a cartwright and wheelwright, whose mechanical genius could see his party through. Bright was one of those sturdy New England men who had mastered a trade and was rock solid in it, and then added two or three more trades for good measure. He had only one peculiarity, and that was his habit of wearing heavy woolen clothing, layers thick, because he always was cold, even on a hot summer's day. On this warm

May day, the man was buttoned tight in his union suit. The man would wear wool on Tahiti, if he could.

Peacock worked his way past gaunt ox teams, heavy wagons with grimy canvas over bows, squalling children, racing mutts, anxious women in blue bonnets and muslin aprons who were amazed that they had walked seven hundred miles from civilization and were still alive; and hollow-cheeked males, most of whom, Peacock knew, were shocked by the tariffs placed on any goods for sale here. Peacock had been forewarned. The price of everything would be treble or quadruple what it would bring in the States. They all had come seven hundred miles by ox team.

There were squinty loungers crowding the veranda, and he thought to begin with them. He approached an affable freckled fellow who looked a bit less forbidding than the others.

"I say, sir. Hiram Peacock here. I'm looking for a certain fellow named Skye, Barnaby Skye. I wonder if you might have word of him."

The gent smiled. "Millard Manville, my friend." He extended a freckled hand and caught Peacock's in a firm and pleasant grip, a sure sign of good character. Never trust a man with a clammy hand or, even worse, a limp one. Peacock could spot a bad apple anywhere. Years in the anthracite and whale oil business had taught him all he needed to know of human nature. This fellow Manville was most promising and his gaze was direct and his demeanor manly.

"And what would you want Skye for?" Manville asked.

"To guide me, sir. I have a need for the very best, a man so reliable and wise to the ways of nature that there will be no failure to get me where I'm going."

Manville sighed, frowned, and looked a little embarrassed. "Well, Peacock, it's not quite like that. I know who he is. Skye hasn't been at this post for some while, just disappeared. And not by getting a client, either . . ." Manville eyed Peacock, and lowered his voice so the rest was confidential between them. "I'm not sure you would want a drinking man like that. Not if you want someone truly reliable and sound."

That didn't sound good. "Well, how might I find him. I'm a good judge of character and I'll make that decision after I interview him."

Manville shrugged. "Beats me," he said. "The bozo hung around here and got into trouble, got booted off the military reservation. That's the last anyone's seen of him."

"What sort of trouble?"

"Oh, I'm not sure. Maybe the bottle again. Maybe he ran up too much debt. Maybe those filthy squaws. He's got two dusky concubines, you know. I hear he lives off them."

"One wife is what I heard. Well, more power to him."

Manville smiled. "That sentiment isn't the usual, sir. Most white people are offended by such things, two women in one small lodge. What's the world coming to?"

"I'll make that decision after I find him. He must be somewhere, unless he was hired."

"If he was hired, I'd hear about it, my friend. I'm going to do you a big favor and warn you away from Skye. He's a bad apple. He's a deserter from the Royal Navy, not even an American. What you want, sir, is a reliable United States citizen, not some low-life border man without a country. He's a drunk, a womanizer, and closely allied to Injuns, not white people. I hear he left London under a cloud."

Peacock nodded.

"What you want is a fine, reliable Missouri man. Now, it just happens that I run a guide service. I have several veteran wagon captains in my employ, and as fine a group of seasoned knights of the trail as you'll ever come across. What might you be interested in doing? We can set a fair tariff, and you can take your pick of some of the finest guides and captains in the entire world."

Peacock dodged all that. "Where might I get more information about Skye? They tell me in Independence that Skye's the only one. I had a long visit with Wyeth, and he told me to get Skye."

"I don't know the name, Peacock."

"If you don't know who Wyeth is, then you don't know much about this western country, sir."

Manville looked faintly annoyed. "I have been twice to California, once to Oregon, captaining three large trains, and I never heard of Wyeth. I never heard of Skye, either, until I got here. Now tell me, where is it you're going. I'm sure to have a man who's been there."

"That's what I want to see Skye about. I'm not sure just where I'm going. It's a matter of climate. I'm a believer in the vision of Ezekiel Throckmorton, whose pamphlet, 'A Salubrious Climate,' is my guide. He, sir, is the rising light at the Worchester College of Hermeneutics. I have in my company, sir, ten consumptives, mostly young. Sad to say, we lost two en route here. Throckmorton recommends a cure based on a desert climate, very dry, neither too hot nor too cold, the air benign, the winters mild. He cites scores of cases in which consumption has been cured with ample bed rest in a salubrious climate."

"Let me get this straight. You're taking consumptive children to a desert place?"

"Exactly. A desert place, but not a hot desert that might blister the life out of these fragile people. Two of them are my own children. I lost one en route. Proximity does it, you know. Let one person in a household become consumptive and the rest will follow. My poor Emma contracted the disease, coughed up her lungs until she bloodied every rag in her drawer, and soon left us, but not before infecting her children. I don't know why I was spared, but I have been. At least for the moment. That may change. I resolved, sir, to do something about it if it was humanly possible. Bringing these people to a land of hope proved to be exacting but not impossible. Most consumptives can walk, you know. It's only in the final stages that they sink. We've walked our way this far."

"You've got a gaggle of sick people in those wagons?"

"I do. It's the most hopeful and rewarding enterprise of my life. With a little help from Providence, sir, we may spare these young lives. There are examples everywhere. Throckmorton researched it, supplied the proofs, and advised what to do. I put great stock in his counsel, and so do several physicians I consulted before we left New Bedford. Would you care to see the text? I have a copy."

"I suspect, my friend, that any guides I might recommend would charge a high fee for so risky a trip."

"Well, that's why I need Skye. He charges very reasonably, I'm told, and we have but little. I've sunk every cent I could spare in this."

Manville ran his freckled paw through his brown locks and smiled. "Well, now, I reckon we're not the ones for you, though I hate to pass by a good price. These men, they're inclined to move too fast for your party. I tell you what. You just head in there and corral the post sutler, Colonel Bullock. He's likely to know where Skye skedaddled to; I sure don't."

Manville cast a worried glance at Peacock's equipage, which consisted of an enameled green wagon drawn by a pair of handsome horses, and a heavy wagon with canvas over bows drawn by an ox-team. The light wagon had a gilded leg-end painted on its box: New Bedford Infirmary Company.

"Good luck to yuh," Manville said. "Seems like I'll end up this day with more offers than I have guides. Never did see such a bunch arrive here in one day. We have our pick, you know."

Peacock watched the man hasten away. He wasn't surprised. Manville smiled too much. Whenever he told anyone he had a group of lungers, they swiftly put distance between themselves and his party. He and Enoch Bright had brought them across seven hundred miles of prairie; no wagon company wanted anything to do with sick people, especially consumptives, so they had traveled by themselves. But he had expected that too. Getting to Fort Laramie was not difficult; that was the known world, and he had mastered all he could of it for months beforehand. The sickest lay in the green wagon. The healthiest walked. The ones in between walked when they could and rode the tailgates when they were weary. There had been sickness all the way: bloody spittle, coughing, chest pain, furious fevers that came and went, night sweats, and some of them hardly ate a bite.

Twice they had paused beside the trail as it wound through prairie beside the Platte River. Enoch Bright had dug a shallow grave, and they had lowered one of their company into the hard and unforgiving clay. One was Doretta Milbank, a sweet girl of sixteen, on the brink of womanhood until she coughed her lungs out, fevered and died in central Nebraska. The other was his own second son, Raphael, twelve years of age. Each day he sickened. Then he stopped eating, gasped for breath as he lay in the green wagon, and one evening he just slid away, his eyes open, staring at his pa. Peacock could not think of it without coming to tears.

He headed into the sutler's store, his heart heavy. Maybe this had been utter madness. Maybe he should have let them all die in the cold damp salt air of New England. Maybe he shouldn't have bet on something he knew so little about.

He pushed such doubts from his mind and hiked through ransacked shelves and casks and bags. Already the migrating crowds had gutted this store's merchandise. Its proprietor, in shirt sleeves, with a black sleeve garter, sat at his desk, looking haggard. This was the Colonel Bullock that Wyeth and others told him to look up. Maybe he would have word of Skye. If Skye was not the scoundrel they were saying he was. Men changed, and maybe Skye had too. But Bullock would know.

seven

The sutler rose at once, and Peacock beheld a graying man with a Vandyke; erect and civil.

"Colonel Bullock?"

"At your service."

"I'm Hiram Peacock, and I'm trying to locate a certain Barnaby Skye. I gather you might know of his whereabouts."

"I might. Why do you seek him?"

"To guide me, sir. He comes highly recommended. In fact, from what I was told, there's no man in all the West who can match him."

"Sit down, sah, and let us talk. A bit of brandy?"

"No, not just now, thank you. You see, I'm taking a group of consumptives to the desert, two of them my own dear children. Every minute counts."

"Consumptives, you say? Lungers?"

"Exactly. I've a rolling infirmary out there. I have it on the best advice that desert air is the only known cure, and desert air is what these poor wretches will have if it is within my power."

"Tell me about this, Mister Peacock."

The Massachusetts merchant did, in great detail.

"And what happens when you reach this remote desert place? You must still subsist yourself and your patients."

"I've laid plans, sir. We shall have an irrigated farm. I have enough to get started. I have a letter of credit as well, which ought to guarantee some supplies for a few months."

"You will put the consumptives to work? Instead of bedrest?"

"No, my hired man, Enoch Bright, and I will do what we can, and I may be able to hire more help."

"All in a remote desert place? I'd advise you, sah, to establish this infirmary close to a city."

"And be driven away? Let me tell you, Colonel, how the thought of a colony of consumptives excites dark passions in the breasts of others. It must be remote. There is no choice in the matter."

"You yourself are not sick?"

"I wish I could tell you I don't have it. But I suspect it may take root in me."

Bullock sat, silently, until Peacock wondered if he had drifted away. But then the sutler reached some sort of conclusion. "I'm not sure, Mister Peacock, that Barnaby Skye is your man. His wives are Indians, and Indians are unusually vulnerable to white men's diseases."

"I'm aware of it. Quarantine is the expedient. They need only to guide us, ensure our passage. They need not even be close at hand. They could stay far ahead of us if necessary. Sir, if I may, I would like to interview this man and let him decide. And for that matter, I'll wish to examine him and draw my own conclusions. The local comment about this man was not as favorable."

Bullock grunted. "Rivals. All right, saddle up."

"Right now?"

"I have a competent clerk. Let's be off."

Swiftly, Peacock unhitched one of the Morgans from his light wagon, saddled it, told his company he would be gone awhile, and met the colonel in front of the store, under the hooded gaze of a dozen curious men.

"I am a great admirer of Justin Morgan's horse," Bullock said, surveying the fine chestnut that carried Peacock.

"This one has drawn our light wagon seven hundred miles and doesn't even show it," Peacock said.

They rode straight through the post, across the weedy parade, past adobe warehouses and plank barracks, until they reached the North Platte, which was roiling its angry way east, charged with spring runoff.

"We will have to ford," the colonel said, heading upstream. A mile later they hit a broad gravelly stretch where the water rippled over rock, and the colonel turned his horse into the water.

"A little dip at the far side will wet your boots, Mister Peacock."

The dip never reached the Morgan's belly, and then they were urging their mounts up a steep, obscure trail that led into pine-carpeted hills. A great silence wrapped them. It struck Peacock that this trail was so furtive that it was no trail at all, and he wondered where he was being led and why Skye's camp would be this way. But at last they topped a forested ridge and descended into a grassy valley, not more than two or three miles from Fort Laramie. And there, in that peaceful flat, was a tan lodge with a smoke-blackened top, some grazing horses, and some savages.

The visitors attracted attention, and a burly man with a

battered top hat awaited them, a rifle loosely held in hand. Beyond, around a small fire, were two slender Indian women, one with gray in her jet hair, the other much younger. She was holding an infant.

Peacock knew somehow that he was being intensively surveyed, and didn't mind it.

"Gentlemen," said Skye, "it's our pleasure."

"Mister Skye, sah, let me introduce Hiram Peacock. He has a proposition for you. This, sir, is Mister Skye, his wives Victoria, who's a Crow, and Mary, who's Snake, and yonder is a horse unlike any other on earth, and his name is Jawbone."

Jawbone clacked his yellow teeth and sawed his head up and down.

Peacock lifted his slouch hat. "This is a landmark in my life, Colonel. I've never before been introduced to a horse."

A gesture from Skye urged them off their mounts, and Skye watched as Colonel Bullock collected both reins.

It didn't take long for Peacock to make his mission known. He watched the deepening skepticism in the guide's eye and knew this mountain man might well turn him down.

"We are halfway there, sir. We can't turn back. We must forge ahead but we don't know the country. Delay would be fatal. Would you consider guiding us?"

"How do you transport these sick people?" Skye asked.

"A light wagon, well made of the finest hickory by a master, drawn by the two Morgans that double as saddle horses. The wagon's so light one horse can draw it. There's room for four reposing in it, and the healthier ones ride the tailgates or walk. Some lungers do walk, you know. We've a large wagon drawn by an ox team of three spans that carries our tents and supplies."

"And what do you want of me, exactly, sir?"

"Take us to a place of healing, Mister Skye. Take us to a place where the air is dry and clean and warm. Where there are no vapors rising from swamps, no miasmas from vegetation. Not too hot, for heat kills, and not too cold, for cold is even worse. These young people can scarcely draw a breath, but the best advice we've found is that a mild desert place is their salvation."

"Getting there is only the beginning, sir," Skye said.

"We have tenting to shelter us, a plowshare, seed, and rakes and hoes."

Skye plainly doubted. "And how many will survive past the first winter?"

Peacock understood and had no good answer. "Consumption is a slow death, sir, but near the end it often hastens its course, and the time of death comes with shocking speed, the person suffering terribly, unable to breathe, coughing up blood and lung, fevered, aching in every bone, his mouth and throat ulcerated, desolated by the loss of all hope and the rejection of all prayer.

"If they die out here, wherever we end up, they will die in dry warm air, not in some cruel northern climate that sends the damps straight into their bones. Whether or not you guide us, we will go on, for we live not only in our bodies, but also by our visions and hopes, and it is in us to live in the desert with hope as the spirit that quickens us."

Skye gazed at the distant pine-clad ridges.

"You talked to Wyeth. What did he tell you. Did you have a place in mind?"

"The Virgin River, Mister Skye. He said we should go to the Virgin River on the edge of the great southwestern desert and there we would find the very place we are seeking. Jedediah Smith passed that way when he went to Mexican California.

59

There are river flats that might be cultivated and irrigated with waters diverted from the river. Some of the local Indians do just that. There's a mild dry climate. There's wood and grass. It's on or near the California Trail, the southern one, so we would not be isolated. It fits the very model described by a scholar I trust who has examined the disease and its cures."

Skye thought about it. "I've never been anywhere near there. The Virgin River is far from any settlement that I know of. You think you'll survive there, isolated, far from supplies, from food and clothing, from meat, from medicine? From roving bands of Paiutes who may or may not be friendly? From outlaws and brigands and desperadoes?"

"Yes, sir, that is our plan."

The colonel turned the talk in a new direction. "I told him, Mister Skye, that American Indians are vulnerable to the diseases of white men, and surely that includes your wives, and that it must be considered."

"And my response, Mister Skye, was that you and your ladies need not come close to my party. We are self-contained. All the evidence suggests that the disease is transmitted by close contact, but who knows? Saliva, touching, whatever. And we would quarantine ourselves for the sake of your family."

Skye looked doubtful.

"There is something else not yet discussed, Mister Peacock," the colonel said. "Mister Skye's services are not cheap. I'm his agent and negotiate for him, but perhaps you can deal directly with him now."

"We budgeted two hundred dollars."

The colonel shook his head. "Two hundred dollars. That doesn't even begin to make it a proposition for Mister Skye."

"It's what we budgeted. It's what we will pay."

A great quiet fell over them. Skye obviously got much

more, especially if the prospects were grim. A breeze stirred his unkempt gray hair.

"We have some maps, crude as they may be," Peacock said, breaking the silence. "We come from New Bedford, on the Atlantic coast. We made our way from Independence to here. We will make our way to what, for us, is a biblical Zion, a place of refuge in the benign air of the desert. We will find our way without a guide. Thank you for your time, Mister Skye. You have many admirers who speak in the highest terms of you."

He turned toward his Morgan gelding.

"Wait one moment, Mister Peacock," Skye said. He turned toward his women. "Victoria, Mary, we have the chance to help bring some very sick people to a place of healing. They have a white man's disease. It would be dangerous for you. This disease destroys lungs until people cannot breathe, and their lungs fill up and they die. It would be dangerous for our boy as well."

Mary deferred to Victoria with a small nod. Victoria walked slowly toward Hiram Peacock. "The people of all the world are one people, and the sickness of your people makes my heart heavy. If there is a place of good spirits, let us take them there."

"That will be our reward," Skye said. "We'll get by. We always do."

Peacock had no words in him. He just nodded. But then he stepped forward and clasped the small hands of Victoria, the young hands of Mary, and the big rough hands of Skye.

"Mister Peacock, you've got yourself the finest guide and counselor in the world," said Colonel Bullock. "He will get you to your home in the desert, and he won't leave you until you are settled there and he knows you are safe. Count yourself blessed."

eight

A deal, then. Skye felt uneasy about it. Disease came in the night, murdered the innocent, and crept away to strike others. But what if he led the sick to a place of healing?

He stood there, in that quiet pine-girt valley, aware that Peacock was examining him even as he was examining Peacock. The New England man wore old-style clothing, gray broadcloth knee britches, black cutaway, a stock at the throat, shoulder-length salt-and-pepper hair, at present tied into a queue, and wire-rimmed, square-lens spectacles that somewhat hid those bright, curious blue eyes. But he had that sturdy Yankee forthrightness about him that Skye liked. There was no subterfuge in this man.

Peacock might be a New England whale oil merchant but he had gotten his sick people from the Atlantic coast to Independence, and then had brought them seven hundred miles west on an overland trail, all on his own. This was no pilgrim, to use a term much favored by the Yanks.

"Just to be clear, Mister Peacock. We will be traveling the

California Trail part of the way, over ground I know, but then we will turn off, go through the Mormon settlements, and plunge into country unknown to me or my wives. I don't know those Indians, mostly Paiutes, nor have I the slightest experience with the Mojave tribe lower down. They don't have the traditions of the plains tribes. The Paiutes are known as masterful camp robbers. I'm telling you this so that you know exactly who and what you're employing."

"Mister Skye, you're the man we want. You'll receive a hundred in gold now, and a hundred upon delivering us. The second hundred will be held in escrow by Colonel Bullock."

Skye nodded. "When do we start?"

"At once. This ordeal is weakening my people. So let's be on our way."

"All right. By the time you're ready there at the fort, we'll be ready too."

"You mean you can break this camp just like that?"

"Just like that, mate."

"Come along," said Colonel Bullock. "When Skye makes an appointment, he keeps it."

Skye watched the two men trail their horses up the steep grade and vanish into the jack pine forest. Behind him he heard the sigh of falling leather. The women had already unpinned the lodge cover and let it slide down the lodgepoles. It took only a few minutes to load the poles, pack the robes, put the kitchen into parfleches, saddle their stock, and put out the cook fire. Mary lifted the richly quilled and beaded cradleboard bearing the tiny child, and slid it onto her back. The boy peered quietly at his father from within his nest.

Skye clambered onto Jawbone, felt the unruly horse quiver under him. He steered his family up the same anonymous slope taken by the Yankees. Worries crowded his mind. Was this the dumbest thing he had ever committed himself to? How sick were those people? What sort of courage did they possess? He just had done something he tried never to do: commit without knowing the character of those he would guide into the unknown West.

He would not back out. He had given his word, and now the only course was to make the best of it. He and his wives led the packhorses through the silent jack pines, then down a long grade into the valley of the Laramie River, and at last raised the post, which was hemmed by high bluffs. He and his quiet ladies soon plunged into a plain bustling with wagons, people, livestock, and racing dogs. They stared at Skye; they always did, noting his battered top hat, quilled leather clothing, meaty face, and weathered countenance. And they studied his Indian wives, and this time, they peered at that infant in the cradleboard Mary was carrying over her back. Why did he evoke such silence? Had these Yanks never seen a mixed-blood family before?

Hiram Peacock was waiting near the sutler's store, looking grand in his cutaway. His wagons stood well apart, and there was a strange emptiness surrounding them. Skye knew at once that none of those westering people in the other wagon trains wanted anything to do with a company of sick people who had a lethal disease, and they were giving the New Bedford company a wide berth.

In a swift moment of recognition, Skye knew what he would face in the trail. On the veranda of the store, the usual loungers squinted darkly at Skye and his wives, and at Peacock. Skye ignored them.

"Mister Peacock," he said, "we're about ready."

"So are we. I'd like you to meet Enoch Bright, my second-in-command. He's a master mechanic."

Skye shook hands with a bright-eyed skinny male, who smiled slightly but said not a word. The man wore layers of clothing, though the day was unpleasantly warm. The fellow had big scarred hands, capable hands, Skye thought. The man could probably put a turnip watch together blindfolded.

"I've got the wagon hubs greased," Bright said.

"I guess we're set, then. I'll check with Colonel Bullock, and we'll be off."

"He's been paid on your behalf," Peacock said.

"Good."

Skye slipped into the store, which now had little left to sell to the migrants, and found Bullock clerking.

"We're on our way, Colonel."

"Mister Skye, there are things to watch out for, and I am not talking about rattlesnakes or wild Indians."

Skye smiled and waited.

"I've been listening to this crowd. They're calling it a plague company, sir, and there are plans afoot, whispers, talk of keeping it from grass and water, and maybe things even more sinister. Watch out."

"I will."

"Now, there's something else. You've been out in the villages so you haven't any word of it. A war's brewing with the Mormons. The army may move soon. The Saints are resisting federal control. It's all about polygamy and who runs the Utah Territory. Washington thinks it's lost control. There's some hotheads in Utah, and they're raising a militia. And you'll be plunging right through the middle of it. I think you'll be all right, but a word to the wise . . ."

"I see. Well, we're hardly a menace to the Saints. But hotheads can cause trouble. As always, Colonel, you have gone beyond all friendship on our behalf."

The colonel straightened himself up, his gaze level, his beard jutting forward. "Godspeed," he said. "And mind my words."

Skye passed the silent bunch on the veranda, well aware of the thoughts teeming in the heads of that crowd, and headed across the no-man's-land to his new company. He beckoned his ladies to join him, and soon the New Bedford Infirmary Company was joined by Skye and his wives.

"It's time to introduce you," Peacock said. "Come. We'll start with the sick wagon."

Within the light wagon were four young people, presumably the sickest, lying side by side, with just enough room. Forward were bedding and gear.

Skye approached, while his wives hung back several yards.

"This young lady, on the right, is my daughter Samantha," Peacock said. "She's thirteen and eager to be on the trail. She's a very brave traveler. Samantha, this is our guide, Mister Skye, and his family, Victoria and Mary Skye, and that's North Star in the cradleboard."

Samantha nodded. She was obviously seriously ill, her young features gray. She clutched a bloodstained rag. She wore a grimy gray dress and woolen stockings. Even as they stood there, Samantha began coughing, and heaved up bloody sputum that she wiped away. Skye couldn't imagine how he would get this girl to a desert place six or seven hundred miles away.

Then the girl smiled up at him, her gaze upon him as if he were her guardian angel, and Skye resolved then and there that somehow, some way, he would take Samantha to a desert place and see her healed.

"And this is my neighbor Peter Sturgeon. He's nigh onto twelve, and he plans to be a cooper. He's got the penchant for it. But life's given him a little detour now. Peter, this is Mister Skye, and over there, Mary and Victoria."

The boy was gaunt, with great black hollows under his eyes, and had a feverish look about him.

"You'll get us there," the young man said hoarsely, and Skye knew that the consumption had ruined his vocal cords.

"Now these are Grant and Ashley Tucker, neighbors of ours, and twins. The pair are twelve, and they're going to get well together, aren't you?"

They were brother and sister, and both had that gaunt gray look of a consumptive in the final stages of the disease. They were each wrapped in a brown blanket.

The twins, emaciated and miserable, stared up at Skye silently. Skye hardly knew which of these four they would be burying first.

The other patients were either sitting on the lowered tailgate of the supply wagon or standing patiently.

The Skyes met Anna Bennett, an eighteen-year-old beauty with chestnut hair and a direct assessing gaze, sitting on the tailgate. Eliza Bridge and Mary Bridge joined Anna on the tailgate.

An older youth standing nearby proved to be Sterling Peacock. He looked like his father, but for the dark patches under his eyes.

"Sterling is my son, my heir if anything goes wrong, and is an able surveyor. But now he has to lick this disease. We're going to get you back on your feet, aren't we, Sterling?"

"I'm already getting better," Sterling said hoarsely. "It is a pleasure to meet you, Mister Skye."

But then a cough seized him, and he spat up blood into a pink-stained rag. And when he stopped coughing, he had a question for Victoria.

"Are you going to heal us with Indian medicine?" he asked hoarsely.

"Hell no," she said.

"I thought Indians have medicines for everything."

Victoria grinned. "Hey, I got stuff to try, eh? Goddamn white men, they don't know nothing."

Hiram Peacock listened intently, and then smiled.

Two ambulatory young men, Lloyd and David Jones, both in their twenties, completed the entourage. The Jones brothers seemed the healthiest, and indeed were sharing the burden of making and breaking camp, and acting as teamsters.

But there was a long road ahead.

"Are you ready, sir?" Peacock asked.

"If you are, Mister Peacock."

Victoria and Mary sat their ponies quietly, letting Skye lead this small, fragile party westward, away from the safety of the fort and into the unknown. Skye turned back to watch the party form behind him, his women and his packhorses bringing up the rear. The Jones boys steered the teams, Lloyd beside the foremost oxen, David beside the pair of Morgans drawing the light wagon. Peacock and Bright walked. A stray cloud threw a deep shadow over them just as they were abandoning Fort Laramie, but the sun still shone on the crowd before the sutler's store, who were all watching with reproachful silence. No one waved.

nine

Hiram Peacock waited until his entourage was well clear of Fort Laramie and working through the black hills before engaging Mister Skye. The guide rode ahead a little, his battered top hat shielding his weathered face from the summer sun, his skin stained dark by a lifetime lived outside. That blue roan devil was a menace and Peacock intended to heed Skye's warning to steer clear of it.

Still, questions seethed in his mind: who exactly was this man who had been entrusted with the life and safety of this company of the sick? Maybe Skye was equally curious, because he soon dismounted and left Jawbone entirely free, not even holding a rein, and settled in beside Peacock, his stocky legs laboring a bit to keep up. Jawbone spurted ahead, intending to lead this parade.

"Why, Mister Skye, I was hoping for your counsel. I should like to acquaint myself with your practices on the road, and what you think is wise policy in this country."

"Well, Mister Peacock, we've a mutual curiosity. It happens I have a question or two. There's something I need to know."

Peacock nodded.

"Did you have trouble on the trail before you got here?"

"You mean about the disease? Not really. I made a point of informing the companies ahead and behind that we had invalids with us. Generally, they appreciated it, and gave us a wide berth at night when we all were camping."

"Did any company give you trouble?"

"Oh, now and then. One captain threatened to shoot our stock unless we moved far from the spring where we were staying. I moved at once. I understand how people feel about a deadly disease."

"Were those all the threats? Any serious threat? To hurt you, to drive you off the road?"

Peacock pondered it. "No, not that. But some were unfriendly, especially the ones in a hurry who passed close by when we were burying one of our children. They always wanted to know what caused the death, and I always told them."

"That reminds me, Mister Peacock. You introduced us to ten young people with the disease. Is that the whole roster? Are you or Mister Bright sick?"

"Mister Skye, I may be the next one. I thought I had escaped even though my beloved Emma lies in her grave and all my children have it. But about the time we started from Independence, I found tiny red specks in hand whenever I coughed, and I suspect the clock may be ticking for me, though I have no real proof of it. I feel well enough. Two buried. Ten ill. Only Enoch seems to resist it. With that pressing on me, I hope you'll forgive me for being in a hurry. The sooner we settle in the desert, the better chance we have."

"I'm glad you told me. I'll want to keep my family apart. On the road to Laramie did anyone stalk you?"

"Stalk? Us? Why, sir, even those who didn't like the company of invalids didn't stalk us. Why do you ask?"

"Because we're being stalked, and have been since Fort Laramie."

"Stalked, sir? I've seen no one."

"Across the river a rider appears now and then and vanishes, but the man is not moving faster or slower than we are."

"Stalked? Why would anyone stalk us?"

"In that wagon is a deadly cargo."

"What would they do?"

"We'll have to see. I imagine before long we'll know."

"Are we in danger?"

Skye sighed. "Let me deal with that."

"When did you see this stalker?"

"I didn't. My older wife, Victoria, signaled me."

"Signaled? I never knew it."

Skye laughed suddenly, a great rumble rising out of his barrel-shaped torso. "That comes from a long marriage."

"Is this stalker dangerous? What is he up to?"

"When I have an opportunity, I'll find out."

"Find out?"

"I'll catch him at it and see."

"Mister Skye, I don't want trouble, not with so many sick people."

"Sometimes the best way to avoid trouble is to confront it, Mister Peacock. Now, I need a few more things from you. How often do we rest? When do those young teamsters need a break?"

"Every hour or so. Their lungs don't afford them much air, and they tire."

71

"What about the ones sitting on the tailgate?"

"They sometimes rotate with those lying in the green wagon. Even sitting on a tailgate wears them down to nothing."

"And the sickest?"

"I sometimes carry them in my lap, sir. I take my turn on the tailgate."

"And when you rest, do other companies pass you by?"

"Often they do. I try to find a place well off the trail where we can let them pass us easily."

Skye seemed to absorb all that. The man certainly had questions and wanted answers.

"Tell me more about this sickness, sir. We had lungers in England and in the Royal Navy, lots of 'em, and mostly they died."

"The agent, or exciting cause, is unknown, Mister Skye. But it causes the growth of tubercules, or hard capsules containing the diseased flesh within the body, and not just the lungs. The disease can lodge anywhere. It often lodges in the mouth and throat but most any other place is possible, and this ulcerates the flesh. Some people resist and live quite a while; others succumb swiftly, unable to breathe, coughing their life away. The worst is called miliary consumption, and it's terrible. That person is doomed to die within a few weeks. That's how we lost a boy, Ephraim, on the road. He went straight downhill. It's a mystery, why God permits it."

"Do you blame God?"

"He leaves my prayers unanswered, Mister Skye."

"And what heals, if anything?"

"In Europe, they claim cold alpine air does it, and they flock to spas in the Alps. Here . . . all the evidence points to the desert. Dry, warm, and a lot of bed rest. There is no other known cure. No herbs or teas or roots or powders. No mustard plasters or emetics or cold compresses. No magical drafts that one may sip and be healed. No exorcisms, no bell, book, and candle. No dealings with the devil. Only the desert air, sir, neither too hot nor too chill, dry air, and a warm cot. That's why I'm bringing these desperate young people two thousand miles from their homes."

Skye pointed. The stalker sat his horse in deep shade across the river, mostly shielded by juniper brush.

"Know him?"

"I don't have the eyes to tell you that, sir."

"We'll find out what he's about."

They reached a widening of the narrow trail, and Skye pulled his party aside and up a gulch a way to clear the path for companies that followed. Immediately the two young men, Lloyd and David Jones, dropped to the ground and stretched out as if dead. Skye knew he shouldn't be shocked, but he was. The youngsters sitting on the tailgate curled up on the ground, suddenly oblivious to life around them. It had been all they could manage to sit up for an hour or so. Skye hastily studied the area for snakes and thought to warn Peacock about curling up on the earth before checking it out.

He hiked back to the green wagon, admiring its light hickory construction, and peered in on the sickest four, who lay in the shade of the bowed canvas top, staring up at him from fever-blasted faces. Skye had the sinking feeling that this was a fool's mission; these children should be safe abed somewhere, anywhere but here, with hundreds of miles of lonely and dangerous trail ahead of them.

Enoch Bright was checking the Morgans for fistulas and anything that might hamstring them, running a knowing hand over the horses' withers, flanks and legs, pasterns and stifles.

"Are they in good shape, Mister Bright?"

"They're Morgans, sir. They'll do what's required. Justin Morgan should get a gold medal."

"That's a fine wagon."

"Yes it is, three hundred pounds lighter than any of the same size. I used hickory and ash, strong as steel. See those oversized wheels? They'll get our patients through three feet of water."

The wagon was a work of genius, and its maker was along on this trip, which consoled Skye. Things broke down on the road.

"Are those Jones brothers all right?"

"No, none of them are all right. But they carry on. They get more air flat on their back like that than curled up. It's air they're wanting. Ten minutes like that and they'll have some air in 'em."

"Should they rest rather than walk?"

"They all should rest."

"Will this trip kill them? That's what I'm trying to say."

"If it doesn't, something else will."

"Mister Bright, you have a wisdom of your own."

A wagon company rounded a slope and rolled into sight, two men on saddle horses were leading, followed by four wagons pulled by ox teams, and behind them a gaggle of scrawny cows, herded by children. The leaders saw Skye's party resting upslope from the trail and hesitated.

But Hiram Peacock headed full sail straight toward them, his cutaway coat flapping open as he walked. Skye thought he ought to follow. There could be trouble.

"Gentlemen," yelled Peacock, "we're a company with sick people in it, and we trust that you'll keep a safe distance."

The lead men, their faces shaded under wide-brimmed

slouch hats, eyed the whale oil merchant silently and studied the wagon and cart drawn apart from the trail.

Then they studied Skye, and observed his family, and finally the youths sprawled on the ground and the others slumped below the tailgate.

Skye was close enough now to see those faces hidden in the shade of their hat brims, and he knew these were two of Manville's guides. And there could be trouble.

"Lungers, eh?" said The Cork. "Someone ought to shoot the whole lot."

ten

kye braced for trouble, but trouble passed by. This party was entirely young men, probably headed for the goldfields of California. None of them wanted anything to do with a company of consumptives, so they kept as far away as they could.

Two more wagon trains followed, both of them composed of families, and Peacock afforded them the same warning that he had given the first company. These people stared, curious, at the sick in Peacock's company, stayed well away, and continued on their way. They were all too travel-worn to afford the slightest kindness to Peacock. Skye absorbed all that. Most of those westering people were decent sorts, people who in other circumstances might give aid to the sick or at least comfort them, but not on this trail where a thousand troubles beset them and competition to reach the goldfields drove them.

Skye made note of it.

"Is this how they dealt with you on the road to Fort Laramie?" he asked Peacock.

"Oh, mostly. Some were friendly enough. Few had been out long enough to deal with all the troubles, the break-downs, the collapse of livestock, the sicknesses. I'd say the farther west we've come, the harsher we've been treated."

It made sense, and it wasn't good news.

At a nod from Peacock, his beleaguered group started west again. The Jones boys seemed to have revived, and prod-ded the ox and horse teams to life. Enoch Bright had seen to the needs of every patient while they rested, bringing water to each.

Through all this Victoria and Mary kept their distance at the rear, observing the ritual of the trail. That was fine with Skye.

They rolled along the North Platte, sometimes cutting over steep hills that tired the oxen. But eventually they left the Black Hills behind them and emerged on an arid, sagebrush-choked plain with little grass. Even as dusk approached, the heat built, and the trains ahead of them left a smothering powder in the air that could only do more damage to those in this traveling hospital.

Still, it was not a bad day. He rode ahead, looking for grass for the stock, but found none. The great migration had chewed every blade. Then he spotted a steep brush-choked coulee sinking toward the pewter-colored river, saw at once that it had been ignored and that ample grass might be found under the canopy of sagebrush above it.

"Here," he said.

In short order, the company had pulled well away from the main trail and camped on a rise next to the brush-choked gulch. Enoch Bright and the Jones brothers knew what to do, and soon the stock was watered at the river and turned loose in the brushy gulch to graze.

That's when Skye spotted the lone rider, the stalker, in the shadows across the Platte. The man sat his horse, didn't move, and probably imagined he was invisible behind a wall of sagebrush and rock.

As planned, Mary and Victoria put up the Skye lodge at some distance from the consumptives. Victoria was crabby about it. "We're taking them, and I don't even know them," she said. There was something in her that was reaching out, wanting to befriend those sick people.

There are moments in life when one feels helpless and this was one. Skye also wanted to befriend the sick people now that they were making camp and gathering around a cook fire, but he couldn't. None of his family could. The health of that infant in his mother's cradleboard, the health of his vibrant young Shoshone wife, the health of his old companion of the trails, Victoria, all stopped him.

"I'll be back," he said.

Victoria eyed him sharply, watched as he boarded Jawbone and slid his old Hawken from its sheath, and nodded. In that nod was a whole unspoken colloquy: she was there if he needed her. She knew exactly what he would be doing.

He rode through dusk, heading for a ford they had passed a half mile back. The dusk almost cloaked him; he didn't much care whether it did or not. He reached the river, eased down to the bank, and urged Jawbone ahead. The blue roan horse hated cold water, clacked his teeth, sawed at his rein, turned and glared reproachfully at Skye, and then stepped daintily into the flowing river, which soon tugged at his hocks. But it was an easy passage, and in two leaps Jawbone bounded up the mud bank to grass, shook, almost unseating Skye, and then stood stock-still while Skye studied the silent, gloomy riverside brush, now sliding into the oblivion of night.

There was no evening song here. No birds trilled. He slid off Jawbone. The horse would lock there, wait, ready for anything. Skye slid his Hawken into its saddle sheath, preferring his ancient hickory belaying pin, that ship's fitting so often used by limey sailors in a brawl, and walked through the brush, making no sound at all if he could help it. But not even the most experienced man could avoid the occasional snap of a stick in areas like this, deep in the debris of sagebrush as tall as Skye.

Across the river a cook fire bloomed, and he could see shadowed men he knew to be Peacock and Bright hanging a kettle on a support rod. The young people, already wrapped in blankets, lay listlessly near the cart. In the background rose two ghostly tents, probably erected by the Jones brothers, ready to shelter these ill people from the dews and damps of the night.

Skye's night vision was still good even in his fifties, mostly because he made a point of discerning things in the dark, registering shapes and shadows, so that the whole wild world was stamped in the back of his mind. He liked working in the dark, and could find his way better than most men. Better than a Yank ruffian posing as a guide, for example.

He worked upriver, gliding from cottonwood to willow when there were trees, or sliding forward, crouched as low as the surrounding brush, so he would not outline himself against the clear, starlit heavens. He had last seen the stalker directly opposite the camp. He might be there, or more likely he might be clear down at river's edge, a hundred yards closer, a rifle shot closer.

Ahead, the dark bulk of a horse shifted: its head went up, and it snorted and sidestepped. Skye froze. He heard nothing but the pumping of his own heart. The stalker was not on the horse. A slow, careful study of the immediate area suggested that the stalker was not nearby, either. Skye edged forward again, found a pebble and tossed it, and got no response. The stalker was down at the river.

Skye decided to leave the horse alone, tempting as it was to free the animal. The horse might give the game away. Skye took his time. When one is stalking a stalker, time is an ally, haste is an enemy. The man's horse had turned to stare at Skye, ears pricked forward, which might tell an experienced wilderness man something. But Skye doubted this was an experienced man.

It was time to wait, to study the shifting shadows, to listen for the crackle of footsteps returning from the river. The night was soft and the air was kind, and only a few mosquitoes found him there. He let them bite.

The crack of a rifle told him he was too late. A thump rose from the riverside, fifty yards distant. The ball had struck flesh. He had heard balls strike flesh all too many times. Skye slipped forward, straight for the river, barely concealing his passage. Across the river he heard shouts, and dread welled up in him. He heard the crash of footsteps off to one side, too far for him to reach, the crack of boots on debris. Skye whirled, raced toward the man's horse, saw a shadow climb onto it and spur the animal away. Skye followed, aware now that the man wouldn't be looking behind him, but would focus on getting out of the brush and away.

Doggedly, Skye followed. The man slowed down up ahead, preferring quietness. But he was still gaining ground. Skye began to trot. He had never been a runner; his stocky beefeater body wasn't made for it. But now he trotted behind that horse, fearful of losing his quarry in the dense dark, but the horseman had slowed to a leisurely walk. Skye saw him looming against the starlight, slipped to one side, and brought the belaying pin hard against the man's shoulder. Skye felt it strike home and heard the man howl. A rifle clattered to the ground. The man cried in agony, spurred his mount into a frenzied gallop, and vanished into the stygian darkness.

The old belaying pin felt fine in Skye's hands. It had been the favored weapon of British seamen for generations, and it was as familiar to him as his old Hawken. In the distance, hooves clattered over turf, and then all was silent. But Skye swore he heard a sob out of the night.

He tripped on the rifle and picked it up, not knowing what sort of weapon it was. It hefted well and was unfamiliar to his hand. Spoils of war. It took him a while to orient himself. Where was the river? Where was Jawbone? But the North Star steered him, and he worked his way to the riverbank, and then easterly toward his patient horse. Jawbone sawed his head up and down, as if to tell Skye that this business had required his services, and that horseman would not now be fleeing if Jawbone had been around.

"You're right. I'm not always very bright," he said, and quieted the stallion with a gentle hand.

He rode to the ford, splashed across, feeling the tug of the stream on Jawbone's hocks, and then the horse plunged up a grade, shook off water, and headed toward camp.

Skye dreaded what he would find there.

"Hello the camp," he said, fearful that Peacock or Bright might shoot.

"Skye! What is this? Come quickly," Peacock said.

Skye hurried toward the fire where people were gathering. He saw Victoria and Mary, and felt a flood of joy sweep him. They were all right.

"What was that shot, sir?"

"The stalker, Mister Peacock."

The whale oil merchant sagged. "That shot killed my Morgan," he said. "Killed my prize horse. Killed me, in a way."

Skye waited, saddened, but there was no more.

He found Victoria and hugged her, and Mary and hugged her.

"We'd better put out the fire," he said roughly.

eleven

bitterness flavored the night. Enoch Bright scratched a lucifer, lit a bull's-eye lantern, and motioned. Skye followed. The mechanic led him into the brushy gulch, the lantern throwing wavery light on sagebrush and juniper, until they reached a hollow near the river. There one of the Morgans sprawled awkwardly.

He held his lantern in a way that let Skye see the neat bloodless hole in the horse's chest. Bright growled softly, knelt, unbuckled the halter, and slid it off the Morgan's head.

"What's the justice of this?" Bright said. "Killing an innocent horse. What crime was this horse guilty of, tell me? Nothing. This animal had no sin in him, sir. Justice is the most important thing in all the world, the highest and noblest of all ideals. And here is an innocent whose life is stolen from him."

"I hadn't thought of that, Mister Bright."

"Now, sir, if I were to go off and kill that man's mother, who's innocent of all crime save for giving birth to that cockroach, that might be revenge, but it wouldn't be justice. Because not even that fiend's mother deserves such a fate. Killing an innocent, sir, now that's the devil's own wickedness. Come along; you've seen enough. I will not have us indulge in morbid excitement here."

Skye found himself gazing tenderly at the handsome chestnut Morgan horse, and they slowly made their way upslope, past the other grazing stock, and returned to the campfire.

Peacock stalked sternly, round and round in a circle. "What am I going to tell the young people, tell me that? Some degenerate has shot our horse? And why was this deed done? Can you tell me? It's an outrage. This West, sir, this West is criminal. That Morgan was a saddle horse, fourteen and a half hands, but the pair had been trained to perform all things for us. That pair, Mister Skye, would draw the cart and pull the plow through virgin land wherever we settle. That pair would help us cut irrigation ditches. The life of my hospice rested in the bosom of that dead horse. The scoundrel will be whipped, I say. I shall thrash him personally and without quarter. And after he is thrashed, I shall confiscate enough of his possessions to replace what was lost."

Skye peered into the darkness around the two tents, and saw solemn young faces there. Someone would have to talk to those sick young people, tell them that others on this road to California meant them harm.

"I must tell them. Look at them, staring at us. What shall I say?" Peacock said.

"There is only truth," Skye said.

"Truth. That they're pariahs? That people on this trail mean to destroy this company because they suffer, through no fault of their own, an illness that fills others with dread? Truth, is it?"

"Perhaps they know that about themselves. There is no

justice, I'm afraid." Skye eyed those pale faces. "How close is safe for me, Mister Peacock?"

"Who knows? But I think one can get close out here. This is open land, where the air blows clean."

The two walked toward the tents that held those consumptive young people, though Mary and Victoria held back.

The Jones brothers, healthiest of these afflicted young, awaited them, almost as one would await emissaries.

"David and Lloyd, a stalker has shot one of our Morgans, as you may have surmised. Mister Skye here chased him off but the damage is done. You know why. I don't need to tell you. We'll carry on, and somehow we'll get to where we're going, and I'll live to see each of you healed or gaining ground in a place where that is possible."

"That horse . . . not that Morgan," said Lloyd.

"Because we're sick?" asked David.

"Someone's afraid, so afraid they don't think about you or your suffering or your hopes. They want distance between themselves and us," Peacock said. "Get ahead of us where it's safe; leave us behind. Slow us down. Stop us."

"We've lost a horse. But that stalker won't be coming around again. I nailed him. I'll get you to the desert, and keep you as safe as I can," Skye said.

"If I wasn't sick, I'd go after him too," David said.

"Good, David," Peacock said. "You boys are my strong arm. We'll tell the rest now."

At the wall tent housing the women, Peacock paused. "I'll address them, Mister Skye."

The merchant stood outside the tent and began a quiet monologue to those hidden within. He chose an absolutely candid approach, telling them that consumption plainly terrified some people. Someone among the wagon companies had attempted to slow this party. But it was time to endure, to dream and hope, to believe that somewhere ahead would be a place of healing, their refuge, and they would all arrive there someday, somehow.

Skye marveled that the merchant could be so eloquent. He soon quieted these young people, some of them his own beloved children, and then emerged into the night.

"It'd be well, Mister Skye, not to get too close to me for a while. I shall wash, as always, but the nature of transmission is unknown; we know only that close contact is dangerous."

"I will do that, sir."

"Will you post a guard tonight?"

"In a way, yes. My horse, Jawbone, is a dozen sentries rolled into one. Let there be even the slightest change in the rhythms of the night and Jawbone will nudge me awake with that big snout of his."

"I wondered about that horse. Why you keep it. Now I'm getting a lesson," Peacock said.

"It's a mystical brotherhood. I haven't the faintest idea why Jawbone and I are comrades in arms. Perhaps he was my brother in some previous life."

Peacock laughed.

"He is an army," Skye added.

Peacock stopped, stared at Skye, and at the mysterious roan horse standing placidly nearby, looking stupid and lop-eared. "So I was told in St. Louis," he muttered.

The night passed peaceably. Even before dawn, Bright was building a cook fire and then stirring porridge. The man was a marvel, the sole person on earth, apparently, who rose even earlier than Skye.

The sick young people had worked out a whole protocol

of caring for one another. The weakest did the least to wash and comfort and feed others; the stronger ones saw to the needs of the most desperate. Skye watched quietly, aware that these young people, some of them fevered, others in pain, many of them chronically coughing, most of them desperate for air, somehow managed to sustain themselves through a hard, endless journey.

Bright lifted his kettle and carried it to them. They had their own eating bowls and spoons, and he ladled porridge into each. These utensils were kept separate.

Skye watched them thoughtfully, wondering if he would ever get to know these youngsters or breach the invisible wall between him and them. Who were they? Did they dream of good things?

With the faintest hint of dawn breaking the eastern horizon, Skye patrolled the outlying bluffs, but there was no trouble there.

He caught Peacock. "How are you going to proceed with only one Morgan?" Skye asked.

"How level is the land here?"

"There are some long grades."

"The wagon's heavy. I need the three yokes of oxen I have to draw it. On level ground, the living Morgan can draw the light wagon. We'll need to do something when we reach a grade."

But Enoch Bright had already begun doing things his own way. He drilled a hole in the wagon bed, crafted a kingpin, and soon hooked the light wagon's singletree to the rear of the heavy wagon, and then yoked the oxen.

"On grades, I'll use the Morgan to give the oxen an assist," he said. "I'll keep steam in the boilers, Mister Skye."

Skye and Hiram Peacock watched without objection as the mechanic rigged things his way.

"I know who the chief is around here," Victoria said. "It ain't you. It ain't that Peacock."

Skye laughed.

He had spent a quiet night in his lodge with his family. His son crawled around on the thick buffalo robes spread across the earth, while Mary and Victoria heated some stew for them all.

"Why did a man kill that good horse?" Mary asked. She was worried.

"White men have memories of plagues, of times when most of us get sick and die. We are afraid."

"And he kills a horse? Does this take the disease away?"

Skye answered sadly: "No, it takes us away. It was intended to stop or slow this party."

"White men are crazy," Victoria said.

Now a great malaise lay upon this small company of the ill, and Skye felt it as the day quickened.

It occurred to him that he had not examined the booty of war he had taken the previous night. He had stowed it in his saddle sheath.

To his astonishment it proved to be a new Sharps. A brass vault in the stock held its unique caps and balls. He poked and probed and aimed and dry-fired. How he had longed for just such a weapon but had never been able to afford even a tenth of the cost. He would learn how to use it, and maybe with luck he could replenish the caps and balls at Bridger's Fort, or Salt Lake.

Even as they prepared to move, another immigrant train whipped by them, its people frowning and cold. Word had passed up and down the California Trail. Skye sensed there would be more trouble, but there was little he could do. Hiram Peacock was the ambassador. Maybe he could quiet all these people.

Skye and his women fell in, and they started west once again, toward a fate no one could know or even guess.

twelve

They were slowed. Three span of oxen weren't enough to drag that supply wagon and the light one behind it. Skye saw it, and so did the rest. The beasts would give out eventually unless they were relieved of their burden.

Still, they toiled along the North Platte River, pausing frequently. Other trains passed them. Clearly, word had spread back and forth. Some sent riders forward to inquire.

"This is a plague party," one rough man announced.

"It is a party with some consumptives, sir," Peacock replied, as quietly as he could.

"Poisoning the water!"

"Have you proof of it? Has anyone ahead of us taken sick?"

"Plenty of sickness along this trail, and you're the cause. Fresh graves, that's all we see."

"From consumption gotten from us, sir?"

"It figures, that's all I'm going to say. What right have you to poison the road with sickness?"

"We're taking sick people to a place of healing. I think you'd like that done for you if you had the disease."

"I don't and I won't unless I catch the devil's own from these filthy squaws. This is the damnedest outfit ever to come down the trail, spreading your sickness. Why don't you turn off and let decent people by?"

Skye bristled but held his peace.

Peacock smiled. "We're here, resting. Go on around, get ahead."

"We'll certainly do that, and a curse on you!"

The fierce man kicked the ribs of his gaunt horse and forced it back toward the wagon train waiting two hundred yards distant. Skye watched as the man gesticulated wildly, waving an arm in the direction of the New Bedford Infirmary Company. Several of them collected firearms from their wagons and posted themselves between the train and Peacock's party, for what purpose Skye could not fathom. But fear exacted its own madness.

Then the party of outraged migrants thundered past at almost a gallop, the oxen slobbering and foaming, the sentries forming a wall between their party and Skye's, as if somehow Peacock's wagons and people would descend upon them all and inflict disease and death upon them.

But they passed. And Skye sensed that this would not be the end of it. A sort of hysteria had gripped the companies on the trail this time, whipped by wild rumor and their own hardship. For it was true that the trail took its toll, and there were graves everywhere, fathers, mothers, grandparents, children, all hastily wrapped in blankets and buried in shallow pits, with a few words mumbled over them, before the weary travelers toiled west once again.

Still, that encounter was the worst of the morning. Another

company of Philadelphians gave Peacock's party wide berth but sent an emissary over to see if they could help.

"Yes," Skye said. "A span of oxen if you have it. I have a Sharps rifle to trade for it."

Victoria heard it and stared.

"We have not one spare animal, sorry," the Pennsylvania man said. "But I hope you succeed. I lost my mother to the galloping kind, the consumption that suddenly destroys a mortal. We're Friends. I'll ask ahead about spans of oxen and what you're offering, if that would help."

"It would, sir," Skye said. "And who are you?"

"Lethbridge, sir. Salton Lethbridge, and this is the Bryn Mawr Company, Oregon bound."

"I am Mister Skye."

"That's a name to reckon with, or so I'm told."

Skye smiled. "People know more about me than I know about myself."

Lethbridge laughed, and trotted his chestnut horse toward his company.

That was the only company that day that showed some civility or mercy. The rest passed with a curse and a whip.

They struggled on, resting frequently, until they reached LaBonte Creek at sundown. There were two companies camped there, but room for more upstream. Unlike most camps in that barren land, this had abundant firewood and even some grass in the moist bottoms. The weary oxen and the remaining Morgan needed both.

Skye surveyed the quiet camps, seeing people settling down for the short summer's night, taking care of livestock, cooking, doing the endless chores.

"We'll go upstream. It means another mile, but we'll have the camp we need," Skye said to Peacock.

There was a way around these bustling camps near the trail, and Skye took it. But no sooner did his weary company turn off the trail than the shouting began, and distant men collected, armed themselves, and began hiking toward Skye's company, spread out in a military assault line.

More trouble.

"Keep moving," Skye said. "Get to good ground upstream."

"You're more of an optimist than I am," Peacock said, but he motioned his weary assemblage forward along a hillside trail that plainly had seen use in recent days.

There was shouting from the approaching men.

"Keep moving, don't stop," Skye said.

Peacock shook his head, but he continued.

Skye peered about sharply. Victoria had strung her small bow and was ready, a quiet ace in the hole. Enoch Bright focused intently on the oxen and ignored the mounting hubbub. The Jones brothers stuck dutifully to their teamstering. The other young people stared, sick with fear.

"I say, stop or we'll shoot!" bawled a bearded man in a slouch hat, probably the captain of one of the wagon trains.

Skye turned Jawbone straight toward the man.

"We are heading for the free campground upriver. Is there a problem?"

"The plague party! You're going nowhere."

"I don't know of any plague in our party, sir. My name is Mister Skye. And yours?"

"Captain Reece. You're going to go back where you came from."

"Or?"

"Or face the consequences."

The consequences were considerable. There were now

about thirty armed men, rifles ready, with more rushing forward.

"What consequences, sir?"

Reece paused a second. "Try it and see," he snapped.

These men were beyond argument but Skye thought things needed to be said. Peacock had stopped his party. Enoch Bright at last turned to face this mob. The young people, peering from under the wagon sheet, looked scared. Victoria had slid into shadow. No one paid any attention to her.

The all-male crowd milled at a distance, not wanting to get closer to the sick. Beyond, at the camp, women and children collected to watch. Now the second company, just upstream, was alerted and more men were racing toward the open field where all this was building into trouble. Thirty rifles now, another thirty soon.

"Our young people are tired and need to stop here. They're consumptives, and need all the rest they can get."

"Get them out of here!" someone shouted.

"If they were your children, sir, would you be saying that?"

"I don't have plague children."

"They need food and water. A safe place to sleep."

"Go back! You will not infect us!"

"You will not be infected if you keep apart."

"You will infect the water above us. No, squaw man, no. That's final. Go!"

Skye lifted his top hat and settled it. "Mister Peacock," he said softly, "proceed."

Peacock seemed scared. As well he should. Skye was scared. The children were frightened. His wives looked resolute but he thought Victoria might be whispering her death song.

"Yes, Mister Skye," Peacock said, and proceeded. Enoch

started his ox team. The wagon rolled forward, followed by the cart.

Scores of rifles lifted, their barrels pointing straight at them all.

"Would you kill the sick children?" Skye asked softly in the deepening taut silence.

"No, squaw man, just you."

"We'll kill your oxen," another shouted.

"I see," said Mister Skye. "We will proceed. Go ahead, Mister Peacock. They plan to kill me. And after that, your oxen, and then it'll be up to you to care for the sick and weak."

Skye had to give the merchant credit. He bawled at the oxen and the wagon again rolled forward.

Behind, in the cart, soft sobs were eddying out on the meadow.

"Men, do your duty!" the captain yelled.

Men aimed rifles. Peacock stopped.

Then, at his urging, the sick children slid one by one to the ground and stood beside the wagon, gaunt, fevered, their pale faces tear-streaked. Sterling Peacock helped Samantha Peacock stand. Eliza Bridge and Mary Bridge slipped off the tailgate and stood, shyly. Grant and Ashley Tucker slid to the grass, unable to stand for more than a few moments. Peter Sturgeon sat down in the grass also. And Anna Bennett stood, proudly.

"Bring Samantha to me," Skye said quietly.

When her brother half dragged, half carried her to him, he dismounted from Jawbone, lifted her into the saddle, where she clung, her breath labored and her small face pinched and wet with tears.

"Come, let us put you to bed, Samantha. You are a brave girl, and soon you will be in a good place, where the dry, warm air will give you life again," Skye said.

Hiram Peacock, brave man that he was, hawed the oxen to life and the wagon rolled forward, inching past the company of angry men, following a rutted road that took them wide around the two camps. Enoch Bright led the Morgan horse on foot. The cart followed, the Jones brothers hawing the oxen, and then Skye's wives and ponies.

One by one, the angry travelers lowered their rifles.

No shot destroyed life and hope that moment. In a few minutes they reached an open glade, settled there, the children bundled in their blankets, their tears washed away. The horses were picketed on adequate grass. A fire sprang up, and soon would heat some broth. Skye carefully washed at the creek, and returned to camp.

Victoria and Mary abandoned their cook fire, slipped close to him, each catching a hand, and held him.

thirteen

amantha didn't wake up. A while after the rest had stirred in the early dawn, someone realized that the girl lay still.

Hiram Peacock shook the girl, who lay curled up in a bloodstained blanket, but she didn't stir. Her mouth formed an O, and her body was chill. She stared up at him from sightless eyes.

"Oh, Samantha," he said. "Oh, my little one."

He knelt beside her, absorbing once again the triumph of his ancient enemy, death. Then he turned to those solemn young people who had gathered around the wagon and shook his head. Samantha had survived only thirteen years, robbed by an insidious disease of all the joys and comforts of life; robbed of adulthood, robbed even of childhood, because she had been sick for three years.

Two beloved children dead this trip. They had buried his youngest, Raphael, near Fort Kearney. Now his second-youngest. He slumped against the wagon, almost unable to go on.

Had he driven them to their deaths? Had the ordeal of travel worn them to nothing?

He felt the need to walk away and be by himself for a time, and he did, hiking down to LaBonte Creek, apart from the silent camp. It was late. The other companies had already departed, leaving only this group of fragile mortals beside the creek.

He heard Enoch Bright quietly explaining things to Skye; heard him command that preparations for travel be halted. Then Hiram slipped through river brush, scaring up red-winged blackbirds, and settled on a log beside the slow, tiny stream.

Death had visited this bright morning.

Emma, Raphael, Samantha. Sterling, his oldest, still lived but the youth's lungs were daily under siege. As were his own lungs, he supposed, but there had been no further sign of trouble after the tiny spots of blood speckled his handkerchief for a few days. Everyone, every dear person in his household, was a victim of consumption. Would this cruel disease not let him alone? Would it take his surviving son too?

Why now? Had it been the horror of the evening before? The horror of having armed men threatening them for the crime of being sick? Had her weakened body and spirit recoiled against that desperate confrontation when it seemed possible that the whole company of the sick might be massacred? The hardships of the road seemed to erode the decency of people. Those men with rifles were simply trying to defend themselves and their families and were so caught in their passion that they almost murdered innocents.

There are things one never knows, and he could never know what stole the life of his girl. Maybe the child was all worn-out. That was the most fatal of all diseases, just being worn-out. He thought he would die someday of being worn-out.

They would have to bury her in some shallow grave and head west once again. He had wanted more for her; he wanted to give her a chance. Had he done something foolhardy, taking them on this endless journey? No! In New Bedford they would have sunk, day by day, without hope, only to lie for an eternity in the family plot. But every hour of this trip they lived with hope! Even Ephraim, the neighbor boy who was the first to die, had been filled with hope until he perished near Fort Kearney. She had hope! Sterling still had hope! He himself had hope! He had bought her hope!

He watched the morning bloom, the breezes pick up and rattle the sedges, and then he returned to camp. Enoch had settled Samantha on her grimy blue blanket, there on the yellow clay, and straightened her out and folded her thin arms over her chest and combed her hair. There were no caskets here, only a hasty hole in the earth and a blanket to cover her. Someday soon there would be nothing left, not flesh, not bones, not a stone at the head of her grave.

Peacock knew he must take charge again. There was not time to grieve. Other frail lives depended on him.

"We will carry on," he said to those gaunt youths. "We will reach a place of healing."

He rummaged a spade from the supply wagon and headed toward a gentle bower that might be a fitting place. But his spade bounced off the hardpan. Enoch Bright showed up to help, but Peacock waved him off. This was his own task, and he would not share it. He moved closer to the creek and tried again, this time in a brushy place, but the sun had cracked and dried the gumbo clay, turning it to granite, and he made no progress there. A sweat was building in him, and his own weary lungs were laboring.

Skye found him there, panting and leaning on his shovel.

"Sir, I think we may have to carry your girl a way before we can find a proper place," he said. "This isn't a fitting place. It's July, and the clay's turned to cement."

"This is where she died; this is where . . ." He let it hang, and gulped air.

"Yes, it is fitting," Skye said.

Victoria watched all this from a safe distance, and then approached.

"Mister Peacock? Would you listen to some old Crow woman?"

Peacock nodded and wiped sweat from his brow. He had been indescribably wearied by only a few minutes of banging that spade into the unyielding earth.

Victoria settled herself in the grass, which evoked curiosity in Peacock.

"My people, they do it another way," she began. "When someone starts on the spirit road, they are on a long journey that takes them up through the stars where they walk on spirit moccasins."

Peacock could no longer stand. He settled in the grass beside her. Off a way, life in the camp seemed suspended, and faces were turned toward them.

"We put our dead ones up in a tree, on a scaffold we build. That's our burial."

"Well, now, I can't even think of that. I want a proper Christian burial, Missus Skye."

She seemed almost to ignore him. "We wrap them tight in a robe or a blanket along with their spirit things, their medicine bundle, their bow and quiver, everything they need for their long journey. Then we lift them up, very gently, onto this platform we've lashed to a big tree, and sit beneath the tree awhile saying good-bye to the one whose name we must never speak again, for this person is on the spirit road.

"So we give this person not to the cold earth, but to the sun and the wind, the dews of night, the stars above, and the moon. We give this person to the blistering heat of summer, and the north winds of winter; to the rains of spring and fall, and the showers of summer, and the snows that settle over that robe and bury it in cold. So this person returns to the seasons, the air and wind, and sometime, long time maybe, these fall down and this person returns to dust, and becomes part of the earth again. Maybe this is good, eh?"

They sat there in the breeze-tossed grass, there beside LaBonte Creek. He couldn't say yes to this; he just couldn't. It wasn't the way he had lived and believed. And yet . . .

He stood, slowly, his aching lungs recovered for the moment, and lumbered slowly toward the sagging wagon, found the axe, returned with it, eyed some cottonwood saplings, and began to hew one down.

"You rest, sir," Mister Skye said, materializing at his side.

"I must do this. I'll let you do it in a minute. Or Mister Bright. The man is a genius with wood, you know. But let me cut this first sapling. It's my task, this first one."

Peacock soon felled a slim sapling, and carefully limbed it, and it felt right to do that. Then he handed the axe to Skye and settled on the ground to watch.

Swiftly Skye felled saplings while Victoria limbed them with her hatchet, and soon a platform grew in a majestic cottonwood whose limbs spread wide. Pole after pole was readied and lashed into the platform, until at last an open-air casket, its bottom wooden, its top the leaves above and the dome of heaven over that, was readied.

Peacock watched Victoria kneel beside the quiet body of Samantha, and realized the danger.

"Madam, no, don't risk your life," he said. "I will prepare her."

She looked up at him. "I am safe. We believe that when the breath is gone, the sickness is no longer there. Is there anything you wish to send to the spirit land with her?"

He thought of poor Samantha's small possessions, and remembered Emma's ring. Samantha's mother had given her a thin silver ring. "Yes, I'll get something for her to take with her."

He found Samantha's little bundle in the cart, found the ring, and brought it. Victoria ran it through a thong and tied the thong around the girl's neck.

"Samantha, this is for the husband and marriage you never had," he said.

"That is a good gift," Victoria said, straightening the girl's collar.

Then she drew the old blanket over Samantha and began a detailed binding, wrapping thong around and around, until Samantha had been encased.

"I will lift her," Peacock said.

Skye looked about to offer help, but this was something the merchant needed to do himself. The girl weighed nothing. She had shrunk to seventy pounds or so, and he found himself gently carrying the blue-blanketed form toward the great and comforting cottonwood, and then lifting her above his head and sliding her onto the poles.

Again he gestured Skye off, and worked Samantha's body around until it lay straight and true on its resting place.

The others materialized then, unbidden but knowing. Bright carried the Book. Skye summoned Victoria and they stepped back. Let the sick ones, the family and friends, gather close.

Peacock watched Skye and Victoria retreat, watched Mary and the child in the cradleboard join them perhaps thirty yards distant, and then Bright was ready.

"We have gathered here this hour to say good-bye to Samantha and wish her a good journey on her walk to the stars," Bright said.

Peacock stared, astonished.

"She will walk among the constellations, pass by the Big Dipper, and come to the North Star, that unmoving beacon in the heavens by which we set our compass and measure our progress through life. She will find others on the star-trail, maybe new friends like these who have guided us. She will not be alone as she walks. Someday she will become a bright star and we all will know which one, and see how she shines," Mister Bright said.

Hiram Peacock had never heard such a funeral oration, and listened to Enoch Bright sing a song as ancient as the wind.

fourteen

They rolled west that afternoon, and encountered few trains. The overburdened oxen required frequent rests, and during these interludes other companies passed them by. Yet there was none of the fear or dread in these trains that had oozed from the earlier ones. They waved cheerfully in passing, or one of their number paused to visit, exchange news, and learn what might lie ahead.

Skye reasoned that these later trains never got word, and didn't know about the consumptives. News did travel back and forth among the various wagon outfits nearby, but the New Bedford Company had fallen well behind the ones that had left Fort Laramie about the same time.

And something else: it was now very late to reach either California or Oregon. Any train that had come only this far west faced brutal Sierra snows or harsh Oregon winter. So these were stragglers, people slowed by problems like the Massachusetts company.

Still, there was trouble brewing. The weary livestock could not drag the wagon and cart much farther. Not even harnessing the remaining Morgan to help drag the wagon up hills helped. And there was more.

"Mister Skye, sir, we've been so slowed down that our larder is diminishing sadly. It's taking many more days than I was advised to prepare for."

"Then we'll have to go on half rations, Mister Peacock. If you're hoping we can hunt our way west, don't think it. There isn't a deer or antelope closer than ten miles each side of this road, if that."

"I take it we're still a month from Salt Lake," Peacock said.

"At least that. More if the livestock give out. But Bridger's Fort isn't so far."

Other companies passed by, and Skye took to bargaining with them. He offered the Sharps rifle for a span of oxen, but he got nowhere at all. One Tennessee captain, who seemed to know a thing or two, summed it up:

"Sirrah, you ain't get your head straight you think you can get livestock for that piece of steel. Oxen, they're the gold out heah. They's none. You have to get to Salt Lake to get oxen. The Mormons, they fatten them up. Soon as some train or other cuts wore-out oxen loose, the Saints git 'em and drive 'em down there to Deseret and put the feed to 'em. But they don't come cheap. No sirree. You'd better git ready to cut off an arm or a leg to buy a span of good fat oxen."

Then an apparition appeared. Two wagons, each drawn by six mules, racing west at a fast clip, the jingles on their collars singing a merry tune.

Skye intercepted them. He drew Jawbone alongside the lead wagon, where a gent with a battered straw hat and a corncob pipe and a tuft of beard held the lines, and his plump wife sat beside him.

"Mister Skye here, sir. I'm looking for livestock."

"Happy Mikaelsen here, my friend, and this is my little woman, Marletta. Now, I'm fresh out of livestock."

"But you're trailing a pair of mules behind the other wagon."

"Those are rotator mules, Mister Skye. There's always two mules hoofing it loose behind. Every couple hours, they go back into the collars and two more lucky cusses get to waltz a while."

"We need them and would buy them."

"Whole world needs 'em. No, Mister Skye."

"They're fat; how do you do that?"

"Oats. I says to the missus, we'll take oats and nothing more. Oats are a two-gaited chow, good for animals, or good for gruel. We got two boys to feed, and they get gruel. We got stock ain't getting much grass, so they get oats."

"But you'll run out soon," Skye said.

"Not until we hit the Columbia, and then those wagon beds turn into flatboats, and we're home."

"Over the falls?"

"They've got Injun porters, we're told. Portage around the falls. They get the mules for pay. Probably eat the whole lot for dinner."

Skye saw how this would go, and laughed. The mule-drawn wagons jingled ahead and were soon out of sight.

Skye slowed Jawbone and drifted back to his own lumbering company.

"No luck, Mister Peacock. I think you'd better plan on abandoning that wagon."

"We can't! That's the hospital. It's lighter than any cart on this road. Bright built it, hickory, ash, the planks planed down, the spokes lathed down, everything light as a spiderweb."

Skye saw how it would go. "All along this road we've seen discards, chests of drawers, trundle beds, trunks, tools, harness, anything to save weight. You'll need to throw out everything you can throw out before the oxen give in."

Peacock eyed Skye sharply. This was a familiar decision, a decision every company heading west had to face.

"I must do whatever is required for the sick, Mister Skye," Peacock said.

"Think on it," Skye said.

The North Platte oxbowed through arid flats carpeted with sage. These baked in the heat of July, making the air close and hard to breathe. Skye wondered how those young people could breathe when even healthy people found the hazy air unsatisfying. There were gnats and flies now, sometimes swarming over these helpless passengers who either lay in the cart or sat stoically on the tailgate of the wagon. A thunderhead built in the west, lost in white haze. Skye felt sweat pool under his arms and evaporate in the brutal dry.

Still they rolled west. The weary oxen plodded through thick powder, step by step, dragging the wagons behind them, slavering from open mouths, their tongues white and caked with clay. Bright was rotating the oxen, changing wheelers and leaders to even the load. But not even his careful management was keeping these overworked animals from sliding into exhaustion.

They halted at dusk at a place that had not seen an immigrant camp and had a little miserable grass poking from under the sagebrush. It lacked firewood but Skye thought he and his women might collect enough debris for a small quick fire. No other heat would be needed that evening when the heat lingered in every rock and the clay itself, and no fresh breeze brought the slightest relief.

His women did not raise the lodge; not a cloud lowered over them, and only the thunderheads over distant mountains even hinted at the possibility of rain. Skye didn't like the place. It seemed naked and defenseless. But he had, over a lifetime lived out-of-doors, ended up on thousands of such spots, alien and mean, but all that could be bought from the natural world before dark.

The youngsters who could walk headed for the river to wash away the miserable grit that caked their hair and faces and clothing. Skye watched them wend their breathless way to the bank, slide down to the much-diminished river, and hesitantly try to clean themselves. The Bridge sisters did it best, bravely splashing the murky water over themselves. Peter Sturgeon seemed worst. He slumped at the bank and stared into the turbid water, too exhausted to do his toilet. Anna Bennett, always one to do things her own way, stood at the stream bank and did nothing, and Skye intuited that she would perform her ablutions in the cloak of darkness.

Skye unsaddled Jawbone and led him down to the river and straight into it. Jawbone felt his way toward the middle, where current tugged at his hocks, and then slowly capsized until the water roiled over his back and neck, driving gnats and flies out of the mane. Jawbone, at least, knew how to deal with this oppressive heat. Eventually the great blue roan stood, shook, splashed to shore, and shook himself again, scattering a pleasant rain over Skye, who laughed. Jawbone snorted and bared his teeth in triumph.

Mary unlaced North Star from his cradleboard, cleaned his bottom with fragrant sage leaves, and let the child stretch on a buffalo robe, free at last from the binding that had pinned him for hours. Then she nursed him quietly, her gaze first on

Skye, then on her boy, and there was a small tender smile on her face.

The oxen drank, stood quietly in the water, their tails switching at flies, and then lumbered up to graze on the flat, their big snouts poking under the sagebrush to snap at grasses there. Skye's ponies spread out, ruthlessly tugging grass from the thickest sagebrush, somehow finding grass hiding under the prickly sage that most domestic animals would miss or ignore. The whirling flies and gnats and mosquitoes were terrible, pestering the horses as well as the whole company, but there was little anyone could do except dip neck-deep into the river.

A distant wagon train rolled by on the trail, not stopping to turn off at this unlikely place, but Skye could see that these people were curious about what fools might camp where there was no wood and so little grass, at least to the untrained eye.

Victoria watched them hurry on.

"They are all in such a hurry. What will they do when they get there? They will turn themselves into slaves. Dammit, Mister Skye, you belong to a mad people."

"We live in the future; you live in the present," he said. "They dream of gold."

But she was drawing lodgepoles out of the bundles they carried.

"I will make a travois for my pony, and I will walk," she said.

Skye nodded. There were no lodgepoles here and no place up the trail to cut them. If she began building travois, they could no longer raise their lodge. But it had to be done. A travois for her pony, another for the Morgan horse that Bright was using on upgrades, and the wagon could be lightened.

She laid out poles, dug into her rolls of thong, found her hatchet, and began chopping the crossbars. Skye took over that task while she bound the bars to the longest lodgepoles.

That drew Enoch Bright.

"Two travois," he said.

"One for my pony, and one for your Morgan," Victoria said testily. She had not consulted with him about using the Morgan to draw a travois.

"Three travois," Mary said. "The boy will ride on one. I will walk."

"Three?" He stared.

"It is good."

"Between four and five hundred pounds off the wagon, sir," Skye said.

Bright peered owlishly at them. "When I invent a fly-catching trap, you will get the first one."

fifteen

They reached one of those message centers that dotted the trail. This was a sandstone cliff and it was plastered with notices, mostly daubed on the rock with axle grease.

Some were instructions. Others were death notices or changes of plan: Eliza Jones, d. Aug 15, 1847. Ella, taking Hastings, Gilbert. Columbus Co. July 28, 1849. Amy Quill, go to Sacramento. Bloomfield Train, June 30, 1850. Lost Eddy, contact Vasquez, Bridger Fort.

Skye paused as he always did, learning what he could from what sufficed as a post office. Here people were lost and found, warnings were posted, deaths announced, and advice given.

Older messages had faded in the sun and wind and rain and were often overwritten by newer ones. A fresh one, the black stain of axle grease bold in the yellow rock. "Plague party ahead, Green Wagon. Many dead." It had a crudely drawn skull and crossbones.

Skye studied it, knowing trouble was brooding. Peacock pulled up beside him and spotted the new message.

"I'd hoped we were past that," he said.

Bright and the wagons appeared. The youngsters on the tailgates studied the cliff. Finally Skye's family.

"What the hell does it say?" Victoria asked.

Skye told her and Mary.

"Well, hell, we got grease and we cover it up."

It was a temptation. But the real trouble lay ahead, not behind. At Fort Bridger, probably, or at the Saints' Great Salt Lake City. Word traveled forward.

"Too late," Skye said.

Lloyd Jones, gaunt but still teamstering, studied the message. "I feel like I've been put into a debtors prison. There's no way out," he said.

"We'll push along," Peacock said. "Let's not borrow trouble."

The whale oil merchant had a steely resolve that Skye admired. They would deal with trouble as it came.

They drove west for several days. The oxen were slowly gaunting in spite of the lighter load, and Skye hoped fresher animals would be available at Fort Bridger, or at least some grain. He would trade that Sharps for fresh livestock or grain, whatever it took.

Twice more they found warnings against the plague company daubed into rocks, and once on the side of an abandoned wagon. Someone ahead was making a major case out of it, whipping up trouble. Each time they came across one of these warnings, the young people grew more and more distressed.

The Tucker twins burst into tears. Eliza and Mary Bridge could not comfort them. Sterling Peacock scowled, and threw pebbles at these terrible notices, daubed in oversized letters in an effort to dominate the message areas. Pete Sturgeon, too weak to do much but lie in the green wagon, learned of it and buried his head under his blanket. But Anna Bennett was a different sort.

"Next camp we see, I'll go visiting and watch them run from the wicked witch," she said.

No one laughed.

Skye stared helplessly from a distance. The quarantine separating him and his family from these consumptives was carefully observed by the sick and the well. Skye and his women were washing themselves far more than usual too.

Victoria needed to have each sign read to her; not just the ones warning of a plague party, but the rest. She was a great student of the ways of European people. But Mary absorbed herself with her son, with cooking and camp-tending, and keeping the travois loads balanced.

Few parties passed them because they were the stragglers now, and only one company seemed to notice the green wagon. They whispered to one another, pointed, and hurried past while Peacock's little company rested beside a tributary creek. Maybe it would come to nothing, Skye thought. Most of these companies bound for California or Oregon were, after all, far ahead now.

July days, and then August days slipped by without incident. By traveling slowly, resting frequently, and sparing the oxen as much as possible, they struggled westward without any breakdowns. If even one ox died or failed, they would be out of luck. Fort Bridger loomed ahead like heaven itself. It would be the place to trade worn oxen for fresh. There would be blacksmith services, wheelwrights, skilled men with tools, as well as everything anyone would need, all for sale. The post had been started by the old mountain man Jim Bridger and his partner Luis Vasquez, but the Mormons had gotten hold of it and now ran it as a lucrative business catering to the migrants. Just now it looked like some sort of heaven to Skye.

According to the gossip along the trail, the Mormons were trading two worn oxen for one rested ox, which Peacock could not afford, but the Sharps would make the difference. Skye was prepared to trade it for two rested oxen and wouldn't take less. That Sharps was some gun, all right. He wished he could keep it, but the welfare of the company came first.

They reached the Sweetwater, struggled through Devil's Gate, entered a land of slopes that wore hard on the oxen, a land denuded of grass by the migration. The livestock starved. Still they struggled west along the one little river in all the West that enabled the migrants to go to Oregon and California. They were climbing now, but so subtly that the Massachusetts people barely noticed, though Skye observed the distant peaks of the Wind River range. This was a naked land, inhospitable, barren, and cruel. The higher they progressed, the less able the young people were to breathe. The air in this high country was thin and unsatisfying, and the consumptives suffered.

Then one day Skye halted the party on a barren slope. Far to the north lay high country; off to the south the land was enveloped in white haze.

"This is South Pass, the continental divide," he said. "You hardly notice. From here, the waters run to the Pacific. We'll start descending to Little Sandy Creek, and then we have a bad stretch we must cross at night. Then we'll drop into the Green River valley, and it'll be heaven. But I must warn you. We're in for some tough going. The sick will have to walk or the livestock will quit and die."

They stared solemnly at him, absorbing more bad news.

They started downslope in windless heat, the sun's blast radiating from the very earth. Soon they were parched. Skye urged them onward.

"We'll hit the Little Sandy soon. You can see the valley from here even if you can't see the creek," he said.

But those around him could see nothing in the white heat haze. He rode onward. At least the oxen didn't have to pull hard; not the way they had toiled up the long slopes to South Pass. The country was so large it seemed frightening, and there were brooding clouds over distant mountains, waiting to pounce on the unwary.

The heat was oppressive, and in spite of the dry air, man and ox sweated. The trail was so well worn here it cut a deep notch in the desert. They were never out of sight of debris, abandoned cargo left by desperate companies. Peacock took to looking for food in all the junk, especially grain or flour, but wily captains of other trains had raided the discards for every useful thing.

They rolled into the anonymous valley where Big Sandy Creek ran, barely two feet wide but still cool, cool water. Skye turned his party upstream a little, hoping for grass but found nothing. They would water here, rest, and then tackle the long night passage to the Green River valley.

The oxen and Skye's ponies slowly lapped up the water and kept their muzzles in it, tonguing it occasionally, sometimes standing in the same spot for ten or twelve minutes at a time. Then they stood still, miserable, their eyes accusing their owners of starving them.

Two other trains came and went, but Skye waited for the cool of evening, waited for his animals to recover as much as possible in that cruel heat. Then at twilight he steered them west across a blinding white desert. There would be no water until the next day sometime, depending on how fast they moved. He had a canteen. Peacock had one small cask, mostly for his sick young people. There wouldn't be enough to water any animal in a meaningful way.

They were lucky. A chill August breeze descended out of distant mountains, freshening the air, invigorating the stock, and even helping the consumptives a little. They all did better than Skye imagined they could, plodding through starlight, and then by the light of a thin moon, into the unknown. At times Skye could barely see the trail but it had been carved so deeply into the caliche that he was never lost for long. As the sun lit the east, they descended into a branching valley, ever downward, past arid cliffs, and finally, in the middle of morning, into the lush valley of the Green River. Somehow, miraculously, they had survived intact. He once again turned them away from the trail, hoping to find good grass. There wasn't much, but it would do. They spent most of that day recovering beside this River Jordan that had become their salvation and baptismal font.

Skye thought to put a few miles on that evening, and they progressed through complex country, with the trail branching off in various directions, cutoffs, shortcuts, who knew where?

He was feeling pretty good. That dry run to the Green River was probably the cruelest lap of the trip, and now it was behind them. Ahead, not far, lay Bridger's Fort, brimming with salvation and hope and renewal.

Then they hit another sign, daubed on the turnoff that would take them to Salt Lake City. This was the famous Hastings Cutoff, which steered the California-bound trains south and into a waterless desert that was brutal on livestock, especially now when the heat was high. It was a graveyard to many a dream and hope, but it could save time if a traveler was superbly equipped with grain and water and fresh stock.

A sign had been erected there to guide travelers. "Welcome, friend. Bridger's Fort straight ahead. Oregon stay right. Hastings Cutoff straight ahead. California via Spanish Trail, straight. We have what you need."

"First friendly sign I've seen in a while, Mister Skye."

"Maybe we'll get some oxen," Skye said. "The Mormons are looking for business."

sixteen

*F*ort Bridger occupied a verdant valley watered by Black's Fork of the Green River. It was a bonanza for whoever operated it; the only outfitting and supply post west of Fort Laramie, heavily patronized by overland travelers.

Skye eyed it sourly from a distance, noting that the Saints had not improved it. It slouched somnolently in the August sunlight, without the slightest sign of life. It was a ramshackle quadrangle of utility buildings, and if it had once been fortified, the defenses had long since fallen away. But the flat before it showed signs of heavy use. Its naked clay was littered with debris, dung, and the remains of hundreds of cook fires.

Skye halted Jawbone and studied the post, finding nothing to alarm him. He motioned to Peacock, and the New Bedford Company made its slow way down a long slope to the rippling river, and followed a worn trail on its bank to the post. This was a good place, generous and comfortable, watered by snowmelt from the mountains. It sat strategically on the junction of several great trails west, to Oregon or California via the

Hastings Cutoff, or to southern California via the old Spanish Trail.

A few years earlier the Mormons had driven old Gabe Bridger out, with warrants for his arrest for supposedly selling powder and lead to the Indians. And soon after, they bought out his partner, Vasquez, and took over. The whole Mormon rationale was a little too convenient for Skye's tastes. Whatever actually happened, the Saints held the post now, and did a lucrative business there, outfitting the endless procession of wagon companies heading west each summer.

"Looks all right. Let's go on in," Skye said.

"I'm weary of trouble," Peacock replied. "But I see no warnings here. Nothing but a long flat."

They proceeded along the crystalline river, admiring the glowing valley, and eventually drew up before the silent fort. But now the quiet was broken by the clanging of a hammer on steel. Enoch Bright halted the hospital wagon, and the Jones brothers pulled up the supply wagon, and the young people began to tumble down to the clay and stretch in the sweet sunlight.

"I imagine you and I ought to go in ahead of the others," Skye said to Peacock.

"That is wise."

Skye slid off Jawbone and turned him loose. The ugly roan yawned, stretched, clacked his teeth, and eyed the world suspiciously. Skye and Peacock hiked through the silence, entering the post through a gap between log and adobe buildings, and found themselves in a large yard, naked of even one blade of grass.

But in the center was a forge, with bellows, and at the forge was a burly smith, hammering a red-hot shoe over an anvil.

The man was as powerful as any Skye had ever seen, his broad chest and shoulders ox-strong. A mop of black hair topped him, and a close-cropped jet beard largely hid his face. Obsidian eyes added to the man's darkness.

If he noticed Skye and Peacock's approach, he did not let on to it, but continued to hammer at the horseshoe. Skye saw at once that the smith was widening the heels of the shoe, and expertly employing the various surfaces of the anvil to achieve his goal. The bony spotted horse whose hoof was being fitted, tied to a post, yawned.

Not until the smith was satisfied with his task did he acknowledge the visitors. He lifted the hot shoe with tongs, plunged it into a water bucket, causing spitting and steam, and then laid the shoe on the brick forge.

"I suppose you're the plague party they've been telling me about," he said.

The voice seemed to rise out of the man's belly.

"Yes, sir," Peacock said. "New Bedford, Massachusetts."

"Well, you aren't Saints," the man said.

"No, we're heading for the desert, where my patients hope to be healed by the climate."

The smith nodded, dipped his hands into the water bucket, and shook them off. "You don't look sick," he said.

"The sick are in our wagons, or near them. We keep them apart," Peacock said.

The smith studied Skye. "I've heard of you," he said.

"I'm Barnaby Skye, sir. And you?"

"Morton Rockwell."

They did not shake hands. Skye thought the man's hands could crush every bone in his own, and was grateful.

"I run the post," Rockwell added.

"We're interested in some trading."

Rockwell smiled for the first time, revealing great gaps in his incisors. "Fat chance," he said.

"Because we're a party of the sick?"

"No, because you're the last of the litter. No one heading for Oregon or California's going to get close to there, this late. There's not a thing on my shelves. Go wake up the clerk. Heber Smoot. He's napping on the counter."

"Not a thing? No food?"

Rockwell shrugged. "I've been bought out. We've had four hundred, five hundred wagons this year."

"We have great need, sir," Peacock said.

"So do they all. So do we."

"We?"

"The Latter-Day Saints. We arrived here with nothing. We still have nothing. Let those who starved us eat stone."

Peacock swallowed a response.

The smith gingerly lifted the cool horseshoe and set it down quickly. It was still too hot to touch. "The company ahead of you warned me about you. They said you spread sickness. Plague. People die at every campsite. You would bring a plague down on the Saints."

Some sort of furnace heat radiated from the smith's face, as if he were working himself into a temper.

"Trail talk," Skye said.

The smith smiled suddenly. "I thought so. They were Pukes. Big company of Pukes."

"You'll need to educate me about that word, sir," Peacock said.

"Pukes. Missouri scum, Illinois scum, thugs who killed our prophet Joseph Smith, killed the Saints, mothers and daughters, sons and fathers, and drove us away with only the clothes on our backs. Pukes. They hung around here outfitting, and then they left. I charged them double. Haven't seen another company since, until you. They talked about you."

"Trail talk," said Skye.

"Disease. The Pale Horse of the Apocalypse. Made it sound like you're the ones who'll destroy the Saints. Well?"

"We're passing through, sir," Peacock said.

The smith stared out at the two wagons sagging outside the post, at the sick young people sitting on the clay, waiting for word. "What is it you need?" he asked.

"Food and fresh stock," Skye said.

The smith smiled darkly. "Right off the shelves."

"We're slowed down. Someone shot my prized Morgan horse. We need a yoke of fresh oxen," Peacock said.

"I have none. I'm cleaned out of every spare animal. I've nary a nag nor a mule nor an ox."

"I have something valuable to trade, sir," Skye said. "A new Sharps rifle."

"A Sharps? Did you say a Sharps?"

"I did. It was used by someone to shoot Mister Peacock's Morgan horse."

The smith smiled. "The Pukes told me to confiscate any Sharps that was offered to me. Someone stole it from them."

Skye drew the weapon from Jawbone's saddle sheath. "This?" he said.

"That."

"Who told you that?"

"Their guide. Manville. He's taking them to the coast."

Peacock snorted.

"Did this Manville have anything wrong with his shoulder?" Skye asked.

"No, but the other one, Trimble, had his arm in a sling. It was Trimble's Sharps, I think."

"That explains a lot, Mister Rockwell."

"What's it explain?"

"Who shot the Morgan horse. I nearly knocked the man out of the saddle. Hit him in the shoulder. It was dark. I picked up the Sharps after he fled."

"Pukes," said Rockwell. "Big bunch of Pukes. Two days ahead of you. Their captain is a Puke named Fancher."

The smith lifted the horseshoe and held on to it now, turning it in his big scarred hands. He lifted a hind foot of the tied-up horse, and pressed the shoe to the hoof. It looked good. Then he straightened.

"I don't have any animal I can trade. I had a few we picked up and rested, but they went fast. But maybe I can do something for you. I got a few bags of oats. You want to buy some oats? Keep your stock going with some oats?"

"I would," Peacock said at once.

"Five dollars a bag."

Peacock paled. "Five, you say?"

"Five."

"But I have to buy food for the sick when we get to Great Salt Lake. I only have fifteen dollars."

"Five."

"Buy three bags, Mister Peacock," Skye said. "We'll make do."

Peacock stared sharply at Skye, pulled the bank notes out of his purse, and handed them to the smith.

Rockwell steered them toward a warehouse door, opened it, and pointed toward stacked burlap bags of grain.

"Take four," he said. "Three for your oxen and horses, and one for the sick."

seventeen

Hiram Peacock thought of himself as a shepherd. He was herding a flock to better pasture. Now the trail to Great Salt Lake took his little company through verdant meadowland, but ahead was the formidable range of mountains that guarded the Saints' capital from the rest of the country. Soon the weary oxen would be dragging the two wagons up steep grades. At least there would be ample grass and water, and a few oats to fuel them.

Sometimes Peacock rode the Morgan horse now that it was no longer harnessed. He had walked clear from Independence, blistering his feet, and nearly ruining them. But he had ignored the cruel pain, and eventually his bloodied and pulpy feet had healed after a fashion, but he still walked on aching feet, and sometimes in blood. Mere pain would not stay him from his appointed task, which was to shepherd his ill congregation to a place of healing.

The company had fallen into a pattern. Skye and his women and travois ponies led, and at a safe distance, the wagons followed. Peacock chose to walk this morning, at least until his feet howled at him. So he fell in beside the Jones brothers, teamstering the oxen, one on either side. David and Lloyd were the least afflicted of his consumptives and were a godsend because they helped make camp, yoke and unyoke the oxen, and care for the desperate. Still, Lloyd in particular was subject to convulsive coughing, and he stained an old rag pink with pieces of his lungs.

"How are the oxen, Lloyd?" Peacock asked.

"The off ox in the middle yoke's in trouble, sir."

And so it was. It was doing little actual work and laboring heavily slightly behind its mate, slowing the team. Bad news. They could not afford to lose another draft animal.

"What do you think, Lloyd?"

"It's done for."

All they could do would be to cut it loose and let the remaining five oxen drag the two wagons—until they all dropped. They were on level valley ground, but before the day was out they would begin the ascent. The proper course would be to cut the worn ox loose, abandon the second wagon, and try to make it to Great Salt Lake with two yokes plus one reserve ox tied behind.

"I would like to try something, sir. Put the worn yoke in the lead. This ox perks up with he's out front. It's his nature. He doesn't like eating dust."

Peacock knew plenty of men just like that.

"We'll stop here. We'll do it."

Peacock strode ahead to catch up with Skye and tell him what was afoot. This was a good place to halt, with grass and water.

"Jawbone's like that too," Skye replied.

So the struggling company stopped, and the Jones brothers

watered and briefly grazed the stock, fed the lagging ox a charge of oats, and then made that yoke the leaders. The sick young people wandered to the river, soaked up sun, and clambered into the light wagon or settled on their tailgates.

The result of Lloyd Jones's scheme was astonishing. The lagging ox turned himself into the king of the world and bulled forward as if he owned the trail and never slowed for the next hours.

"Lloyd, you've worked a miracle," Peacock said.

"He's still bad worn," Jones said.

"There are people who'd wear themselves to the nub for something they want badly," Peacock said. "That ox wanted to lead. You want to get well more than anything else on earth, and so you're walking across a continent."

Bright joined them. "That ox has steam in the boiler," he said. "There's food fuel, and there's spirit fuel. He's running on spirit fuel."

"How's the hospital wagon, Enoch?"

"It is self-propelled, Captain."

Peacock laughed.

Bright peered earnestly at his employer. "I swear, sir, the desire of those within it is so large that it propels the wagon. Each young person has only one dream, to reach the place where their lungs might heal. I swear, you could unhitch that wagon and it would slowly roll west, propelled by a force beyond reckoning."

Peacock almost believed him. For a mechanic who loved pulleys and cogwheels, Bright had an oddly adventuresome mind.

Mary Bridge slipped off a tailgate and joined them. She was one of the luckier ones because her consumption came and went, sometimes leaving her feverish, but just as often it seemed to vanish. Just now she was doing well, and her square face didn't seem flushed with fever, the way it sometimes did.

She smiled at Lloyd. "I hear you breathed life into a dead ox," she said.

"He's still pretty far gone," he replied. "But he likes to have all the rest behind him."

"I'm going to walk a little," she said. "You mind?"

"We'll walk to the desert," he replied. "You and I."

Peacock was relieved that all of his company got along with one another. United, they could work miracles. Young Jones had taken a shine to Mary, that was plain.

But as swiftly as she had vacated a seat on the tailgate, David Jones had commandeered it. There was never enough room. It had been worse at first, when there were twelve young people struggling to breathe. But now three were gone . . .

Peacock brushed aside thought of Samantha, lying so still on a scaffold in a cottonwood tree.

This was good country, somewhat arid because the great chain of the Uinta Mountains to the west wrung rain from the heavens. Nothing but ruts told travelers where to go. But those fateful ruts led straight to the next oasis, Great Salt Lake, and they passed through some of the handsomest mountain country in the great West. Ahead rose cobalt mountains, and over them hung puffballs in an azure sky. It was good to be alive at that very moment.

Peacock hastened forward a little to study that amazing gray ox, which had transformed itself into a new animal. It was gaunt. Its haunches were hollowed. Its ribs showed. Its muscles rippled directly under taut flesh. It set the pace, a nose or two ahead of its yoke-mate, proud to be leading the procession.

"I suppose I should call you Christopher Carson Ox," he said. "Out in front, are you? What did it? Was it nutrition? No, not a few oats. Medicine? We haven't doctored you. Yet it was something, something in your ox head that transformed you. I wish I knew what it was. If I knew, I would know the secret of life," he said.

This was becoming a spiritual odyssey, though he couldn't quite say how or why. He had seen the trip purely in practical terms. How did one get a dozen sick and fevered consumptives safely and easily to the desert, and build them a sanctuary there where the soft air would heal them? So he had dealt with it in such a fashion. Get just the right wagons. Just the right livestock. Just the right equipment. Just the right guide. It had been all logistics and calculation, and now this proud gray ox, worn down to muscle and bone, was telling him there was more to life than logic.

He felt almost liberated, as if he were freeing himself from every habit of thought that had imprisoned him for all his years as a coal and oil merchant. Now, suddenly, he was in a world of will and spirit and liberty.

Ahead, Skye's women stopped at a creekside meadow for the nooning and a rest, while Skye pushed ahead to see what lay there, as Skye usually did. The guide took a hard look at every place they stopped, wanting no surprises. This was a benign country and a benign day, and yet Skye never lowered his guard. Peacock wondered whether Skye was overdoing it a little. What harm could befall them? They had scarcely seen a living person since leaving Bridger's Fort, and had seen no Indians at all.

He watched Mary Bridge help the youngest and sickest of the group down to the creek bank where they could sip cool water, wash their faces, refresh themselves. She had been a godsend, a young women brimming with maternal love for those even less fortunate. It was Mary who helped the stumbling, coughing Peter Sturgeon through his daily ordeal; Mary who looked after the Tucker twins, and helped bathe Ashley when she was too weak. But it was also Mary who heartened the youngsters, told them that they soon would be healing, reminded them that they had conquered another day of travel.

His own son, Sterling, was the paternal one among these desperate youngsters. Now Sterling was helping Grant Tucker refresh himself. Grant Tucker had coughed himself down to a skeleton and was too weak to walk, so Sterling had looked after the boy.

They were all living on willpower, all wrestling with the cough, the fevers, the unending pain, the bouts of despair that made them want to curl up and die. It was only hope that kept them going. Somewhere at rainbow's end would be a magical place where they could breathe again, and clamber out of their beds without gasping for air, and enjoy a meal, and walk without agony, and maybe believe there would be a tomorrow.

Anna Bennett was the different one. From the start, she had insisted on caring for herself, letting no one do a thing for her. It was as if her pride was affronted by the disease that sapped her, and she would not surrender to it. Anna stayed much the cleanest, laundered her clothing, washed her hair, combed her dark locks fiercely, and found pride in her ability to fight back. She wasn't a loner, and remained perfectly companionable, and yet there was something that set her apart, something that rejected the communal. During the meals, she often ate by herself, and then fiercely scrubbed her tin mess ware, as if to announce that she would never be a liability or burden to anyone.

Peacock watched her now as she shook out her blankets, scrubbed a spare bonnet, and cleaned her battered shoes.

Then, all too soon, the nooning was over, and Skye's women were collecting the ponies. With luck, they would reach the foothills of the Uinta Mountains by evening. There was something about this day, and their good progress, and the competence of their guide, Skye, that filled Hiram Peacock with optimism. Soon they would settle on the Virgin River, and begin the great healing.

eighteen

As dusk approached, Skye hunted for a good campground. There was wood smoke in the breeze, which made him uneasy. But this was fine camping country, with ample grass and firewood and a rushing creek. Even the weather was perfect, the temperature swiftly falling after a hot afternoon. Except for a few clouds lanced by the Uinta Mountains, the sky was clear.

He rode ahead of the infirmary company, and finally settled on a pleasant meadow that ran alongside the rushing creek. It had been much used by travelers on the Mormon Trail, but it was one of those watered places where the grass sprang back as fast as it was grazed. Cottonwoods, aspens, willows, and jack pine crowded nearby slopes along with juniper and sagebrush.

He signaled to his wives, who were not far behind, and then steered Jawbone along the trail, wanting to know all about the wood smoke. It didn't take long. Once he rounded a bend, he beheld an even larger and greener valley, and here, on both sides of the little creek, were scores of wagons, their white wagon sheets making them look like giant boulders strewn everywhere. This was no small company. At a great distance he saw people wandering everywhere, busy with their evening chores, for the burdens of overland travel did not cease when the wagons stopped rolling.

Even from Skye's perspective, it was plain this was a westbound party, and a large one. And that posed the usual problem. Should he and Hiram Peacock act as ambassadors once again, and let this great party know of the presence of some consumptives? Sometimes that was the right and diplomatic thing to do; but Skye had seen it work badly too. What pained him worse was the possibility that this was the giant train that Rockwell had warned him about, with Millard Manville and his crony, Jimbo Trimble, guiding.

So far, he had not been seen. He quietly turned Jawbone and vanished around the bend, sensing that maybe the best course was to camp obscurely a way back and simply avoid trouble altogether.

He found Peacock settling in. He used a bedroll and slept outside whenever the weather permitted, and under a wagon or sometimes in the supply wagon when the weather was troublesome.

"There's a big camp up the road. Forty or fifty wagons, a lot of people."

"Well then, we must visit them."

"I'm not sure we should, Mister Peacock. I think this is the Missouri crowd that Rockwell warned us about. And Millard Manville and his crony are guiding it. We might well just hunker down and avoid trouble."

"I wouldn't think of it. This whole trip, candidness has served us well. Companies didn't like to camp near us, but at least they were not surprised. And besides, it's the thing to do."

Skye held his peace. Peacock lived by his code, and now he would adhere to his code, no matter what the result.

"All right. You want to saddle that Morgan?"

Peacock swiftly caught the Morgan horse and soon was ready to go.

"We're going to visit the camp up there," Skye told Victoria. She stared, her eyes flinty.

But just as they were about to ride up the creek, two horsemen appeared out of the twilight, coming from the camp above. Skye waited quietly. Camping companies always wanted to know who their neighbors were.

"I believe we've saved ourselves a trip, Mister Peacock," he said.

The two horsemen approached in a leisurely manner, and Skye could make out the brims of slouch hats and the relaxed forms of experienced horsemen. Then, as the pair drew near, Skye knew who his guests were: his Fort Laramie rival, Millard Manville, and his flunky, Jimbo Trimble. This would not be a friendly visit. Skye noted that Trimble kept his left arm in a sling fashioned from a black bandanna. No indeed, not a friendly contact from a neighboring camp.

"Gentlemen?" Skye said.

"So it's you. We thought so," Manville said easily as they dismounted. The perpetual smile was on his freckled face.

"I'm most pleased that you've come by," Peacock said, dismounting. He offered his hand to Manville, who shook it.

Skye waited warily for trouble, but it didn't seem to materialize.

"I've been hoping you'd come for a visit," Peacock continued. "Perhaps you can tell me what's ahead."

"We're just looking things over," Manville said. "Those sick people, are they getting along?"

"It's hard for them, Mister Manville. But I've never seen such courage. They're going to get where we're going."

Trimble had said nothing, and his gaze roved everywhere, finally settling on Jawbone, who stood saddled near Skye, his ears laid-back. He knew an enemy when he saw one.

Light from Victoria's cook fire was swiftly replacing the twilight, as the world turned darker.

Trimble finally pointed at Jawbone, a gesture that Manville picked up at once; he nodded slightly.

"Looks like you've got a Sharps there in that sheath, Skye."

"I do. And I prefer to be addressed as Mister."

Trimble was looking itchy now, and Skye sensed what was unfolding.

"Well, now, I think that's my Sharps. Same brass patchbox in the stock. Most likely it is. It was stolen from me, plumb stolen when I wasn't looking."

"You accusing me, Mister Trimble?"

Manville stood ready, and Skye knew a confrontation was brewing.

"Well, I'm just getting my property back."

"And how do you suppose I got it, if it's yours?"

"Now that's a real question, ain't it? Likely someone made off with it."

"Are you calling me the thief, Trimble?"

Trimble licked his lips and glanced at Manville. It would be Manville's play, with Trimble's arm laid up like that.

Manville smiled easily. "Seems to me, Skye, you should hand it back. A guide taking these nice folk out to the desert really should be a little more careful about how he conducts himself, don't you think?"

"Trimble, your arm's laid up. What happened?" Skye asked.

"I took a fall," he replied. "Now do I get my property back, or do we push a little, Skye?"

"You push."

"Now see here, Mister Skye, if this man's Sharps is in your possession, it behooves you to return it," Peacock said.

Skye ignored him.

"Shoot horses, do you? Shoot a prize Morgan horse, do you? Try to strand some sick people in the wilderness, do you?"

"This is the man?" Peacock asked.

Skye discovered a massive Colt Dragoon revolver in Trimble's fist, aimed squarely at himself.

"Hand over my Sharps, Skye," Trimble said.

Manville was grinning, his hand in the pocket of his duck cloth jacket.

Peacock exploded. "You shot my horse? What sort of wretch are you! You destroyed a great horse. You've endangered my party! You scoundrel, I'll have your hide. I'll report you to authorities and see you punished. When we reach Salt Lake, mark my words, you'll see irons on your legs."

Trimble's revolver never wavered, its muzzle squarely on Skye, even as Peacock bulled toward the man, the tails of his frock coat flapping.

Then everything happened at once. Manville stepped forward, brought that brutal fist up into Peacock's gut, just under the ribs. That diverted Trimble long enough for Skye to land on Trimble, slug him even as a shot sailed by, wrench Trimble's good arm and spill the revolver, and then kick Manville, who was aiming another blow at the toppling Peacock.

Let them see a limey seaman in a brawl. He snatched the Dragoon revolver and hammered Trimble's head with the barrel, lashed at Manville, who was no longer smiling, and landed another blow on Trimble's ear and another on his bad shoulder, which set Trimble howling. He lowered his head and battered that handsome Manville with it, knocking Manville over even as the guide tried to wrestle a weapon out of his pocket. Skye's moccasin smacked Manville's hand. Skye heard something crunch. Manville quit, lay on his back panting, his handsome face gazing at evening stars.

Trimble sat stupidly, holding his ruined shoulder and sobbing.

But Peacock was on his back, his face distorted into a horrible grimace, unable to breathe.

Skye yanked a Navy revolver from Manville's pocket, checked the other pockets, and then handed it and the big Dragoon to Victoria, who rushed to the scene, a nocked arrow in her bow.

Mary collected Manville's and Trimble's horses and led them away.

"You've just donated your horses to my company," Skye said. "And the two won't repay the loss of the Morgan. Now clear out of here."

But both of the guides were too battered to move.

Watching them warily, Skye turned to Peacock, whose paralyzed body writhed on the ground. Skye leaned over him. "Breathe?" he asked.

Peacock couldn't. Skye remembered what Manville's punch had done to him back at Fort Laramie. Peacock stared up, bug-eyed, desperate. Skye squeezed Peacock's chest, and again, rhythmically, until at last Hiram Peacock coughed and breathed, the air sucking in and out in desperate convulsions. Manville's fist had very nearly killed Hiram Peacock.

Skye turned to the two guides. "Start walking. Don't come back. Expect worse if you do."

Manville shakily got up. Trimble didn't. He sat holding his ruined arm, whining. Skye yanked him up, amid a long wail.

"Go," he said. "Or die."

nineteen

kye didn't dare to move Hiram Peacock. The merchant hovered on the knife-edge. His breathing quit for long stretches, only to spasm to life, a desperate sucking and expelling of air. Manville's fist had torn something to pieces in the old man.

Victoria and Mary stared, ready at any instant to pump the merchant's chest, squeeze air out, and hope his desperate lungs sucked more in.

Somehow the sick ones at the other campfire absorbed the events, and soon Sterling Peacock appeared out of the gloom, staring at his father sprawled over meadow grass.

"Pa!" He turned to Skye. "Pa's hurt!"

Hiram Peacock coughed blood.

"What happened?" Sterling whispered.

"Manville and his flunky, Trimble. Tried to get the Sharps back. I dealt with them. But Manville got to your father. It's bad," Skye said roughly.

"How bad?"

"Manville's got a trick. Fist up that pocket below the ribs.

It kills. It almost killed me, and I was watching for it, but I never thought Manville would use it on an old man." Skye saw the shock in Sterling's face. "I'm bloody sorry, mate."

Sterling knelt beside his father, watching the older man struggle for each breath.

"Can't move him," Skye said. "We'll cover him up and he'll stay right here. We're going to have to watch tonight, and hope he starts breathing right."

"I could help you lift him into a wagon, Mister Skye."

"If it rains, I'll ask you. You can help by taking one of the watches. If he struggles for air, you'll need to press on his chest."

Victoria emerged from the gloom with Peacock's bedroll, which she laid out, and then stepped back from Sterling. Skye and Sterling gently slid the merchant onto one blanket and folded the other over him. Peacock convulsed, coughed, and caught some air.

Sterling settled beside his father, two lonely figures at the edge of firelight.

Skye and his women and his little boy rested quietly around their own fire. The women had not erected the lodge this mild night but soon they would. The nights were lengthening, and they could expect autumnal rains anytime.

Enoch Bright showed up. "I've fed the sick, and now what do you want me to do?"

"Pump his bellows," Skye said.

"The scum," Bright said. "I'll bring them to justice."

"Pump," Skye said. Bright gingerly reached over his employer and pressed on the lungs. Peacock convulsed, gasped, sucked in air, and coughed.

"That's it. Keep him going, and pray that nature takes over," Skye said.

"I wish I had a galvanic battery to shock him," Bright said. "I'd give him regular shocks."

"Stay here two hours. Then we'll get someone else," Skye said.

The Jones brothers took the next watch later in the evening, after Skye had come to them with his request. First Lloyd, and then David, stared at the desperate man, whose irregular breaths were alarming. Skye taught them not to permit the silences to go too long. Contract the man's lungs and keep on doing it if they quit.

Skye drifted over to the other campfire, where they gazed solemnly up at him. No one had gone to bed. He saw fear in every face. The man who would take them all to a healing place was in trouble.

"Hiram Peacock's in grave condition," he said. "We need to keep him going. We think he'll be better in the morning."

"What happened?" Anna Bennett asked.

Skye told her as forcefully as he could. It never helped to soften reality. He needed to prepare them for the worst.

She absorbed it quietly. "I'll pump his lungs all night," she said.

"I've arranged watches. If I need you I'll certainly call on you."

"You don't trust a woman," she said.

Skye felt worn-out and ignored her. He doffed his top hat and returned to his campfire, where Peacock lay in his bedroll.

The wounded man was conscious, staring up at Skye. Beside him sat Enoch Bright.

"Take me to the summit," Peacock said. "Show me the desert. Let me see the desert, the healing place, and I will find peace."

"You'll be well soon, Mister Peacock."

"Let me see the desert before I die."

Skye knelt beside the man. "I will," he said.

Peacock spasmed again and closed his eyes.

Enoch Bright wept.

By turns they watched over Hiram Peacock that night, several times pressing his lungs to work, restoring breath to him when it faltered. Manville's fist had done terrible damage, and now Peacock hung by a thread to this world.

But dawn came, and he lived, and with the dawn the last of the watch, David Jones, stood and stretched. There were the usual morning duties, and a meal to prepare.

Faintly on the breeze, they heard the other wagon party hitch up and plod west. Skye did not hasten to follow. He had not yet decided how to carry Hiram Peacock. Probably the gentlest place would be a nest hollowed out of the supplies in the large wagon. Maybe the steady rocking of the wagon would induce breath in Peacock. Or maybe it would kill him. But for the moment, the man who had formed this mission of mercy still lived.

Quietly they yoked the oxen, put packsaddles on ponies, prepared to head west once again. Skye and Bright made a pallet in the supply wagon for their stricken leader, and gently lifted him into it. Peacock coughed, and a film of blood slid from his lips. There was some sort of internal bleeding. And yet he lived. Anna Bennett slipped into that wagon beside him, ready to press the man's chest anytime she thought he was too long comatose. And then they were ready.

Skye headed back to the sick young people.

"We're going now," he said. "We have Mister Peacock on a pallet, and he's being watched every moment. He wants us to keep on going. He told me so. I want you to keep on going, for his sake as well as your own. Soon we'll reach the desert."

None of them spoke. Skye knew they were recoiling from the possibility of Peacock's death, finding themselves out here, far from everything, without their protector.

Skye clambered onto Jawbone, but was stayed. The horse's ears were rotated backward, and then Jawbone craned his long neck around. There was something approaching from behind.

Skye turned to meet whatever was toiling up the grade, and was met with the sound of harness jingles, all of them making a merry tune to the rhythm of the draft animals. Here was a whole wagon company, but unlike any Skye had seen. A couple of gents in slouch hats were leading the parade, which consisted of a dozen freight wagons with high sides, or flatbed wagons. Only one had a bowed canvas top. And poking from these wagons were all sorts of furniture and household goods.

The lead man halted.

"You're Mister Skye," he said. "Recognized this outfit."

"I am, and who am I addressing?"

"Pete Hunsaker, Great Salt Lake City. I'm in the furniture business. Call it the scavenger business."

"You're harvesting the debris from the trails, I take it."

"That's it. It's worth a fortune in my town. Good furniture's rare in the desert, a thousand miles from anywhere else. So's most everything else. I make a good living at it."

"So I see," Skye said.

There were half a dozen men involved in this enterprise. No doubt all of them Saints.

"You got a bunch of sick with you," Hunsaker said.

"Consumptives, sir. We're taking them to the desert. There's some evidence that dry warm air heals them."

Hunsaker grinned. "From what I heard, you're spreading the Black Plague hither and yon."

"It's not transmitted that easily, and the sick keep their own mess and stay apart."

Hunsaker eyed the company. "You've got trouble here," he said. "Two wagons hooked to three span."

Skye nodded. "Plenty of trouble."

"Those saddle horses. Seems to me I saw them recent."

"It's a long story," Skye said. "We acquired them as compensation for some losses we suffered."

Hunsaker was grinning broadly, baring gapped teeth. "Entertain us, Mister Skye. I want to hear it. Those two nags right there were, last I knew, the property of a pair of bunghole guides."

Well, why not? Skye motioned them off their horses, and Hunsaker and some of his men collected around him. The story came easily. Enoch Bright contributed some indignation of his own. But then they turned somber when they found out about Hiram Peacock's condition.

"That gut-punch is a sure killer. I've seen a man die of it, and I heard all about Manville. He's just ahead, you say?"

"With a big company, two divisions of them, Arkansas and Missouri people."

"Pukes," Hunsaker said. "That's Captain Fancher's outfit. They ain't friendly to the Saints, I'll say." He eyed Skye and Bright. "I think you ought to travel with us."

"I think we should too," Skye said. "But we'll slow you down."

"Not if I put my spare mule team on that light wagon."

"You'd do that?"

"I reckon I'd help folks in trouble, like you."

twenty

*I*t all looked mighty good to Skye. Swiftly, Hunsaker's men hitched two stout mules to the light wagon, while the Jones brothers mounted the newly acquired saddle horses, and Sterling rode his father's Morgan. Enoch Bright preferred to walk, and teamstered the oxen.

Hiram Peacock was soon settled in the supply wagon, where Anna Bennett was ready to help him. He would breathe awhile, convulse, fall into ominous quiet, and then she would start his respiration again, with firm pressure on his chest. Skye peered in at Peacock, lying in a nest there, and felt as helpless as he had ever felt.

Skye and Hunsaker rode ahead of the rest, leading the combined train into the mountains.

"Is there a summit? A place where we'll see the desert?" Skye asked him.

"No, we'll be in valleys and canyons the whole way. It's like a plow cut a crooked furrow through the Wasatch Range."

"Maybe that's good," Skye said. "Peacock said he had one

last wish. He wanted to see the desert. He asked me to show him the desert. It's his Promised Land, I guess."

"He thinks he'll die?"

"One last look is what he wanted. It's keeping him alive. The vision of the desert, where all those people might be healed. But maybe if there's no last look, he'll keep on going."

"There's no place I know of," Hunsaker said. "And if he's going to the Virgin River country, like I hear, he's not going to see any of it from up high. That's a long way."

"It's what's keeping him going," Skye said.

"How far ahead are those Pukes? I want to be ready for them if we bump into them."

"They left at first light. They ate breakfast before dawn. Half a day?"

"If we tangle with them, too bad for them," Hunsaker said. "If they've got forty wagons, we'll probably catch up,"

They pushed through a peaceful green notch, beside a tumbling river that plunged over boulders. Skye sensed they were climbing, though he scarcely felt it. Arid slopes vaulted upward into a dry highland. This was the rain-shadow side of these mountains, and only the valleys were grassed.

But they saw nothing of the big train ahead, and as the morning unwound, they wrestled up a steady grade, passing muddy potholes. The oxen drawing the big supply wagon were the slowest of the teams, slowing down the whole combined company.

"What's in those wagons, Mister Hunsaker?" Skye asked.

"Call me Pete. I'll call you Mister. Oh, chests of drawers, bedsteads, highboys, barrels, dressers, stuffed chairs, dining tables, wooden chairs, flour bins, coffee mill, cast-iron pots, a few books, some cotton mattresses, an empty coffin, a lot of castoff clothing and worn-out shoes, harness, saddles and tack, ox yokes, a grist mill, some family Bibles, half a dozen plowshares, hoes, spades, pitchforks, harrows, a double-bottom riding plow, you name it, I've got it. The whole of it pitched out beside the Oregon Trail. I'd have a lot more if the pilgrims didn't chop up half of it for firewood."

"Valuable in Great Salt Lake?"

"You have no idea. I can sell these things for ten times what they'd bring back East. But the Saints haven't much cash, so there's a lot of bartering."

"Saints do a good business from the migrants."

"If it weren't for the wagons passing by, the Saints would still be poor."

"What's this trouble about?"

"Marriage. The Saints say the more wives the better, the government says cut it out or we'll come in and stop you. And that's what's happening. The blueshirts are on the way, I hear. Or will be soon. There's been some troop movements and the federals are sending a column our way."

"And what are the Mormons doing?"

"Making a lot of noise." Hunsaker's grin told Skye a lot.

"Will there be a fight?"

"Some will fight, no doubt of it. If old Brigham says so, there'll be some real battles. And he's sure sounding like a bull moose pawing the ground."

"Is my company in any danger?"

"Anyone not Mormon, I'd say, could get into trouble. But you're not Pukes. That company ahead of us, the Missouri one, now that could get itself starved in Utah."

"They're Arkansas people, they tell me."

"Missouri and Illinois too. That's just asking for trouble. The Saints, they don't forget. They don't forget the killing of Joseph Smith. They don't forget Independence, Nauvoo, getting driven out, and dying all winter long from exposure. No, Mister Skye, they haven't forgotten one bit of it."

All that morning and afternoon they ascended the eastern slope, their view cloistered by valleys and canyons. But late that afternoon they reached the summit, and began a descent. That's when Anna Bennett hurried up to Skye and Hunsaker.

"Sir, Mister Peacock begs a halt here."

"All right," said Hunsaker. "The stock could use a rest."

Skye headed back to the wagon, and found Hiram Peacock gazing up at him. Pete Hunsaker joined them.

"That flat there. Take me there, Mister Skye."

The little flat wasn't far, maybe a hundred yards, but they were steep yards. It actually was a west-facing bench, beneath a craggy red cliff.

"Sir, in your condition . . ."

"Take me."

Skye knew at once it must be done; it was one of those commands that no man could thwart or he would regret it all of his days. He glanced at Hunsaker, who was experiencing the same thing.

"Very well, sir. But there is no view west anywhere near here," Hunsaker said.

Peacock simply nodded.

Some swift commands brought a doubled-up canvas, which Hunsaker's men laid on the ground. Several of them gently lifted the merchant out of the wagon and onto the canvas. Then three on each side—Skye, Enoch Bright, Pete Hunsaker, the Jones brothers, and Sterling Peacock—lifted Hiram Peacock and struggled up the rocky slope, all of them trying their best to ease the journey for him. It seemed far more of a climb than Skye had imagined from the wagon road. But at last they struggled over a lip of rock onto the boulder-strewn flat.

And there, to Skye's astonishment, was a sharp vee to the west, and beyond it a bright glimpse of another country, arid and dazzling, sharp blue and white and gray. The Promised Land.

It was not difficult to pull Hiram Peacock into a sitting position, with his back against a great red rock. A hush fell over them all. Somewhere, still an infinity away, but there in the Great Basin, was the Virgin River.

How had Peacock known of this overlook? Not even Hunsaker, who had been over this trail scores of times, had known of it. There were mysteries beyond fathoming.

They all stood quietly, while Hiram Peacock stared through that notch in the towering range.

Then he turned to Skye and Hunsaker.

"Thank you. I am done," he said.

They thought to carry him away, but Hiram Peacock had closed his eyes, and Skye knew at once he was dead. So did the rest. They stared, astonished. Skye gently shook the man, but it was a superfluous gesture. The man who had led this healing expedition two thousand miles was gone.

Sterling Peacock knelt, pulled Hiram's limp hand into his own, and held it.

"Thank you, Papa. You are the Good Father. You brought us here safely. We'll soon be home. I will see to it."

The youth could not continue, but sat beside his father, saying good-bye. Now Sterling was alone, the last of his family.

In some mysterious fashion, those who stayed below knew what had transpired up on this flat. Those who could struggle toward this benchland had come partway. Now they were clumped together at the foot of the steepest rise. Skye saw Anna Bennett, the Bridge sisters, Ashley Tucker. Only Peter Sturgeon was not present. And somehow they all knew. Mary and Victoria had come, and had kept a little distance from the consumptives. Yes, they all knew. How could they know? But they did.

Skye lifted his ancient top hat from his head, and it was an acknowledgment of death and a mark of respect. The others beside him pulled their slouch hats from their heads also, thus joining Skye in a moment of quietness. It was over. He who had dreamed a great dream had perished.

Skye peered at that vee in the western mountains, feeling the mysterious power of that view. Hiram Peacock had seen the promise of it. Maybe he should stay here, his face turned west, for all time.

There was a way.

"Sterling, would you like to bury your father here?" Skye asked.

"But it's rock."

"Many's the time when I was in the mountains that we buried a man where there was no soil at all, in places like this. We are at the foot of a broken cliff, with many a cleft in it. We can bury him in a cleft, facing where he wanted to go."

Sterling looked doubtful.

"Or we can take him down a way, and bury him beside a creek where there's earth to receive him, son."

Sterling stood, gazing at that bright notch in the mountains, and the sunny blue desert beyond. Skye knew how hard it was for the young man to make such a decision.

"Here," Sterling said. "Facing us. Facing where we will be."

Soon, Hunsaker's teamsters had wrapped Hiram Peacock in canvas, tied it tight, and placed him in a great cleft in the red cliff, where he could gaze forever westward, toward his own. And then they all filled the cleft with rock, until no animal would ever unearth Peacock's bones.

And then Skye descended to where the rest waited, partly down the slope.

"We will say good-bye now," he said.

twenty-one

Skye peered into the faces of those desperate young people, and knew their fear. He pressed the brim of his hat against his chest, somehow turning the moment into an oath of office.

"We've lost Hiram Peacock, but we'll go on. Mister Bright will see to it. My family and I'll see to it. Sterling Peacock will see to it too. We'll proceed exactly as Hiram Peacock planned, and exactly as he described his mission to his son.

"Sterling's in charge now. He's one of you. I'll take my instruction from him and from Mister Bright."

But nothing he said allayed their fear. They were sick, helpless, and without their protector. He could read their faces and see it. He realized just how profoundly Hiram Peacock's vision of health and healing had infused them, and how much they all looked up to him. They would be doubtful of Skye, the man of the western mountains, and there was nothing he could do about it except to take them where they were going.

"Mister Peacock faces west now, where his gaze will watch over us," he added.

"Always assuming the dead see, an unsound proposition," Bright observed. "But I have long speculated that thought is but galvanic energy that is released from our minds into the ether, and if that proposition stands scrutiny, then Hiram Peacock's thoughts must be radiating into the universe, waiting to be recognized and plucked up." Bright paused. "Ghosts. Night visions. Dreams. We'll listen for the man."

The mechanic's odd cosmology seemed to be his alone, and the ill ignored it. But Skye was rather taken with it.

Hunsaker was eager to be off, and his men were standing restlessly, wanting to head to Great Salt Lake, to their homes, their wives and families.

The young convalescents drifted back to the train, pensively. Everything was different now. It was as if no one believed he would be healed now. Only Hiram Peacock's adamant and inflexible belief that the desert would heal them had banished disbelief. But now Skye saw a glumness in them. They had gone from believers to agnostics. And maybe in some, disbelief was slowly twining itself around their hearts.

They traveled uneventfully to Great Salt Lake City, which lay on a plain west of the mountains. It was laid out on the compass, orderly, sunny, and peaceful, almost Mediterranean in the summer sun. It was still more a village than a city, though. It had been erected by journeyman carpenters and millwrights and smiths and joiners and stonemasons, a city rich with skills even if its people were poor. Its very orderliness spoke of a vision they shared, a community of believers safe in this isolated and arid land so far from the rest of the States, which had ejected them. A mighty church was being built to the north.

Mary, who had never seen a white man's city, apart from

the sprawl of Fort Laramie, stared at these orderly rows of white frame houses, some with gingerbread trim, with real glass windows, shake roofs, lilac bushes and hollyhocks, and shaded porches. She lifted her cradleboard until North Star could see these strange things and perhaps glimpse something of his own heritage in this place. The few people walking the streets, women in bonnets and great skirts and bulging bodices, smiled at the whole entourage and stared curiously at Skye's women.

Hunsaker simply took his wagon company through wide clay streets to his shop, a narrow clapboard affair that sprawled back from the street front to an alley behind. There he and his teamsters paused, the oxen sagging in their yokes before the store. A painted sign said "Furniture, New and Used. Household Items. Peter Hunsaker, Prop." This day would add scores of new items ransacked from the trail to Hunsaker's stock of goods, all of them unusually valuable so far from any place where these things were manufactured.

There was an awkward pause. Skye knew that he and Enoch would need to detach their wagons and be on their way. The teamsters were eager to unload, care for the livestock, and go to their own homes.

"Thank you, Mister Hunsaker. You've brought us here safely," Skye said.

"It was what a Saint must do."

"It was what you personally did."

"All right, say that about me. The sick, how can a man not help the sick? Now before we part company, I propose a trade. You happen to have two saddle horses, prizes taken in combat. Now I can sell good saddle horses at a handsome price here. There never are enough of them. You, on the other hand, have a great want of livestock. So my proposition is, would you trade the saddle horses for those mules of mine, currently harnessed to the light wagon? I'm afraid I would have the better of it, offering you a pair of miserable Missouri mules for that brace of saddlers, but if you could see your way clear . . ."

"Done!" said Skye, before Enoch Bright could engineer an objection.

Hunsaker smiled slightly. "Come in, Mister Skye, while I draft a bill of sale. My men will collect your nags."

Skye plunged into the cool dark interior, mostly barren of merchandise because the store could not meet the demands of the Saints for household goods. Hunsaker lit an oil lamp, dipped a nib pen into an inkwell, and scratched out the sale.

He handed it to Skye, and the pair of them clasped hands, and then Hunsaker escorted Skye to the door. Already, his teamsters were unloading the freight wagons.

"We'll go on now," Skye said. "One question, sir: we need to replenish, and have only the Morgan horse to trade. These young people need food. What's a good horse worth, and where do we go for provisions?"

"Good Morgan horse is worth plenty. But I'm no judge of it."

"Where do we go?"

"We're on State Street. You need to go to Fourth. Parley's Dry Goods, or Kimball's Groceries."

Skye swore there was a halo behind Hunsaker's head, and laughed. Their handshake was rough and strong.

Hunsaker was obviously anxious to release his men, so Skye and his party drove quietly south to Fourth, and then east to a cluster of mercantile buildings. Kimball's was a false-front white frame structure with a hitch rail in front. This was a busy place, with women ducking into one store or another to fill their wicker baskets. Skye hardly saw a male on the street.

Skye and Bright entered, and Skye intuitively let Bright negotiate. He thought maybe a limey with two Indian wives might be at a disadvantage.

A bald man stood behind a polished counter. This was no crude frontier store, but a remarkably well-fitted building.

"We're passing through, and would like to trade, sir," Bright said. "What would an excellent Morgan horse bring?"

"I have no use for a horse."

"This is a fine saddler; ride him if you want. And he's well broke to harness and the plow."

"How old?"

"Five, plenty young, and not a thing wrong with him. He's one of Justin Morgan's own stock, purchased for two hundred fifty dollars in Massachusetts."

"Well, you won't get that here. I'll have my clerk look him over. I'm busy. Ah, what is it you want?"

"Staples: flour, sugar, coffee—"

Kimball frowned. "Ne'er coffee nor tea, ne'er spirits shall this store stock."

"Yes, I forgot. But you have flour and lard?"

"In plentiful." He turned to a skinny lad with a prominent Adam's apple. "Cogswell, go try that nag."

The youth ducked through the double doors, studied Skye's women a moment, and headed straight for the chestnut horse at the rail. He picked up feet, examined the hooves for cracks, looked for fistulas on the withers, examined the teeth, lifted the tail looking for bots, and once satisfied, led the horse in a few circles looking for a limp, and then sprang up, riding the Morgan a few hundred yards before returning to the hitch rail.

The youth materialized inside. "He's a fair decent horse but I know the sort; he'll be barn sour, and a stump sucker."

"I'm afraid your terms evade me," Bright said.

"This one'll head for the barn if he can, it takes a stern rein to hold him, and he'll chew on any wood in a stall."

"How do you know that? It's not true."

The youth was grinning.

"Twenty-five for him," Kimball said. "Taken in merchandise, no cash."

"A tenth? A tenth of his value?"

"That's my top and final offer, gents."

He stood behind his polished counter, smiling gravely.

"What's flour the hundredweight?" Skye asked.

Kimball eyed him. "Where are you from?"

"Long ago, London."

"I thought so. I can tell a man's home within a dozen miles, I always say. Flour's twelve dollars a hundredweight."

"Then a first-rate buffalo robe?"

"I have no use for a buffalo robe. Try haggling me and I just raise my prices. Now it's fourteen a hundredweight."

"I can offer you a good Hawken rifle, shoots true."

"A Hawken, is it? Let me see it."

Skye slid outside, into the mild sun and peacefulness of Great Salt Lake City, and pulled his Hawken off one of the travois.

"Your rifle?" Victoria asked.

"One of them," Skye replied, carrying the faithful old Hawken into the store.

"You can have this rifle for a hundredweight of your best flour, ten of lard, ten of sugar, and ten of dried fruit."

Kimball studied it, sourly. "One pound of lard, just one

pound. No sugar. It comes clear from Argentina or some place. And one pound of dried apples."

Kimball looked ready to pitch Skye out the door.

Skye caved in. "All right," he said.

Kimball summoned his clerk, who collected the stuff.

"Want him to carry it out?"

"We'll do that," Skye said.

"We need rifles," Kimball said, grinning. "Saints need firearms just now. You gave it away."

Skye hunkered down inside of himself.

And so they left Great Salt Lake City with only a hundred pounds of flour and little more. He wanted five hundred of wheat and oats and barley, lard, tea and coffee. Skye wasn't sure how he could keep all those sick people fed or clothed, especially in the desert. For that matter, he didn't even know where he was heading. He was in country he had never seen, and among people he only vaguely understood.

twenty-two

The trail south from Great Salt Lake City wound through settled country, much of it irrigated. Skye marveled at how much the Saints had accomplished in ten years. The fields were bursting now with wheat and oats and barley as well as potatoes, corn, cabbages, and other vegetables. Emerald pastures nurtured sheep and a few cattle, poultry, and hogs. Some orderly young fruit orchards promised rich harvests soon. All of this was watered from ditches brimming with diverted river water flowing out of the Wasatch Mountains. This was their land of milk and honey, but its emerging abundance had been wrought from endless toil.

Skye's small party, just two wagons, one still drawn by oxen and the other with Hunsaker's well-fed mules, worked slowly south through mild weather that blistered them only during midafternoon, and cooled quickly in the evenings. They trailed through sleepy farm villages, with a few mercantiles huddled together, and always a temple dominating the village square or the center of the town. Sometimes bearded farmers paused to watch them, their gaze guarded. Few women were in sight, but a row of identical frame houses here and there spoke of plural marriage; a man's several families all in an orderly line along a road. Many had clotheslines strung across their yards, from which dangled breeze-dancing union suits and petticoats and chambray shirts and stiff britches. These caught the attention of Victoria and Mary, who studied undergarments and outer garments with a fascination that puzzled Skye.

Once in a while they ran into traffic. This was Utah's great artery, connecting the villages in the south to the capital. These were sometimes high-sided freight wagons drawn by slobbering oxen, sometimes a spring wagon or a buggy drawn by trotters, occasionally horsemen. They stared at Skye's odd ensemble, the wagons and teams, his wives, his ponies and travois, Enoch Bright teamstering beside the oxen, the Jones brothers beside the mule team, the pale, sick young people sitting on the tailgates. They were oddly silent, sometimes stern, somehow recognizing at once that these were not Saints.

But then a bull-shouldered man with a jutting brown beard driving a black carriage hailed them.

"What you got there, stranger?" he asked of Skye.

"I'm Mister Skye, sir, and these are my wives, Mary and Victoria. We're taking some people to the desert."

"Passing through to California, are you?"

"The desert out west."

"You'll want to go to California and not stop. You'll not want to stop anywhere in Deseret."

"We don't plan to."

"Not for food, not for supplies. You will not talk to people."

"We'll be looking for provisions. We hope to trade."

"What's in those wagons?"

Skye thought the man was probing a little too hard. "Have a look," he said.

"You tell me and tell me now."

"Who am I talking to, sir?"

"It matters not."

Skye lifted that top hat, contemplated it, and made a decision.

"Then we'll be on our way."

He touched heels to Jawbone, who started forward, ready to sink his yellow teeth into this man in the buggy. But a subtle signal from Skye cooled the horse.

"Likely it is you'll regret your insolence," the man said.

The bearded man didn't move his carriage aside, but sat quietly, reining in his trotter, while Skye's women passed to the side.

But as Bright and his oxen pulled up, the man raised a buggy whip.

"Stop there," he said. "Your name?"

"Bright, sir. New Bedford, Massachusetts. And you?"

"What are you carrying?"

"Necessaries, my friend."

"Who are these children?"

"All from New Bedford, sir. We are heading into the desert on their account. Most are adults."

"I know that. Where are the parents of these children?"

"Oh, they're back East."

"Who owns them?"

Bright was taken aback. "Why, I imagine they rightly own themselves."

"They are minors, collected here and possessed by you, or Skye there?"

Bright looked amused. "They were bound over to Hiram

Peacock to be taken to a sanitarium in the desert. It is a plan filled with mercy and hope. But he perished near Fort Bridger, and we're carrying on, friend. I am their guardian."

"Perished?"

"He was killed by a ruffian, sir. A fist to the bellows. The criminal is even now guiding a wagon company a day or two ahead of us. His name is Manville, and it would be a blessing if this territory's constables were to pinch him."

The bull-shouldered man stepped down from his ebony carriage and hiked past the wagons, peering at the pale young people, especially those lying in the second wagon or sitting on its tailgate.

He whirled suddenly toward Lloyd Jones. "You. Who are these children?"

"We're all lungers, sir, making this long trip and hoping the desert will heal us. That was Mister Peacock's vision."

"They look stolen. Have you papers?"

The questioning was finally getting somewhere that Skye could fathom. He turned Jawbone back to this inquisitor and addressed him.

"Mister Peacock was a whale oil merchant whose family was stricken by consumption. He lost his wife and two children to this disease. He was also a visionary, whose studies led him to believe the desert offers hope to those consumed by this wasting sickness. He organized this company, sir, and we intend to follow his footsteps."

"I've heard enough from you, Skye. I was not talking to you."

"It's Mister Skye, sir. And you are Mister . . . ?"

"I am an apostle, one of the Council of Twelve. Harley Peets. I look to public safety in Deseret."

The jut-bearded man smiled, radiating a cruel confidence

as he gained ground here. There was something about him that suggested he was in command, and anyone who challenged him would find himself in serious trouble.

Skye watched warily. This was a moment to be quiet, observe closely, let this man finish his business and be on his way.

The apostle circled the two wagons, peered into the larger one that carried supplies, and finally studied the handsome Morgan tied to the rear of the first wagon.

"I believe that's a stolen horse," he said. "Stolen children, stolen horse. It's the finest horse I've ever laid eyes on. And that says all that needs saying. It's been reported that a wagon company holds a dozen children in captivity."

Skye suspected that the real stealing was about to begin, and he intended to stop it.

"Are you a constable or a peace officer, sir?"

The hulking man merely smiled.

Skye knew he wasn't. This was no official inquiry at all. "I thought so. We'll be on our way now."

Once again, the hulking man deferred to Skye, or seemed to. He nodded, returned to his carriage, and offered no more opposition. Skye's train started south once more, but no sooner had it passed the buggy than the man cracked a whip over the rump of his trotter and plunged northward, his horse bursting away at a clip that could be sustained for only a mile or two.

Skye watched him go. The man had a mission. The Saints were secretive. It was something to ponder. There was something calculating about all this. And those questions sounded like some sort of prelude to trouble, some sort of rationale for seizing Skye's entire party.

They continued uneasily southward through a quiet countryside that was peaceful and sunny, in sharp contrast to the worries whirling inside of Skye's head. Here was an accusation of horse theft. Here was a broad hint that these children were some sort of contraband. And if children and horses were valuable to these people, who had an unending need for horse and child labor, it might be easy to conjure up reasons to detain them. Especially if you were a powerful man.

Something in all this made Skye feel as if his party was being watched as it passed through one village after another: Midvale, Sandy City, Crescent, Riverton, Draper, and then into a great plain with a shimmering lake far to the south. That would be Utah Lake.

They camped beside a laughing creek that flowed into the lake, and while they were enjoying the comforts of a fire and a good rest, a horseman raced by, his lathered horse at a steady canter. They watched the horseman, even as the horseman studied them, but he didn't pause.

The next days they continued southward through slumbering villages, irrigated fields, comfortable settlements: Pleasant Grove, Orem, Provo, Spanish Fork, Payson, Santaquin. The names sounded biblical to Skye.

Each day more dispatch riders flew by in both directions. More were headed south than north. None paused to pass the time of day with the struggling wagon company. None even acknowledged their existence.

The air was dry and warm, and Skye thought the invalids were enduring fairly well. None was in dire straits, though Ashley Tucker coughed miserably and was spitting blood, and Eliza Bridge was suffering hectic fever again. But there was not enough food to last long, and he knew he must try to trade at Nephi, a bleak little town huddled beneath the Wasatch Range off to the east.

He wondered what to trade. Not Peacock's handsome

Morgan horse if he could help it. It actually was Sterling Peacock's **horse now**. Skye had been admiring that docile, eager mare **for much** of the trip and knew its value. In the middle of a quiet **afternoon** he halted his company before a whitewashed **plain** rectangle of a building labeled "Nephi Mercantile." This was farming country. There would be abundant flour, oats, fruit, and produce here.

But it was strange that not a soul was visible on the clay street of the business district even in the middle of a bright afternoon.

twenty-three

The whitewashed mercantile scowled at Skye in the bright light. A raven sitting on a rooftop scolded, shattering the silence. Skye headed toward Bright and the Jones brothers.

"I'll go in here and see what we can do," he said.

He abandoned Jawbone and stood stiffly in the quiet street, recovering the use of his legs, and then headed for the mercantile. He let himself in to the jangle of bells, and found himself in an orderly general store, with shelves well stocked and the air rich with the scents of fabrics, foods, and leather goods. Light from an overhead well banished gloom from the long, silent room.

"Anyone here?" Skye asked.

"You are not welcome here. Please leave."

The male voice rose from a curtained doorway.

Skye sensed what all those couriers were about. "I'm Mister Skye, sir, and I am hoping to buy or trade for some provisions. I'm escorting a group of invalids to the desert. It's our understanding that desert air and rest will heal them. I myself am not sick and you have nothing to fear from me."

"We are not permitted any intercourse with you, sir."

The voice echoed out from the curtained doorway.

"I see. Well, I can understand that. Our young people know enough to keep away. And we do need food. Supposing I bring in Mister Bright, who is himself in fine health, and we select what we need."

"Absolutely not!"

The voice rose sharply.

"Who are you?" Skye asked.

"Harley Pratt."

"Mister Pratt, even if we can't do business, why don't you step forward and tell me where we stand. It'd help me to know what this is all about."

Surprisingly, Pratt did. He was a bald, thin man, sharp Adam's apple, and a look about him of a raptor. He studied Skye, plainly disapproving of the quilled and beaded leather, the unruly locks, and the battered top hat. Even so, he edged around the counter, heading for a place where, Skye supposed, the man kept a weapon, just in case.

"You won't need a weapon here, sir," Skye said quietly.

Pratt froze.

"Just tell me where we stand. We have young people who need to be fed. We need some greens as well as meat and grains. Perhaps you can help us."

Pratt shook his head violently. "It is forbidden on pain of excommunication to have the slightest intercourse with you."

"Why?"

"Because you are a plague invading our land. You are the Apocalypse, the Pale Horse of Revelation. You will take our food and pay us with sickness. Death, disease, famine . . . You

166

and the United States Army are coming to destroy Zion. The prophets have warned us, and we will resist to the last man."

"Do you believe that?"

"I believe what the elders tell me is true. They have received it from the Lord."

"What exactly do they say?"

"That, sir, is for the Saints to know."

"What would you have us do?"

"Turn around and go back the way you came."

Skye knew he would face even more trouble heading that way. "Perhaps you could give me advice," he said.

"Harley!"

That was a woman's voice, and it clanged like a church bell.

"Missus Pratt is telling me she's ready. She has the cow bells in hand. If you don't leave at once, she will ring them, and the militia will arrive."

"What then?"

"They are armed, and will take matters into their own hands."

Skye settled his top hat, nodded, and retreated to the silent street. A breeze whipped a weed down the center of it. How very strange. Not a horse or wagon stood anywhere in sight. Not a soul was walking the boardwalks. But Skye didn't doubt that his wagon company was being observed from a hundred windows. He did not see any weapons poking from those windows, but suspected that they soon would be unless he took his company out of town at once.

He reached Bright. "They want us out of here. Won't sell a thing."

"But why?"

Skye shook his head. "They won't say. Well, yes they will.

They believe I am one of the Horsemen of the Apocalypse; that we have come to spread sickness among them. The rider of the Pale Horse brings sickness. Jawbone is indeed a pale horse."

Bright absorbed that with a shake of the head.

Skye noticed that Victoria, who had a keen sense of trouble, had reached the travois with her bow and quiver, and was ready to help any way she could. He shook his head, slowly, but she glared at this place, her loathing palpable.

They started south again, straight through the brooding town, until at its southerly edge they discovered a livery barn. It, too, was whitewashed, its board and batten siding fresh and clean. Horses stood quietly in a pen. Several buggies and wagons stood in the yard. The double doors in front stood wide open, letting the breezes eddy through a cavernous interior.

The town was mostly behind them. Skye peered rearward, seeing no armed mob. Nothing at all.

"Let's try this," he said. His women nodded.

He rode Jawbone up to the livery barn, slid off, and left Jawbone to his devices. The young people peered at him from their tailgate seats. Some stood. The sickest lay abed in the second wagon, uncaring about delays.

He walked cautiously into the cool barn, enjoying the sweet scent of hay and horses. A loft above enabled the liveryman to fork hay into mangers below. A horse shifted in its stall.

An office stood to one side, so Skye entered. A hostler sat waiting, his arms crossed. He was an older man, with a full white beard combed straight so every hair hung down.

"Go," he said.

"I am Mister Skye. And you?"

"Willard Romney. And that will be the last of this discussion."

"We're heading south to the desert. We're looking for provisions."

"Why come here, then?"

"Over there I see bags of grain. Oats, I believe. Barley. I'd like to trade for some."

"Horse feed."

"Feed that will help very sick young people reach a place of healing."

"I believe I asked you to leave."

"Mister Romney, I can understand why your people want us to leave. A war is brewing. I hope you'll let us trade for food so no one starves."

Romney didn't reply. His bright blue-eyed gaze slowly took in everything about Skye that a gaze might reveal. He said nothing, which encouraged Skye to keep on.

"We have a fine Morgan mare, five years old, from Justin Morgan's own stock, no injuries, good teeth, no fistulas, no splints, obedient under saddle. I'd like to trade her for some of that horse feed."

"Never heard of that line of horses."

Skye stared. Something obdurate radiated from this liveryman.

"The mare was owned by the man who put this company together, Hiram Peacock. He's dead now. The ownership has passed on to Mister Peacock's surviving son who is with us. The whole family save for him has perished. His name is Sterling Peacock. He will sign over a bill of sale."

Romney said nothing, simply stared as if he hadn't heard a word.

"This fine mare was purchased for two hundred fifty in

Massachusetts, and is worth all of that here. What I propose, sir, is five hundred pounds of grain, mostly oats, some barley, and you will receive title to her. She's just out the door. I'd like you to take a close look."

"I thought I instructed you. Are you deaf?"

The liveryman stood abruptly, and in his hands was a fowling piece. He swung the barrel around until the muzzle faced Skye.

Then he nodded toward the door.

"You have a choice. Stay and be shot. Argue and be shot. Linger outside and face our militia, which even now is armed and ready. What will it be?"

Skye nodded curtly. No help here. The town had coalesced into trouble.

He stepped into the barn, then through the double doors into bright sun and silence. Now, a hundred yards distant, stood a group of armed men, wearing the smocks of clerks, the dark suits of lawyers and professional people, the rough britches of laboring people. They formed into a line and began a slow walk.

Skye climbed up on Jawbone, nodded to his women and Bright, and the wagon train rolled southward. The militia continued to follow, step by step, until some unseen boundary was reached that Skye supposed was the southern edge of Nephi, and then no one followed.

At least not at first. After an hour of plodding quietly through peaceful agricultural country, Skye noticed a horseman trailing a half mile or more behind. He called a halt for a rest. The horseman halted, a small dot on the northern horizon, but Skye had a bad feeling about him. From now on, this company would be shadowed.

Skye dropped back to talk to Bright.

"It seems we're not welcome," Bright said dryly.

"It's more than consumption. These people are waiting for war to come. The Yank government's on the move. We're outsiders and suspect. A company that could spread disease is worse. It's biblical talk, brimming with sulphur and brimstone. We're in trouble and I don't know how to deal with it."

Bright nodded. "More of them than us. They've got weapons. I'd say keep on rolling, since I can't think of anything else worth doing."

"We've got the young people to feed," Skye said. "And I don't know how to do it."

twenty-four

They plodded ever southward into a lonely land without sign of habitation. Sagebrush cast a gray coverlet upon the land. There were timbered mountains rising to the east, a vast distance away, but from now on the country would become even drier.

Only a rude trail marked the way, but it was the sole artery connecting the settlements of the north and south.

Behind them was that horseman. When the company halted, so did he. Sometimes he seemed to vanish, but he always reappeared. At night he was nowhere in sight, but no one doubted that the man was not far off, and possibly very close. Who was he?

One night Enoch Bright reported that his wards had a new ailment. Some were bleeding from their gums and their joints were swollen and stiff. Both of the Bridge girls were suffering this new sickness, as well as Peter Surgeon and the Jones brothers.

Skye didn't like the sound of it.

"Is this a symptom of consumption?" he asked.

"None of us has ever heard tell of it."

"How long has this been troubling your people?"

"A few days now, Mister Skye."

"What are they eating now?"

"Porridge, sir. It's all we have left. The dried apples are gone."

"Oatmeal?"

"That's the whole of it. They add a little sugar."

"We're that low?"

"We have a sack of oats, and that's it. Hiram was going to buy things in Great Salt Lake, you know. We were assured there would be ample of everything. Fruits, vegetables, preserves. He was going to get cuttings too, so we could start our own orchards."

Skye gazed into Victoria's cook fire a careful distance away, knowing his own family was not much better off than these sick ones. He still had some pemmican and jerky. The pemmican contained chokecherries.

Here there was little that was familiar to him. He had been watching what his livestock grazed upon, and discovered there was still a little grass hidden under the sagebrush, and something else. They were eating a saltbush, at least he thought that was what it was, including its fruit, which had four little wings. Maybe what was good for stock would be good for human beings.

He returned to Victoria's fire, troubled.

"What?" she asked.

"A new sickness, bleeding gums, soreness of the bones and joints. It sounds familiar. Scurvy is what it's called."

She opened a parfleche. "Take this to them," she said.

It was the last of the pemmican.

He hesitated.

173

"Take it!" she said crossly.

He carried the parfleche to the other campfire, where the consumptives huddled or lay stretched out on grimy blankets.

"My wife wants you to eat this. Divide it up. It's pemmican, a food the Indians make from fat and berries and shredded meat, and she thinks it might help you. It has chokecherries or buffalo berries."

Sterling Peacock took it. "We don't have greens, Mister Skye. And now this sickness."

"Are you sure this is not consumption?"

"I mastered everything my father mastered about consumption. He wanted me to know it all in case anything happened . . . in case he didn't live. It's a disease that destroys any flesh, not just lungs and throat and mouth. But this bleeding doesn't fit."

Skye nodded. "I've been studying what the livestock eat here, and maybe it'll help us."

They didn't look very convinced. But he had nothing else to offer them.

Long ago, in the Royal Navy, he had learned everything there was to learn about scurvy and its cures. Sailors were called limeys for a reason. They were given a lime each day to ward off scurvy, or if not a lime, then a lemon or orange. And most vegetables would do in a pinch, especially potatoes. Somehow it worked. On board, with their daily gruel or ship biscuit, they were never getting enough greens. Was this scurvy? Was it even possible to get it in the middle of a continent?

Mary, who was cleaning North Star, looked up. "I see what the ponies eat, and this plant with the four little wings,

I see how they snatch it, so I collect it each evening and mix it up with things for us. It is in our broth, see?"

She fished some shredded green material from her bowl.

Skye squatted beside her. "Maybe you're keeping us from sickness, Mary."

"It is a good thing to eat," she said.

"I don't know what's good and what's bad here. But you know."

"It is in my heart," she said.

The whole food situation was becoming critical. He had scarcely seen a four-footed animal in this area. Once he saw some desert mule deer fleeing over a hilltop. But this was a land without many animals and he would not be making meat. Not unless he got lucky. Still, he thought he would need to hunt each day. The road was plain; he could leave the navigation to Bright and ride toward those eastern ridges and valleys, where water tumbled out of the mountains, and maybe find an antelope or a deer. Not that either animal would provide more than a meal for so many people.

The next morning he headed into the open slopes looking for the winged fruit of the desert shrub he thought might be saltbush. There wasn't much here. This was sagebrush and juniper country, gray and black in the early light. Still, there was a little, and he harvested it.

"Mister Bright, put this in your stew pot," he said. "It's a green the livestock like, and maybe it'll help us. And look for it along the trail. In country like this, we need to make everything count."

Bright held up the little winged blooms as if they were roses. "Nature supplies what we need if we have the wits to make good of it," he said.

Skye watched him carry his armload of greens to the campfire, consult with Lloyd Jones, who was doing the breakfast that morning, and watched them shred the greens and drop them into the porridge.

Who could say if it would help?

This was the loneliest campsite they had visited, but it had a mildly alkaline spring that fed the foliage marching down a ravine. It had seemed a good place, far from trouble.

Twice in the night horsemen had trotted by on the road below the spring, awakening Skye, who always slept lightly. The traffic never ceased, he thought. It must be urgent if a horseman was cantering along at two in the morning. Had war come to the Saints?

But nothing more disturbed the night. He missed the night sounds of the great plains and the mountains, the bark of coyotes, the occasional howl of wolves, the muted conversations of owls. This was a different and harsher land.

In the morning, he heard at once about Eliza Bridge. She had slid into tears, which welled from her eyes in an unending stream for hours. All her courage was gone.

Bright summoned Skye, who found her lying on the ground near their camp, wrapped in her blanket, her arms covering her face.

"Eliza, it's Mister Skye."

"Leave me alone," she said.

"You would like to go home, I think."

She stared upward at him. He knelt beside her.

"It's a long journey. We've a way to go. And we don't know what we'll find when we reach the desert. We don't even know for sure how many of us will be healed. The man who was leading you and giving you hope died too. He was a friend of your family. And now he's gone."

She said nothing, but at least she was listening.

"You're fevered again. I can see it."

She looked bad, with dark circles hollowing her eye sockets and a harried desperation consuming her faster than her disease was eating her flesh.

"And we're not welcome here. You feel bad about it. It would be so good if these people were kinder to strangers and would help us any way they could. Like Peter Hunsaker. But they aren't doing that. I feel just the way you do, as if we're trespassing."

He could tell that his words were resonating with her. At least she was listening.

"I have little to offer you, Eliza. But don't forget prayer."

"My family doesn't hold with religion. It's futile. This whole trip is futile. How many days down the road will I live? Where will my end come?"

"Live just for today, Eliza. Just for now, and don't worry about tomorrow."

"I won't worry about tomorrow. I have no tomorrow."

Skye had no answer for that.

"Have you ever ridden a horse?" he asked.

"It's not becoming for a woman," she said.

"I'd like to sit you sideways, sidesaddle, on my horse. Jawbone is a fine, proud horse. You can hold on to the saddle. You can watch the desert go by instead of lying in that wagon. Would you like that?"

"I'm too sick."

"For a little while? And see the land as we pass over it?"

She stared, and finally nodded.

He brought Jawbone to her, a crazy, wild-eyed animal with floppy ears, the ugliest horse in the universe.

She let Skye lift her to the saddle and settle her sideways

and let Skye tuck her grimy blanket about her against the morning chill. It was late August now, and the seasons were shifting.

They started out from the alkaline spring a little later that morning, with Eliza Bridge just barely hanging on while Skye led the stallion.

And now they were trailed by two horsemen.

twenty-five

All that hot day the two horsemen trailed Skye's party. Often they were invisible, but then one or another would show up again. They rarely came closer than half a mile and were little more than tiny dots crawling across a monotonous sea of sea-green sagebrush, or slopes black with juniper.

This was still an open land, preserving its virgin ways against the enterprising settlers. Not a single homestead came into view. No cleared brush, no plowed fields, no irrigation ditches, no trees surrounding a house, or livestock grazing in random bunches on cleared land. This was country that was always ushering the wayfarer somewhere else: to the east, beyond countless ridges, rose mighty mountains, arid and yellow and speckled with pine, while obscure desert ridges to the west led into mystery. Who could say what sort of life played out here on the gray and tan slopes?

Skye rode ahead, keeping an eye out for water. The trail was clear, but the distances between water holes or creeks out of the mountains were not clear. For a while they paralleled a dry river that probably ran in the spring but now was a sandy waste lined by chaparral.

And still they came, those dark riders who kept a careful distance between themselves and the slow-moving wagons. When Skye and Bright speeded up, so did the riders. When the train slowed to a crawl, so did the riders.

"Who do you suppose they are, Mister Skye?" Bright asked.

"They seem to regard us as important. We'd be ignored if we weren't somehow important."

"It's this war. Colonel Johnston's column is heading here to end the Mormon rebellion. People in the East don't take kindly to the Saints and their assorted wives."

Skye laughed. "I think it's a dandy custom, Mister Bright."

"I'd rather collect buggies," the New Englander said.

This country was hot, and Skye paused frequently. Eliza Bridge had lasted an hour or so on Jawbone, and asked to return to the wagon. Somehow, the ride put her at ease. Perhaps it was simply seeing the country go by. But as long as she didn't become more feverish, she could bear the journey again.

Skye's women roved far and wide, hunting edible greens, but found little in this bleak stretch of juniper and sagebrush. The whole question of food gnawed at Skye. If they didn't soon replenish, they would have to go onto half rations, which would further weaken the sickest of the young people.

Late in the day they descended into a shallow valley with a green swath indicating a river. Skye sat Jawbone absorbing the startling change.

"The Sevier," Bright said. "It's on the maps."

"Good. That helps me."

The Sevier was on an ancient Spanish route south and west, and vital to the Territory of Utah because it offered well-watered passage north and south. Skye thought it also meant settlements again, and maybe the chance to trade for food.

The Sevier proved to be not much of a river, but it was at least wet, and its water nurtured abundant grasses for the livestock. Skye's ponies as well as the oxen and mules nipped grass whenever they could. But the country was still desolate, and Skye wondered why he saw no farms. Bad soil, maybe.

Then indeed he did spot a homestead on the far side of the river, well off the trail.

"I'm going to take Victoria and try for some food," he said to Bright. "You keep going. Maybe a squaw man and his wife will do better."

"I see no friction in it," Bright said.

He summoned Victoria and explained his mission.

"I bring a travois, yes?"

"All our travois ponies. And we'll take the Morgan for trading."

"Hey, you can trade me for food, eh?"

She laughed. Her people had an endless stock of bawdy ideas and stories.

Bright and Mary, with her ponies and North Star, continued their way along the trail while Skye and Victoria cut off, descended a gulch, gingerly forded the stream, wary of quicksand, and then made their way toward a single forlorn farmstead. It wasn't much of a place, with an adobe house and shed and corral, and implements in the yard.

It looked deserted. Skye slid off Jawbone and knocked on the plank door.

"Yousah?" asked a male voice from the shed.

A red-bearded young man, built like a bull, emerged.

"I didn't heah youse. Shoeing my plow horse and I hardn't git company heah." He stared. "Why mah stars, it's hun Injun."

"I'm Mister Skye, and this is Missus Skye . . ."

"Well, that's a good match. Me, I got no one. All the elders grab the girls, they're knee-deep in fat wives, and that leaves a mess of bachelors hereabouts. Like me. Given the half and half of the sexes, some poor Saints ain't so lucky. But they's promising me sumpin' pretty soon. I hope she can pull like a hoss."

"I think some young lady's going to set her cap for you, Mister . . ."

"Oakshott. Lemuel Oakshott. Ohio-born. Well, if she does, she'll be plain as a cucumber or else the elders, they'll get to her first."

"Mister Oakshott, we're looking to trade for some food, especially vegetables and also grain, and maybe some meat."

"I got stuff all over here, except meat. Haven't slaughtered a hog in some while, needing to take a few to market. But I got potatoes, so many spuds a man can't hardly get rid of them before they go soft. And cabbages, just come in last week, and lots of stuff. What'll you give?"

At last. Skye eyed the empty adobe corral. "We were thinking about maybe one of these ponies. Broke to travois, so they'll pull a plow. Good tough mustang stock."

"That's a deal. How about that one there?"

It was the pony that dragged the travois with the lodge loaded on it.

"We could do that."

"I got stuff there in the shed. Sacks of potatoes, all the rest. You take as much as you can haul outa here and give me a bill of sale for the horse, and I'll put that nag to good use around here."

It happened like that. Skye gave young Oakshott a bill of sale and the pony. Victoria recruited the beautiful Morgan mare to drag the travois carrying the lodge. And both of them lugged burlap and cotton bags of spuds and cabbage and barley and onions and even some maize and heaped them onto the groaning travois. Skye slid two burlap bags of potatoes onto Jawbone's saddle and anchored them down. He would walk.

How swiftly it all happened. Twenty minutes later, he and Victoria and the ponies dragging the groaning travois left young Oakshott to his shoeing, waded the warm river along with the horses, barely avoiding wetting some of the grain sacks, and headed south.

The wagons were almost two miles ahead, and Skye suddenly realized the stalkers were between him and the wagons, and there could be trouble.

"We're going to meet our followers," he said.

"I'll be ready," Victoria said.

"Maybe we can walk right through."

"Dammit, Skye, why do these many-wives people not like the other white men?"

"It's the wives. You get some white men arguing about how many wives they're worth, and you've got trouble."

"Me, I'm worth about ten husbands," she said, and laughed wickedly.

That was the Crows for you, he thought.

Ahead, the two horsemen had stopped and dismounted and were resting their horses. That meant that Bright's company had probably stopped too up ahead.

Skye walked boldly forward leading Jawbone and feeling increasingly cheerful. He'd take a good gander at this pair and their horses and whatever they might be carrying with them.

They saw him and stood suddenly, scowling. Skye walked straight on, and saw the recognition run through this pair. One was big and mean-looking with a squared beard that was combed straight down. The other was thin and ferretlike, with bright brown eyes and a hawk's beak. Neither was armed.

"Afternoon, gents," Skye said.

They nodded.

"You resting up?" Skye said. "We're a long way from anywhere."

They glanced at each other. "Who are you?" the square-beard asked.

"Why, I'm Mister Skye, and this is Missus Skye, and yourselves?"

He paused directly before them.

"We're—"

The other shook his head. "It's a nice day," the square-beard said.

"Say, how far to the next settlement?" Skye asked.

"It's a piece," Square-beard said.

"We're heading into the desert," Skye said. "You coming our way? Won't you join us? Quite a trip, and we're safer traveling together."

Square-beard shook his head. "We pretty much mind our own business."

"I'm a guide," Skye said, "and you are?"

"We work for . . . ah, the president."

"Oh, the president, that's a fine position. What do you do for him?"

The question went unanswered. "Where did you get those spuds?"

"We traded a pony for them back a way. They're a blessing for us. We were just about out of food. Why do you ask?"

"President Young has decreed that no food may be given to outsiders for the duration of the emergency. Some Saint has betrayed the elders. I'd like to know who."

"It was a Good Samaritan," Skye said.

"Who?"

"I'd want no harm to come to him," Skye said. "He helped the needy."

It had come to be an odd standoff. Jawbone didn't like either man, and was slowly clacking his teeth. In a trice, if Skye had let him, he would have plunged into them and knocked them flat. But Skye's hand quietly soothed the animal.

"Come join our party, my friends," Skye said. "Maybe we can share a meal and good company."

But they didn't reply. Skye and Victoria and the horses trudged on while the other two stared. Skye itched to look back, fearful of a back-shooting, but Victoria was better at it. Somehow no one ever looked at her; they were too busy watching Skye. And then the stalkers disappeared behind a bend in the trail.

"They have their secrets," Skye said.

"They mean to kill us all," Victoria said.

Skye had, over many years, learned to heed Victoria's intuition.

The one with the well-combed square beard lingered in his mind.

twenty-six

The invalids demolished more potatoes and cabbage than Skye thought was possible. Even Peter Sturgeon, whose consumption had ulcerated his throat, downed all he could. And the Jones brothers were ready for more even after Enoch's stew pot was empty.

Skye and Bright had loaded the sacks of grain and potatoes and cabbage into the supply wagon, swiftly calculating that they could go two or three weeks on what had been collected from the farmer. With a little meat, Skye thought, it might suffice for the time being.

They camped that night on a flat beside the Sevier River, where Jawbone, the ponies, and oxen and mules could make short work of the abundant grasses. The place seemed safe enough.

All that day his company was shadowed by the gents who had declined Skye's hospitality. Skye saw something in them that troubled him: bright glares, calculating glances, a certain odd eagerness, things he couldn't quite fathom that were rippling through them just under the surface.

The supper hour passed, the stars tolled their bright songs in the darkness, the Utah wilderness stretched endlessly east and west. Once again they were far from habitation, and this country was as untouched as it was before the Mexicans had worked out the trajectory of the old Spanish Trail.

For a change, the invalids didn't simply crawl into their blankets but sat around Bright's cook fire as embers lifted into the darkness.

"I think it's time to force the issue," Skye said to Victoria.

She grunted skeptically. He had learned to heed her skepticism and supposed little good would come of it.

He caught Jawbone and saddled him, and rode into the night, working through a moonless black along the river, relying on the horse to pick his way. He could hardly see his own hands but Jawbone had better night vision than he did.

The two shadowers were nearly a mile back, and had built a little fire deep in a gulch where they would not be noticed. Skye heard their horses snort and then nicker when they picked up Jawbone's scent, and wondered whether these two stalkers would arm themselves. He paused, letting the night thicken around him once again. The other horses quieted, but he suspected that if the shadowers bothered to look, they would find those horses staring straight at Skye, their ears cupped forward.

It was easy. These two weren't expecting company. Skye slid his hand over his belaying pin and walked in. He loomed suddenly out of the black, startling them. They leaped up.

"I'm Mister Skye," he said.

"What right have you to come here?" Square-beard snapped.

The pair of them spread apart, ready to jump Skye.

"I think not," Skye said, checking their hands for weapons. Behind him Jawbone loomed out of the night.

"It's time for some hospitality. Come join us," Skye said.

"Never."

"I think you will."

"We don't have commerce with Lamanites."

"I'm unfamiliar with the term. Tell me," Skye said.

Square-beard nodded faintly toward Owl-beak, and they both rushed Skye. Jawbone snarled, crashed into Owl-beak, and sent him sprawling. Skye's belaying pin snicked out, cracked Square-beard's knee, and then landed just above the man's ear. He tumbled also, howling.

They weren't seriously hurt.

"Let's walk," Skye said.

"Are you constraining us?"

"An odd word, but yes. Consider yourself constrained."

"You are violating our persons. We are sovereign persons and if you insult our persons you'll suffer the consequences."

All this was pouring from Square-beard, who seemed to be the senior one here.

"Well, you've been stalking us for days, and violating our persons," Skye said. "March."

"You'll drag me through hell first."

Jawbone snorted, leaned over Square-beard, and bit him on the shoulder.

"That horse is doomed to hell for violating me," Square-beard yelled.

"What are your names?"

Both men rose slowly, fearful of Jawbone, who clacked his teeth at them.

"Call me the Messenger of the Prophet," Square-beard said.

This was all most peculiar. But his two captives offered no further resistance, other than a simmering rage and watchfulness, and Skye drove them ahead of him through the night, barely seeing the river that was his only compass.

It took them a while to reach Bright's cook fire, and when Skye and Jawbone drove both men in, they gazed fearfully at the young invalids.

"You do not need to come closer," Skye said.

He turned to the young people. "These are the men following us. They decline to tell me why. We will tell them exactly who we are, and I will show them the contents of both of our wagons, and introduce them to my family. This man with the combed beard announces himself as the Messenger of the Prophet, and the other gentleman declines to name himself. They both work for the president, or so they say. I presume it is not the president of the United States."

The pair had subsided into stony silence, and were still looking for a way to make a sudden escape into the cloak of night.

He saw Victoria come as close to the invalids as she dared, and noticed she had her quiver thrown over her back, and bow in hand.

Square-beard exuded rage. The type of rage that radiates heat. The type of rage that teeters on the brink of an abyss. Skye noted it.

"Sterling, please begin. Tell them about your father, yourself, and this wagon company of invalids."

"I am the last of my family, sirs. We're from Massachusetts. We buried my sister Samantha not long ago, and my younger brother Raphael near Fort Kearney. Consumption killed my mother, my brother and sister, and would have killed my father, Hiram Peacock, but he was killed near Bridger's Fort by a man named Manville."

The visitors stiffened.

189

"It was his dream to bring us to a place of healing," he continued. "He sought understanding of the thing that was destroying us, and finally came across the work of Ezekiel Throckmorton, who wrote about the effect of climate on our sickness." He described his father's vision, his belief in desert healing, his studies of consumption, his employment of Bright, organizing the company, spending his last cent on it, collecting the sick and desperate, most of them neighbors, and starting west.

One by one the invalids shyly explained who they were.

"I'm Mary Bridge. My sister and I, we . . . we've just been sick so long. It seemed like a dream, going with Mister Peacock. I believe we'll get well there in the good air. I really do. It is so cruel, stealing breath from me. But . . . but Eliza . . . and me . . ." She couldn't continue.

"Hello, I'm Peter. Peter Sturgeon. I can't get up much, so I'll tell you, this is my last hope. I just want to grow up. If I could get to be eighteen . . . I would like that."

Anna Bennett stood up, lovely in the firelight, and walked directly to the two stalkers. "I am one of the sick," she began. "One of those who are passing through your land. You need not care about me, personally. I will wrestle with my sickness without your help or caring, if you wish. I am simply a stranger, as far as you are concerned, so why care about me? But I care about you. For one thing, I hope that none of you are afflicted, as we are. I think, if we are healed by the desert, you will soon know of it and you'll be able to heal your own. Who am I? I'm a believer in the suffrage of women, taking the part of Susan B. Anthony and my friend Elizabeth Cady Stanton. I intend, as soon as I am well again, to work for the rights and equality of women everywhere."

Square-beard's sulphurous gaze fixed upon her longer

than it should have. She sensed it, and stood prouder and taller. Then the moment passed.

"David Jones here. I'm in usable shape. We're helping out, my brother Lloyd and I. We've got the consumption, but it don't seem so fast as the others. So we're teamsters, getting these wagons west. I guess we'll just pass through, and be out of your hair pretty quick."

Skye watched the men he had coerced to come to this place, and saw not a flicker of warmth, not a hair of sympathy, not a blink of regret. He also had a sense that they knew much of this.

Soon the rest of the invalids had spoken their piece. Eliza, Lloyd, Grant, Ashley. Small hopes, small dreams, desperation, and maybe a miraculous future.

But if it had any impact on these burning-eyed men, Skye didn't see it.

"And Mister Bright?" Skye said.

"Me, I'm no sicker than I ever get. I hired on, mostly because Mister Peacock, he's a hero of mine, and also I saw how I could keep the wagons and equipment up and running, and how I could keep the world running too. A mechanic, that's what I am, and now I'm a mechanic of body and soul too, I imagine. I'll say, sirs, if this company finds healing, the world will follow. You'll see a miracle in the desert."

Skye took his visitors around to the other cook fire, away from the invalids, where Mary sat quietly on a robe, with their child.

She stared up at them, uneasily, as they approached the wavering fire.

"This is my younger wife, Mary. She's Shoshone, one of Chief Washakie's band. And here is my son, who bears two names. His English name is Dirk, and his Shoshone name is

North Star. You have met my wife Victoria, of the Absarokas, my lifelong companion. I'm a Londoner by birth, and then I led a trapping brigade for the American Fur Company, and was in the robe trade, and now I guide. It's my privilege to take these struggling invalids to a place of hope."

The visitors stared with expressionless faces, their sharp gazes leaping from the sleeping infant to Mary, then to Victoria, and back to Skye.

Skye showed his visitors the supply wagon, with its food, kitchen supplies, rolls of canvas, implements, and tools.

"There it is. You've seen the entire outfit. You know who we are, what we do, what our intentions are. I'll take you back to your camp now, and if you are peaceable men, men of goodwill, you'll take all this to your president."

"You have it wrong, Skye," said the square-bearded one. "I am not a peaceable man. And I have nothing but ill-will in me. You are Lamanites. You insulted my person. Anyone who holds me captive, even for one moment, one second, violates me. You have held me under your powers for an hour, and for that you will be placed on the list, the very top. It is the unforgivable offense, this captivity, for which there is no forgiveness. And for this insult to our persons, sir, I pronounce your fate. The doom of everyone and everything in your company."

Skye listened closely, not only to words but to the icy, seething soul behind those words, and he knew he had made a grave mistake. And no one could tell him what a Lamanite was.

twenty-seven

An ill wind brought sharp cold that night, and Skye knew that summer was over and they must hasten. It reminded him that he had no lodgepoles and ought to cut some. That would prove no problem just here, where cottonwoods, willows, and sycamores dotted the Sevier River basin.

The next morning he found green saplings that would suffice. They were not as sturdy as the lodgepole pine so loved by Victoria's people, but they would do. These grew arrow straight and amply tall, so he hacked down the nine needed for his family's small lodge. Wordlessly Victoria limbed the poles and dragged them to the travois. They added weight, and Skye hated to do it, but he had Mary and North Star to think about, and cold fall drizzles that could destroy health.

It took very little time to cut the poles. Bright and the invalids watched, at first not grasping what the Skyes were doing.

"Seasons," Skye said.

"I was thinking we've been slow and need to hasten before we get caught in a storm," Bright said. "Hiram has a roll

of canvas in that wagon, and we intended to put up temporary canvas houses in the desert until we could build better."

"It's a good plan. But it's September, and from now on
things could change."

They started later than usual that morning and continued
along the well-worn trail. A horseman passed them by with
scarcely a glance, and then another who kept his distance,
making a wide loop around Skye's company. Skye couldn't
see the man but kept thinking it was the Square-beard, en
route to foment trouble ahead. It puzzled him.

Still, the day progressed peacefully, and now the midday
temperatures were pleasant rather than hot.

Late that day they reached a considerable village, which
lay somnolently beside the river, flanked by peaceful hills on
either side. It was the first settlement of any consequence in
miles. And even as they approached town, a cluster of armed
men blocked the road. Victoria quietly slipped her quiver
over her back, and took up her bow, but Skye feared that a
fight would be a disaster for them.

The plunging sun turned each of those men into a silhou-
ette, an utterly featureless human male, black against gold
and blue. The light blinded Skye, and he tugged his hat lower
so the brim gave him relief.

A leader of some sort, his face in deep shadow under the
slouch hat pressed low on his head, waved his rifle.

"No farther," he said so softly that Skye could barely hear
him.

"Well, all right, we'll go around town," Skye replied.

"No, you're going back the way you came."

"I see. And where would you expect us to go?"

"Away. It matters not where."

There were ten or twelve men here, all of them with long

194

guns of some sort. Some were fowling pieces, the others were rifles. The shadow on their faces was so deep they might as well have been masked. They looked determined, and there was no prospect of persuading them to open the road.

Mister Bright hurried forward. "What's the trouble here?" he asked.

"There's no trouble unless you cause some, and then there will be trouble you won't ever remember," the slouch-hat man said.

"Have you reasons?" Skye asked.

"You've been told, and that's reason enough."

"Would you really do this to invalids?"

"You are Lamanites. We will defend our land."

"We're just passing through."

"How about if we circle well away from town?"

"Men, prepare to do your duty!" the man snapped.

At once, every rifle and fowling piece was lowered and aimed, most of them directly at Skye. He saw the muzzles of half a dozen weapons pointing his way, and found the threat persuasive.

He smiled and lifted his topper. "Very well, we will turn around, and a fine afternoon to you, gents."

He started to wheel Jawbone, who was trembling with his own wild rage, when he spotted the square-beard standing well back of this skirmish line. Skye nodded, waved his hat, and plunked it down on his graying hair.

It took some doing to turn the wagons, and Skye feared a misstep would unloose a murderous blast. But these resolute men were not hasty, and watched carefully as Bright and the two Jones men gradually wheeled the caravan around. Victoria, seething but showing none of it, Skye thought, turned the travois ponies, and eventually they were all headed north.

Skye's back itched. Now they were at the back of the wagon train, and Bright was ahead, and Square-beard was back there, watching every step.

After a mile or so Skye ventured up a knoll and found the town's sentries still there, gathered on a hilltop where they could mark the progress of Skye's company. Skye studied the rambling Sevier River, and thought he saw twin tracks ford it. It was growing dark by the time they turned a bend and left the sentries behind.

"We'll head for the river," Skye told Bright. "I thought I saw a ford back a bit."

"Ford?"

"If we camp on the road, we'll probably have visitors. Let's use the dark to good advantage. I'm going to explore a little."

Skye rode through twilight, uncertain whether anyone was watching but willing to take the risk. This was a cloudless evening, and stars were piercing through the dusk, one by one. He reached the river, scaring up a large animal he knew was a mule deer, and walked southward along its flats, looking for the faint two-rut mark upon the earth.

He missed it the first time, but something bade him stop and go back, and then he did find the faint mark of wagons descending to the river, and the same marks barely visible on its far bank. The trouble was, this country was so anonymous that if he fetched the company here, he would miss this place in the thickening dark. So he slipped Jawbone toward the bank, which was a gravelly flat. Jawbone hated crossings, and shivered, but Skye urged him into the shallow river, and found good hard gravel underfoot. Jawbone didn't even get wet above the hocks. It was a fine ford. Skye took Jawbone up the far bank, which was another reach of gravel, and rode a little into the unremarkable hills there as night settled. There was plenty of firewood and deep cover on that far shore, and the place was as safe as any—if he could find the ford again. He worked back in the twilight, found the ford, crossed the river, and then dug his red bandanna out of his britches pocket. He found a stake, drove it into soft earth a few yards from the ford, and tied his bandanna to it. Then he headed back to the camp, where the invalids were washing themselves and stretching.

"It's good," he said to Victoria. "We'll cross the river. I put my scarf on a stick."

She nodded, and began preparing to travel once again. The night was cold, but lit by a lingering twilight in the west, and Skye managed to find the ford again, recover his bandanna, and await the creaking wagons. Victoria splashed the travois ponies across, finding easy passage, and Mary and North Star followed, with Bright's ox-drawn supply wagon first.

"Solid, shallow, and an easy grade on both sides," Skye said.

Bright removed his boots and then took his oxen into the river, crossing without trouble. The Jones brothers splashed the mules and their wagon across easily. Somehow or other they had made it, and gathered on the far side of the river. Skye rode ahead in a pleasant, if chill, night, found a grove of trees well hidden from Redmond by a ridge, and thought it would be as good a place as any.

"What are we going to do, Mister Skye?" asked Lloyd Jones.

"I don't know. I wish I did know. I don't know how bloody mad these bloody damned people are. I don't know what they think. I'm hoping to work around this town. I don't want any trouble."

He was seething. All he wanted to do was get sick people to safety, and he'd gotten caught in a war. He felt like attaching a white flag on a pole and walking straight through. Let them violate a white flag if they would. And yet . . . it had come to that. They would.

They slept undisturbed. The young people looked distraught. Not even potatoes and cabbages solaced them this time. Would they wander the desert hills until they all died? This time it was Eliza whose tears flowed down her shadowed face in the flickering firelight.

At first light Skye looked around carefully. It was always the most dangerous moment in wilderness. And yet it was hard to imagine these sturdy, hardworking Saint settlers who wanted only to be left alone descending on them. But then he remembered Square-beard, another sort of Saint altogether, with something smoldering in his eyes.

So he slipped out of his robes in the half-light, studied the hills, and paused. There, on a ridge to the south, was someone standing in plain sight. The person didn't seem to notice Skye's camp because it lay in deep shadow. But that someone was hunting, and Skye knew his company was the prey.

He nudged Victoria. She nodded, slipped out of her robes, pulled her quiver over her shoulder, strung her bow, and vanished into the woods. A brushy gulch would take her to the very foot of the ridge where someone was watching and maybe a hundred more were armed and readied just over its brow. Skye quietly awakened the rest, told them to find cover in the thick brush away from camp. Who could know what sunrise would bring?

twenty-eight

A skinny man emerged from the morning gloom, followed by Victoria, her bow drawn and an arrow nocked. The man was not silent.

"Who do you think ye air, ye blawdy bitch! Treating me like some bloomin' pincushion, are ye? Damn blawsted demon!"

He paraded straight toward Skye, who stood waiting, while Victoria resolutely kept her bow drawn. He spotted Skye, exhaled, straightened himself up, and marched forward.

"Ye be the owner o' this savage? Ye bloomin' spawn of the devil, what do ye want of me, stealing me from my morning prayer, eh?"

The stubble-jawed skinny wretch was plainly furious. And that flood of words, so familiar. Could it be?

"East End, is it?" Skye asked.

"East End, Cheapside, how the 'ell did ye know that, eh? And stop this savage from sticking an arrer into me arse, eh?"

"I'm an East Ender," Skye said.

"It makes sense, that it does," the skinny fellow said. "Do what ye will then, get out the 'ammer and knock me over the noggin. There's not a tuppence in me britches, so the joke's on ye, ye scum."

Skye started laughing. "East End, all right. How'd you get all the way from London to here?"

"Wouldn't ye want to know, before ye knawk me on the noggin."

"I'm Mister Skye, and I know your parish, friend."

"Friend, is it? Don't call me a friend until this savage puts that arrer back in the bag."

Skye nodded to Victoria, who eased the drawn bow and restored the arrow to the quiver.

The gent watched all this with plain relief. "East End? You don't make the right noises."

"It's been a long time. I was a seaman in the Royal Navy, courtesy of a press gang."

"Now ye be talkin'. 'Alf the queen's navy gets pressed from the East End. Now, by God, ye make some sainse."

That was true.

"You're a long way from London," Skye said. "I'm Barnaby Skye. And you?"

"Mickey, Mickey the Pick."

"A noble profession, Mister Pick. Most of the citizens of East End could pick a pocket before anyone found it out."

"Well, that's me. On'y thing was, the bobbies was swarming all the whiles, a-lookin' for me, the cutpurse. and if I got snatched, it's transportation to Australia. So I ware looking for something, anything, and here's this Immigration Society, it's run by the Saints, the Mormons, steerage across the sea and passage to this Americer if I join up. So all of a sudden, me, Mickey the Pick, ain't I a Saint, and here I yam."

"A Saint?" Skye marveled.

"Most of the time, matey, most of the time."

"This is your place?"

"Yep, the elders, they said Mickey, laddie, we've got a nest for ye, and showed me this piece of ground, and I like it, mate, I plumb like it. They start me with some hogs and ducks and geese, and that's it. I'm a hog man, a pig-sticker."

By now a crowd had collected. Mister Bright listened, the Jones brothers studied, the invalids clustered shyly, Victoria squinted, Mary smiled uneasily, and Jawbone jammed his snout into Mickey the Pick and whoofed.

"By blawdy 'ell, Skye, ye got a party here. These here dusky women, they belong to you?"

"I belong to them, you might say. They're my wives. Behind you is Victoria of the Absarokas, named in honor of our monarch, and Mary of the Shoshones, named in honor of the Virgin."

"Well, 'ell, the elders promised me a wife or two, myself, but they ain't shown up with none yet, because ever' time they see a comely one, they snatch her for themselves. Been three years now, since they promised me one, and I'm getting a little testy about it, blawsted bishops. I should have me two or three by now."

"You have breakfast yet, Mister Pick?"

"Mister Pick! What sort of talk's that, eh? Mister Pick, me arse."

"A notion of mine, sir. In this New World, I want to be Mister, not just Skye. That's what's here, a chance for ordinary people to get ahead."

"Where do I know that name, Skye, eh, matey?"

"My father was an importer and exporter. He had an East End warehouse and offices."

"I know the place, I do! Once they left the doors unlocked and I nipped a few bolts of nankeen and got a few quid for 'er."

"That still your business?" Skye asked.

Mickey the Pick sighed. "I could make more quid with a rock in a sock than raising hogs and ducks. But the Mormons, they don't much go for sapping the wayfarer. You know what I was doing when this here mean ol' savage woman aimed that arrer at my arse? I was praying. Each day I go to greet the dawn, and go to tell Gawd I like this pretty land, and how He's treated me right. That's what I do, this old East End laddie."

Mickey the Pick said it so softly Skye had to strain to hear the man.

"You're a Saint, then, a real Saint?"

"I don't know whot else to be. No bloke's got a purse to pick around here. They got lots of things, but not a quid in their britches. So I'm giving 'er a chance. By Gawd, this here Mormon outfit, they're collecting the likes of me from all over the world and settling us here." He eyed his silent auditors. "Now, laddie, tell old Mickey what you're doing here? So far from the road, eh? Up to no good, are ye?"

It would take some explaining.

"We're taking these young people to the desert to heal, Mister Pick. They're from the East Coast. They're consumptives, and we think maybe the dry desert air is what heals them."

"Croakers, are they! 'Arf the East End's sick with it. They say 'ardly a soul lives beyond forty in East End, and most don't make thirty. My ma and pa, it sent them to their grave. Sisters too. Me, not me. I'm too mean."

Skye introduced the whole party and told what happened. "Armed men stopped us. Turned us away. We just wanted to pass through. They called us Lamanites. What's that?"

"Ye air Lamanites all right. Dark-skinned. The Indians, they're Lamanites. Rebelled against God. Sons of Laman. God gave 'em dark skins as a curse. They're the Antichrist, them Lamanites."

"We're the Antichrist?"

"Or spies or Missouri Pukes or people from Independence or Nauvoo, Illinois, causing trouble."

"You've learned Mormon history, then."

"I'm tired of the 'istory. I live right now, not yesterday. They don't just tell us, they say 'ere's how ye got to think. Ye gotta believe this or that or some other they tell you. But old Mickey, he does his own thinking."

"I should warn you, Mister Pick, that we've been shadowed."

"That don't scare no East End laddy none. I've seen 'em in town, all 'ot-eyed and suspicious. But any East End lad could show 'em a thing or three. I don't have no regular sap, but a rock in a sock, it's just dandy, and I could lift their purses without half trying."

"We're looking for a way around town, some way that would put us back on the road a few miles below town without anyone knowing."

The skinny fellow stared. "Gawd sent you here, I think."

"We could give you something for it," Bright said.

"Give me something! What, consumption? Me, I'm joining up this here outfit. You just pressed me."

Skye started laughing. The others were puzzled.

"You have to know the East End of London, mates," Skye said. "We've added to our company. Mickey the Pick is joining us."

Pick doffed his formless hat. "I'm fetching you to this place in the desert, that's what this bloke's up to. I'll bring

203

some ducks and geese in my cart, and maybe some suckling pigs, sell off the rest, and 'ere's to you Lamanites."

This was a brave and impulsive man, Skye thought. And an asset. They stood around staring, as the day brightened and the sun climbed over the eastern hills.

"I'll hike to my 'ouse if this savage don't put an arrer in my arse. It's that way, maybe a 'arf mile. By the time you get there I'll have a skillet full of eggs ready for some serious eating."

"I'll walk with you and help," Victoria said.

"Sure enough, your majesty," he replied.

That puzzled her, but she gamely collected her pony and led it as she started off beside him.

When they did reach his farmstead, Skye was astonished to discover a thatched cottage with stucco sides. It was the first thatched roof he had seen in North America, and Pick had used river sedges for the thatch. Fowl wandered everywhere, chickens, ducks, geese, but Skye saw no hogs. Still, this place was not far from the river bottoms, and he surmised that the hogs made their living down there.

A battered cart sagged into the ground, and a pair of burros yawned from a pen.

Bright took one look at that cart, pulled out his tools, and set to work. Pick eyed him warily at first, and then began smiling as Bright anchored a loose iron tire, splinted the cracked singletree, and greased the axles.

Mickey the Pick and Victoria soon had a mountain of eggs and porridge ready, and the invalids ate a meal such as they hadn't had in months.

"Now, I've been scheming, Skye. It's a shifty thing, getting you blokes around the town, and I'll have to guide you. Don't try it yourself; you'll be spotted. It's wartime and they got themselves a militia. There's a place where we'll be right across the river from town. I've got to load up my cart, get some breeding pairs into cages, drive some 'ogs to market, and fetch a few quid. It's a big job. So you go on ahead, and I'll fetch up behind ye in a day or two. I've got a bit of business, maybe sell the place 'ere and tell the elders they owe me a couple of women. Then, whiles they're thinking about their sins, I'll come along behind ye and we'll get these blokes to the desert."

That sounded like a plan.

twenty-nine

*T*he bloke took over. Skye watched, flabbergasted. Mickey the Pick collected two breeding pairs of squealing piglets from a sow and stuffed them into a slat-sided cage. Then he snatched ducklings from their mother and stuffed them into another cage.

"There's some meat, guv'nor," he said, and dropped the cage into the supply wagon. "Feed 'em or eat 'em. Now, youse get yourselves ready whiles I git you a few eggs for a supper, and I'll steer the outfit roundabout those hills. This little trip will take most of a day, and it'll drop ye at a ford a few miles below town, and ye can cross her, watch out for a swampy spot, and git onto the road. I'll cut back here and close down this bloomin' bedbug castle and catch ye down the trail some-wheres."

Soon they were off, Mickey the Pick leading them through hills until Skye scarcely knew where he was. But then Mickey halted.

"We've come past town, matey, and now you're all by your lonesome. I'm going to ship out. Drive meself to town, sell the lot, load my stuff in my cart, and get me arse outa there."

Skye extended a weathered hand, and Mickey the Pick clasped it, grinning like a monkey.

All that autumnal day, Skye's party worked south along a faint two-rut trail, probably cut by Mickey's own cart. Skye rode ahead, looking for trouble, but Mickey's route wove around quiet juniper-dotted slopes and Skye never found a spot where he could see the river from the trail, much less the main road beyond it.

Then the trail veered down a gully toward the little river, and Skye could see the silver glint of water ahead, and beyond that, the main road on the far side. So they had dodged the little settlement. But he thought to cross that creek under the cloak of darkness, so he called an early halt well out of sight of travelers. This was good grassland, and the horses and oxen would profit.

They had skirted town but what about the next settlement, and the next and the next? Skye wished he could find an alternative route, but he had invalids with him, and that meant the main road where wagons could go.

They feasted on eggs cooked on a tiny fire Victoria built from dead juniper limbs. The invalids seemed somewhat better, having had some changes in diet the last few days. Skye thought maybe their scurvy would be conquered if they could get enough cabbage and potatoes. But now he was seeing in them a deep weariness. They had traveled too long and were too worn out to go much farther. They were a long way from the Atlantic coast. Even David and Lloyd Jones, the strongest of the invalids, were plainly at their limit. And Skye had no help for them.

But there was this, he thought: the air had changed. They

had passed some invisible line between climates, and this air of southern Utah was different, dry and mild, with the scent of sun-pummeled cedar in it. Cactus and creosote bush and juniper abounded. This air had pungence, a balm for lungs. It was an odd thing, this change in the air. He could not fathom why this air was different, why this air seemed to come from some other corner of the world. Where had it changed? Maybe there was something to the idea that lungers could heal in the desert.

Skye saw his son lying on a robe, and he picked up the little one, who was still a feather in his hands but gaining a little weight at Mary's breast. The infant was enjoying the balmy air, and stared up at Skye with bright brown eyes. Skye felt a great wave of tenderness. Here was a son to take his name, his nature, and Mary's nature into the future. But only if this little one escaped sickness and the thousand things that befell children as they grew.

Mary was cooking some of the potatoes. He handed the child to Victoria, whose face reflected joy and pain at once; the pain of being barren, the joy of being a mother to this child, even if it was not the issue of her loins. Then, at last, she set the boy back on the robe, with a small caress of the boy's black hair.

"The sick people, they are pretty damn sick," she said.

So she had noticed too.

"No one wants them. This new sickness, it is because these Saints don't let them pass. I do not understand this. Damned paleskins. I'm glad I'm me," she said.

After a hearty meal for man and beast, Skye and Bright started the wagons down the last grade to the meandering river, found what looked to be a crossing, and Skye took

Jawbone out into it. But the horse hit a pothole and floundered toward the far bank. Skye held a big hand to the horse's neck, quieting him. Then Jawbone tried again, upstream twenty yards, and found shallow footing all the way across.

"We need to stay upstream, here, a little," Skye told Bright.

That was all it took. Mary and Victoria took the travois ponies across, along with the Morgan mare, while Bright watched, and then the wagons came along, and just at twilight they were all safely back on the main road and riding south in deep silence. Skye planned to ride into the night if he could. And maybe find some sheltered spot to camp. He wondered about Mickey the Pick, an East Ender who knew little of the wilds. Where and when would this little Londoner find them? If ever?

They camped on a flat below the trail, next to the Sevier River, and met with no trouble that night. The following day they made their way south without hindrance, and Skye thought maybe there would be no more difficulty. But then they came to a hamlet called Aurora, a farming community drawing its irrigation water from the little river. It seemed a peaceful place. There were people in the village, farm wagons, women with wicker baskets under their arms, bearded men in brogans and rough trousers and homespun shirts. They stared as Skye's party approached, studied Skye on Jawbone, squinted at Skye's wives, the ponies and the travois, examined the two small wagons, the oxen and mules, and the young people riding the tailgates.

Then, shockingly, they all turned their backs. Some giant hand had spun each citizen of this hamlet around, children too, so that not a face was visible to Skye's party. They were being shunned. It was a grave insult. It was the opposite of a welcoming. It needed no explanation. Skye and everyone in his company understood. Skye's women stared back, flinty of eye, angry at this reception.

Bright hastened forward. "I've a mind to stop right here for a spell," he said. "Let 'em keep their backs turned for an hour or two."

That was Bright for you, Skye thought. But it could not be. Their obligation was to the invalids; get them safely to the desert. And provoking these people would gain them nothing. These farm people were not armed and had not formed a militia. So keep on going, never pause, and show no fear.

"They knew we were coming," Skye said. "I imagine we'll see more of this."

"I've never seen so much backside," Bright said. "It's like viewing the world from behind a one-bottom plow."

They wove slowly past the half-dozen whitewashed commercial buildings, a general store, a smithy, livery barn, feed and implement dealer, and something that looked like a temple rising on a hilltop. What looked to be a school stood near the temple.

But then they were free of that place and moving slowly through stubble fields. These people had long since harvested their grains. A few cattle and some hogs roamed freely, gleaning a living after the harvest.

"Is it my imagination or is this air different?" Bright asked.

"It's different. I've been thinking that somehow Hiram Peacock knew the air would be different. Maybe he even would have an explanation for it. It feels like velvet."

"I'd like to invent a machine that tells me why this air is more to my liking than the air a hundred miles back."

David Jones joined them as they walked. "I think they

didn't much care for us," he said. "Maybe I don't care much for them."

Something in the young man was spoiling for a fight. He and the others had been insulted and shunned once too often.

Skye smiled. "We're in the desert now, Mister Jones. It won't be long before we'll be building a home for you and letting the sun do its healing."

The answer obviously did not satisfy the young man, but he drifted back to the mule team. If his thoughts were those of the rest of the invalids, there was bitterness riding the wagons.

Skye took them south well into the night, and then found a riverside flat for a camp. But even before they had unhooked and watered the teams or completed their chores, teamster music filled the air.

"Bloomin' burros, move your butts." The familiar voice rose out of the darkness. A cart with squealing wheels howled through the night.

Skye clambered up a grade and intercepted Mickey the Pick, and steered him to the campsite.

The cart was alive. Crates of something or other filled it, along with a bedroll. These creatures, fowl apparently, flapped and fluttered in their containers, and squawked now and then.

Mickey steered his howling cart straight into camp.

Bright listened to the squeal, headed for the grease pot hanging from his wagon, and set to work on Mickey's axles, even before greetings had been exchanged.

"I'll not listen to that hour after hour, day after day," he muttered.

"Skye, my bruvver, I did it. Sold the 'ogs on the hoof; got a few quid and a few more for my croft. Sold the whole lot to a widower I know, lost three wives in a row, and prefers 'ogs and 'ens."

"You drove all the hogs to town, Mister Pick?"

"Mister Pick is it, yeeeow, ye miserable bloke. No, I sold 'em the right to collect the porkers himself, and any loose goose he might find around the place. I fetched me twenty dollars for the lot."

That seemed low to Skye, but it was cash in a barter economy, and maybe the best Mickey could manage.

"I got a bit of news, matey. Ye know what's rufflin' their feathers? Big train full of Pukes, Missouri men they say, a hundred forty of them, rolling through here two days ago. Fancher's the captain, the very devil of a hater, they say. He's fixing to kill every Saint he can or drive us out of here. Him and his company, wagon after wagon after wagon."

Skye wondered about all that. Was any of it true?

thirty

They set out in a great quiet, never seeing a soul that day, or the next and the next. The settlements had vanished. The arid country was as empty as it had been before the Saints swarmed in. The meandering river bisected an anonymous valley, with distant snow-dusted ridges to both sides. Fall had arrived in the mountains, even if summer lingered in the bottoms. But Skye could always feel change of season in his bones, even when it was not yet apparent to anyone else. They were running out of time.

Mickey the Pick had taken to walking beside Skye in the van of this small procession. Jawbone fended for himself, and Mickey's burros seemed to know they were to follow him. There had been a sudden fraternity blooming between the two Londoners, and Skye enjoyed hearing the music of Mickey's tongue, something he had not heard since his days in the Royal Navy.

"Now, Skye, bloke, these Saints, they're two sorts, and we're facing the worst. The ones up at Great Salt Lake, they're a bit more reined in, but these southern ones, they're a wild bunch, full of bad memories, let me tell ye. They've not got a law to their name, other than what they make up when they need one. The lot'd as soon kill ye as look at ye. And they don't take orders from old Brigham, neither. They're like a nation inside of a nation, and we'll have to tread mighty light. Just a little word of warning."

"I was hoping we were done with them. It's pretty quiet."

"That's because this isn't land they favor. Now down south, there's good sheep country in the valleys, and a man can grow squash and tooties."

"What's this war about?"

"Gawd help a bloke for trying to explain it. I'm as dumb as a turkey about this war. But it's mostly about wives, matey. Wives it is. The Americers, they're saying no more than one to a customer, and the Saints, they're saying up yours, go to 'ell, ye buggers."

"What about Deseret?"

"Deseret? Haw. Some of the Saints, they want to carve out a little empire all their own, see? It's Yank turf, it is, but that don't stop the bastids. Old Brigham, he was territorial gover-nor until the Yanks tossed him, and now all the 'otheads, they're spoiling for war and stirring up the Indians too."

"Tell me about that."

"The Saints, they've spent a lot of time playing footsie with the redskins. Buttering 'em up like, with gifts and all that, but at the same time settling in the river bottoms where the Paiutes raised squash. So the Saints, they give 'em pie and mash, and got the tribes in their pocket. Not only that, but they got the tribes to do their fighting for 'em. This federal column heading 'ere, they're going to meet up with a few hundred Paiutes and they're going to get their arse whipped, because the Saints have armed those Paiutes into some dandy little cavalry, or so the blokes tell me. Me, I don't trust a thing I'm told. They by damn holy promised me a wife a year ago and never delivered. A man needs a woman. I should have me about three now. How come did I join the Saints? That's how come. And now the bloomin' elders, they got in ahead of this little East Ender, every chance they had, and probably laugh when they think about it."

"Where are these Paiutes now?"

"All over the hills, bloke. We could run into five hundred of the devils any moment."

"You're a Saint? Is that enough to quiet them if we do?"

"I'll damned well tell 'em a thing or three. I'll tell them here you are, two wives, a true Saint by 'ell. Not a Mericat in the lot. That's what they call Yanks, Mericats."

"What if they've been told otherwise?"

"Ain't you the worrier. I'll give 'em some little porkers and hens, and they'll sit their arses down and start a cook fire."

Skye laughed. Ever since Mickey the Pick joined the party, the day's worries had dissolved in humor.

What's more, Mickey had not hesitated to mix with the invalids. He was often back there gabbing with them, telling them about London's East End, telling them that the bad air of London, thick with coal smoke and fog, sometimes in deadly combination, knocked off consumptives at an alarming rate, and that was why he was going to get them all to good air.

"Mister Pick, what do you plan to do when we find a place on the Virgin River?" Skye asked.

"Mister Pick is it? A low and coarse insult is Mister Pick. I'll damned well get these poor cobs settled and start me a 'og farm and build what needs to be built and start the wretches to healing. You know what heals 'em up, bloke? A horse laugh and a toddy."

"A toddy? And you, a Saint?"

"Me, I'm a special kind of Saint, call me Jack."

"Jack Saint?"

"Haw!"

Each evening Mickey the Pick fed his fowl from the stores of grain, or let them pluck a living from the brush for a while, and did the same with his little porkers. Skye saw the value of it at once. Someday these breeding animals would provide meat for the invalids.

The Sevier River continued to take them south through open arid country, but the distant slopes were dark on top, revealing the presence of pines. This trail would take them to California if they wished to go that far, providing adequate graze for the livestock, firewood, water, and safety.

But all that could change in an instant. Skye was too much a man of the wilds to trust a peaceful place too far.

That night, at his own family campfire, he asked Mary what she knew of the Paiutes, the numerous tribe that inhabited the Utah country, and which her Shoshones knew well.

"Ah, a good people," she said, her face aglow. "I know their tongue a little. It is like my own. I maybe know their talk like this."

She held two fingers up, a little apart.

"They grow things in the river valleys. Maize, squash, melons, seeds. They eat agave, the great plant of the desert. They collect piñon nuts and kill small game. They eat eggs and lizards and snakes. Rabbits, little animals of the desert."

"Mickey says the Saints converted them."

"I know nothing of that. They honor a spirit, Coyote, that I know. They live in small family groups around springs.

Long ago the white priests came and took children away, and then the Utes and Navajos took Paiute children away."

"You can talk with them?"

She nodded. "I think so."

"Are they warriors?"

"Oh, no, they are a quiet people. Sometimes my people trade with them. They have nothing and they want robes and furs and trade with us for squash and melons and nuts and seeds."

"Could they be turned into an army by the Saints?"

"Ah, no, Mister Skye, I don't think so. They have too many headmen. Each in a little village, little hunting band."

"The head of the Saints, Brigham Young, is threatening to send a whole army of Indians to stop the Yankee column. He said the Yanks won't even get close to here."

She frowned. "I do not know this thing. Everything changes. For a woman of the People nothing is ever the same now."

Change was coming too fast for all the tribes, Skye thought. He had a dark premonition about the future of them all.

Food, then. If there was trouble, greet the starving Paiutes with food. That was what he got from Mickey the Pick, and now Mary. It was hunger that drove them, hunger caused by the usual dislocation of the tribes from choice land by whites, in this case the Saints.

The wagons progressed ever southward through a deep desert peace, day by day. The land was changing. Now there was cactus and wax-leaved shrubs and everything had thorns. Desert plants had their own fierce defenses. And the air continued to change in some ineffable way. If anything, the world grew more silent. Arid country could make a man think he was deaf.

One eve, Enoch Bright dropped in at Skye's campfire.

"You know, the cabbages and potatoes are putting a little bloom on our invalids," he said.

"I hadn't noticed. One of my sorrows is that I can't join your people or bring my wives to their camp. There's no help for it."

"Well, take my word, this air, this quiet, this better food, it's working some good. I take it that people are like furnaces. You can build a fire with most any wood, but put in a good seasoned hardwood, some ash or hickory or beech, and you'll see a fine hot flame. You feed some good hard food to these people, and they build up steam until their safety valve's whistling."

"Well, I hadn't quite thought of it that way, Mister Bright. And what do you think about the stock?"

"I've been studying on it. These grasses here, mostly dried and brown, make better fuel than some of the lush green stuff we passed by. This desert fodder puts some heat into their furnaces. Our oxen, oh, they're lean and worn all right, but rightly muscled up and ready for more. Christopher Carson Ox is still leading the parade, skinny as he is. And the mules, tough as lions, and they yank that wagon along as if it's a feather. Mickey the Pick claims that his burros do better around here than up north."

"And the wagons?"

"We have loose tires. This dry air's shrunk the felloes and I'll need to do a little smithing if it gets worse. For now, I've driven a few wedges into the wheels to keep the tires tight, but the same desert air that's making life better for our invalids, it's starting to give me some aches and pains."

"How about you? You've come across a continent."

"I was talking to Mickey the Pick about that just an hour

ago, Mister Skye. We're not tired. That London man and I, we think alike. I'm stronger than when I started. I'm Hiram Peacock's steward, you know. He said, before a few witnesses, if anything happened to him, I'd be in command and he'd entrust me with carrying it through. Well, that's my fuel, Mister Skye, good seasoned hardwood in my own furnace, and it's making steam, all right."

thirty-one

They arrived at Parowan, the most important settlement in southern Utah, one chill September afternoon. The town lay in a wide valley and was surrounded by excellent farms.

Skye saw nothing that troubled him. The trip south had been peaceful and the clouds of war had vanished. Parowan boasted broad streets and practical frame houses, and was already a solid city that displayed the genius of the industrious Saints in its orderly buildings. Hollyhocks and lilacs and rosebushes furbished the yards and added grace to this austere settlement. Life here in an arid land might be hard, but familiar flowers softened it and turned their town into an Eden. The city slumbered in a cool bright afternoon, paying no attention at all to wagon traffic on the artery connecting southern and northern Utah.

Skye rode warily ahead of his company, hoping that the troubles were past and they could proceed unimpeded to their refuge in the desert. They weren't far now; in a few days

Bright's company would be camped somewhere on the Virgin River, and beginning to erect some winter quarters.

He would see about food. Always food. He did not yet know how this company would feed itself. It had no money, no time to break ground and plant crops, no meat, no fruits, and spring planting was a long time away.

Skye thought he could trade another of his ponies for quite a bit of food, and as he led his company through the sleepy streets, he looked for a general store, and settled on one across the broad avenue.

"We'll look for food, Enoch," Skye said.

"Fuel for the boilers," Bright replied.

The main street had two or three false-front mercantiles, plain but serviceable, plus a few lesser buildings that housed a clothier, a smith, a harness shop, an apothecary shop, an implement dealer, and a livery barn. Beyond, lay a somnolent town square, with a stone temple dominating the far side. Substantial houses lined the square.

Victoria and Mary studied the place; white men's towns always fascinated them. The few people on the streets, mostly bonneted women, gazed discreetly at this odd company.

A small shake of Victoria's head sent a silent message to Skye. She didn't trust this place, and was letting him know it.

But he saw little that alarmed him, and stiffly dismounted, leaving Jawbone to stretch, clack his yellow teeth, and slay dragons.

"Let's see what we can do at the Parowan General Store," he said to Bright.

"A real store; not a mirage," Bright replied.

They had not seen a store for weeks.

But even as they started across the clay street, a party of

three men hailed them. These were all dressed in black broadcloth suits, and Skye thought they might be officials of some sort.

He paused, awaiting the Saints.

One wore a small nickel-plated circlet.

"Marshal Klingonsmith, sir," the man said.

A homely one, Skye thought, as he shook hands.

"I'm Barnaby Skye, sir; guiding this company west."

"Ah, then you've got the sick people."

"I'm Enoch Bright, in charge here. Pleased to meet you. Yes, we're taking some consumptives to the desert to heal. It's a remedy that holds great promise."

Bright shook hands with the marshal, and then with the others, who proved to be a deputy marshal named Tanner and Bishop Higbee, a balding, bespectacled man with a receding chin hidden by a close-cropped beard.

"We've heard you're coming," Klingonsmith said. "It's not a good time, you know. Our people aren't happy to entertain Gentiles."

"And that's what we want to talk to you about," the bishop said. "There's Indian trouble ahead. The Paiutes are stirred up, and we think it'd be fatal for you to proceed."

"Why?" asked Skye.

"They've been treated badly by California companies. That's what we hear. So we thought to warn you."

"What companies?"

"A large train a few days ahead of you. They've got the Paiutes stirred up. We don't know much more, but we thought to pass along a friendly warning."

There were a lot of ways a company could stir up Indians.

"Where are the Paiutes now?" he asked.

"Who can say, sir? West of us, we believe," Klingonsmith said.

"What do you want of us?"

"Camp a day or two here. When it's safe, we'll send you on your way."

Skye had the odd sensation that this was an order, even if it was clothed as a suggestion. "We're hoping to find a suitable place and put up shelter before it turns cold, sir. These people are very sick."

"Children, mostly, I'm told."

"Young people, from twelve into their twenties."

"Women, I'm told."

"Four. All from New Bedford, Massachusetts. The company lost two."

"We would like to meet them," the bishop said.

"You're welcome to meet all of our company, sir. They're consumptives, and it's necessary for you to keep some distance."

Skye shepherded them all to the two wagons, where the young people had collected. All who could escape their pallets stood, awaiting what fate brought them.

But first, his family.

"This is my Crow wife, Victoria Skye, and my Shoshone wife, Mary Skye, and my newborn, who carries two names. Dirk, after my English father, and North Star, a name given to my son by my wife's people."

The bishop smiled dismissively. He was not interested in Indians or a half-breed child. Instead, he beelined for the consumptives, who stood or sat on the tailgates of the wagons.

Bright made the introductions. "Now, let's start with Eliza and Mary Bridge. Eliza's seventeen, Mary's nineteen.

They're daughters of Ethan and Geneva Bridge, New Bedford. Geneva, their mother, was sick with the consumption herself, and wasn't strong enough to come here. Their parents sent them with us."

"They are without a guardian," Higbee said.

"I'll get to that," Bright said. "Now we have Anna Bennett. She's eighteen. Her father's a Congregational minister. She's had the consumption for three years and has suffered more than a plenty. She asked to come along, thinking it might do her a good turn. It was hard; she left behind a lad she's promised to. She told him she'd fly to his arms just as soon as the desert air did its work."

The bishop eyed Anna too long, Skye thought.

One by one, Enoch introduced the consumptives, taking a moment to make each of them a person with hopes and dreams, for the benefit of the bishop.

Skye listened carefully. He did not detect the sort of rank hostility here that he had discovered earlier among the Saints. Higbee was assessing each of these people, the Jones brothers, Peter Sturgeon, the Bridge sisters, the Tucker twins, and Sterling Peacock with quiet gazes.

But there was something else, something hidden, something Skye wondered if he would ever fathom, that was transpiring here. At last, after the somber bishop had met the entire company, he addressed Bright and Skye.

"Come, let us sit in the shade," Higbee said.

Skye and Bright followed him to a storefront with a roofed boardwalk before it. A log bench stretched across its front.

With the gesture from the bishop, they seated themselves.

"It's the war," Higbee said. "In the eyes of some of the Saints, you're the enemy. It doesn't matter that you're transporting unfortunate souls to the desert. You are Gentiles. From here on, if you insist on traveling, you will encounter people who burn within, whose gaze takes you for a Mormon or for an enemy. The Paiutes have been stirred up against you, and there is nothing I can do about it. The fire that eats these settlers south of here burns fiercely on the memories of all the persecutions. And not just Illinois or Missouri, either. These people remember every persecution in New York, Ohio, Pennsylvania, Iowa, and elsewhere. As God is my witness, they will take you for enemies too."

"I have nothing against your people," Bright said.

"Ah, of course. And I'm sure Mister Skye doesn't either; he even shares plural marriage with us. But try to tell that to the firebrands south of here. Try telling that to a settler named John Lee, who carries in his bosom every wrong ever done to the Saints, and intends to avenge every wrong. He's organized every like-minded fool in southern Utah to fall upon the Gentiles, and he's not waiting for a war with the government, either."

Skye pulled his venerable top hat off, letting the dry air cool his hair. "You are saying?" he asked.

"I am saying it is not safe. Not just because the Paiutes are stirred up, but because, I regret to say, there are fanatical men in our ranks."

"Are they here in Parowan?"

Higbee nodded. "Here, everywhere, and they have couriers. They know your every step, sir. And the fact that you carry innocents to the desert to heal does not spare you their wrath. Some call you Lamanites, the dark-skinned tribe who fought the true faith; others say you're the Pale Horse of the Apocalypse."

"We're virtually unarmed," Skye said.

"Believe me, that would not spare you. Men with burning brands wounding their souls stop at nothing."

"What do you suggest, Bishop?"

Higbee peered into the bright street, where the New Bedford Company, what was left of it, waited patiently.

"Forgive me, sirs. You may not like my proposal, though for me it gives the promise of great joy. The only way for you to achieve safe passage is to join our church. For each of you to become a Latter-Day Saint."

thirty-two

The bishop's proposal hung in space, turning the world upside down.

"Of course," said Higbee, "I would entertain only a most earnest conversion. If I could win the soul of just one of your company, heaven and earth would rejoice."

The marshal, Klingonsmith, looked faintly discomfited.

"I could catechize your company for an hour, and let them make their own decisions. It would need to be a most sacred commitment. But I believe it would be the gateway to joy, and your company would find the pearl of great price."

"I don't have enough steam in my boiler," Enoch Bright declared, which puzzled the bishop.

Skye hardly knew how to respond, but decided to see about the consequences. "We already have a Saint in our company, Mister Pick, who agreed to help us reach the Virgin River. Would that not suffice?"

"Sadly for you, sir, it would not. The Saints have made alliances with all the surrounding tribes, and now with the threat of war hanging over my people, the tribes are stirred up. The presence of a Mormon in your company would not forestall trouble. From what I hear, the Paiutes are quite beyond the control of our LDS people."

"You mentioned that you have your own radicals, looking for trouble."

"We do. And your membership in my congregation would guarantee you safe passage. I might add, Mister Bright, that you intend to settle on the Virgin River, in the Territory that the Saints have reserved for ourselves. If you hope for cooperation, and foodstuffs, and help, you would be very wise to join my church. That will open the doors. Your invalids will be fed and sheltered and protected, as we would protect our own. And land would be set aside for your sanitarium."

"We have a Saint. Mister Pick. Can he trade for food here?"

"I'm afraid not. The president has embargoed all trade with Gentiles because of the impending invasion."

"He's a Mormon."

"But the leader of this company is not. Mister Bright is not. And, I take it, Sterling Peacock, who inherited the company, is not." He shook his head regretfully. "I'm so sorry. I can't defy the apostolic command."

"Did the big company ahead of us obtain food here?"

"Not a bushel. Not a peck, not a pint."

All this angered Skye. "You're saying you won't protect us? You won't quiet the Paiutes? You can't even keep us safe from your people? A company of invalids?"

Higbee stiffened. "We did not provoke this war, this invasion." Then he softened. Skye sensed that this Saint did not want to see the New Bedford Infirmary Company in harm's way. "There is an absolute way to protect your women . . . from whatever might befall them. Let them marry Saints."

"Marry Saints?" Bright exclaimed. "You just blew my safety valve."

"The Saints believe marriages are forever, and continue on in heaven. No Saint would violate the wife of another. Let them marry."

"And stay here? With strangers chosen for them?" Skye asked.

"Let them continue to your healing place. We can marry them by proxy. I am sure Marshal Klingonsmith would rejoice to receive wives destined for him in heaven."

"Proxy, you say?"

"Our own women will speak as proxies, yes. The ceremony is closed to Gentiles. You may proceed on your way, each of your invalid women carrying with her a record of her wedding. Let them enjoy their marriage after this brief life ends, and their glory in heaven begins."

Skye knew the bishop's offer wasn't for him. He had started life, so long ago, as an Anglican, and had absorbed its liturgy as a boy. Now, five decades later, all that liturgy had been stripped away. But there remained a hard kernel of faith and belief, the vision of God he knew would never leave him.

But the bishop was waiting, smiling blandly. Skye thought it was one of the strangest moments of his life; safe passage guaranteed only to those of the bishop's faith.

It really was Bright's decision to make, and he made it.

"Bishop Higbee, matters of conscience are up to each person. I will exempt only our two youngest, the Tucker twins, who are twelve and not ready to make such choices. You may present your ideas, both the religious and the practical, and it will then be up to each of our invalids to decide." He smiled slightly. "You might even acquire a bride or two."

"It is I who take the risk, sir," Higbee responded. "One false heart would offend my very soul."

This was not Skye's business, but the result would be. A company with some Saints in it might well be safer, if Higbee was right, than one without any Mormons. And Higbee was surely right about the settlement on the Virgin River. If there were Saints in the New Bedford Company, there might be succor through the long first winter.

Enoch led the Saints to the wagons, where the isolated invalids perched on the tailgates or rested within. The oxen slumped in their yokes, and the mules yawned.

"Come, gather around," Bright said. "This is Bishop Higbee, and he's going to talk about what we do next. Beside him is Territorial Marshal Klingonsmith, and Deputy Tanner."

The young people collected warily.

Skye had to give the bishop credit. He began with a tribute to the courage of these young people who were fueled by a vision of healing. He said his people had made the same desperate odyssey across a trackless waste, often in winter, to escape persecutions that were, in a way, not unlike the disease afflicting them.

Higbee turned to the perils ahead, and also to what might be expected if these sick people settled in Utah Territory, which the Saints had reserved as their sanctuary. "We're much alike," he said. "We, too, have sought our Zion here in the Southwest."

He turned delicately to war, to the feeling among the Saints that they were about to be invaded, transgressed, denied their beliefs. And from this he candidly discussed the prospect of running into firebrands and fanatics, whose memories of the great persecutions burned fiercely. And he discussed the Paiutes, allied to the Saints, who were, even now, stirred up so much the Saints could not quiet them.

"Now I will talk about my beloved faith, and my beliefs, and how they might bring you a life of joy and salvation, what we call the pearl of great price."

In swift, sure cadences he outlined the beliefs of his people, their history, a word about Joseph Smith, the Book of Mormon, and the flight of these people to this, their own Promised Land.

"I invite you to join us, first and foremost to the joy of the heavens, and also for temporal purposes, your comfort, safety, and security in the future. You've heard my appeal, which I offer with a joyous hope in your salvation, and you've heard both the spiritual and temporal purposes this might achieve. It is my hope and belief that once you reach your destination, all the world will smile upon you, and you will walk away with new lungs, new hearts, and the prospect of a long life."

It was an eloquent talk, touching both practical and spiritual concerns.

"Are there questions?" he asked. "Will anyone step forward?"

Anna Bennett had one. "Can Mormon wives marry more than one husband?"

"No, that would separate the woman from God."

"I'm a feminist. I believe in equality. I won't embrace a religion that gives me one iota less liberty than a male."

"Ah! We think that upsets the natural and godly order of the universe, as handed to us by our prophet," Higbee said. "But I know there are many young stalwarts here who would gladly take you to wife."

Anna laughed, and Skye sensed this interview was deteriorating. But then Sterling Peacock stood, looking determined and not unlike his father.

"This is my company. It was my father's company. It is my responsibility. I will assume that responsibility. I accept."

"I rejoice to welcome you, Mister Peacock. But I want your most sacred pledge that your purpose is spiritual, not temporal. Utter that pledge before God and man, and I will welcome you into our congregation after a brief instruction."

Sterling Peacock stood resolutely, his pale gray flesh showing the havoc of the sickness that was slowly ruining his whole body. Skye saw no desperation or indecision in him.

"I pledge it," Sterling said.

"Pledge what?"

"To accept your church, the Latter-Day Saints, as my faith, and to accept its doctrine."

"So help you God?"

"So help me God."

Why did Skye feel troubled? He could not say.

"Are there others?" Higbee asked. "Would you care to meditate on it awhile?"

There were no others.

"Young ladies, there is yet another way you can assure your comfort and safety, in the now and in the forever. Marriage."

The Bridge sisters stirred. Plainly, the idea intrigued them.

"It is my holy office to bond Saints in matrimony. I should be most pleased to marry you lovely women to Marshal Klingonsmith here. It would assure you of your safety and comfort throughout the territory, as well as union with a man of great integrity and distinction."

Lloyd Jones intervened. "Would you marry me to a Mormon woman? And would that ensure my safety?"

"I will ignore your impertinence. There are none available, and I could not unite one of our own to a Gentile."

"I'm still waiting in line for mine," Mickey the Pick said.

Higbee stared coolly at the little Londoner.

Skye caught the glance between Mary Bridge and Lloyd Jones, and knew what it was. So there had been dreams all along.

The subject of Mormon matrimony vanished, and Skye found himself wondering about Sterling Peacock, and what was passing through the gaunt young man's mind, and heart and soul.

thirty-three

*S*terling Peacock followed the elders, and was soon out of sight. Skye saw various people collect at the distant stone temple on the square.

Hiram Peacock's son was trail-worn and sick, and carried a grubby rag, into which he would spit up the bloody debris from his lungs and throat. And yet he walked away from the company in pale dignity, a great earnestness upon him.

Whatever would befall him was not for the New Bedford Company to know. This was something private, between the Saints and young Peacock, but Skye surmised it would involve instruction, acceptance, confirmation, and prayer, the essential elements of a step into a new faith.

The company tarried on the broad avenue that cut through Parowan, all of them silent. Somehow it was understood among them that a man's change of religion was not to be discussed; neither was it to be approved or disapproved. And so they all waited in the mild September sunlight, through a ticking afternoon. For this plainly was not a hurried ceremony, and the Saints were taking whatever time was required.

Skye looked to his horse, checking Jawbone for hoof bruises and other troubles, while the Jones brothers examined Christopher Carson Ox and the other oxen, and Enoch Bright examined his mules, hoof by hoof, leg by leg. The animals were gaunt and worn, and half starved because this desert offered so little feed. And yet the company would soon settle on the Virgin River, where the livestock could recruit.

Skye could not know what was passing through Sterling's mind and heart, and thought he ought not wonder about it. A man's faith was, ultimately, his own, and not the business of others. Still, Sterling's decision had surprised Skye. There had been no warning, no cue that such an event was forthcoming. Skye could not remember anything that Sterling had said or done along the road that separated his faith and belief from the rest of these New Englanders.

The sickest had returned to their pallets, shaded by the canvas of their wagon, while they all waited for Sterling to return to the company. If he would return. Skye wondered whether Sterling might choose to abandon the company and live in Parowan. This was desert enough for a man with consumption.

People on the street did not greet them, but hurried by, unwilling to make contact with these Gentiles, and Skye was reminded that this was wartime, and these people felt besieged and threatened.

The invalid women were using the rest break to freshen themselves. Their trail-grimed clothing was in tatters, and stained from the endless tramp across the continent. They needed fresh, but there was no clothing to be had. Lloyd Jones and Mary Bridge were deep in talk, of some sort, and Skye realized that the two had formed some sort of bond; their terrible sickness had not prevented them from a liaison. That, Skye thought, doubled their need to be healed.

Then, late in that afternoon, the Mormon churchdoors swung open. Skye could see the elders shaking hands with Sterling, and then the young man walked alone to the New Bedford Company. His appearance surprised Skye: Sterling wore a fresh shirt and trousers, and had scrubbed away the trail grime that had covered him.

Now they all stared. Had this young man been transformed? Was he still Sterling to them? Would things be different?

"I am free to trade at any store," he said to Bright and Skye. "The embargo does not apply to me. I've decided to trade one of the rolls of canvas for whatever we can get for it. We'll make do with less when we reach the Virgin River. You'll have to carry it for me."

Skye nodded. Each roll of canvas ran two hundred pounds. He summoned the Jones brothers, and then Skye, Bright, and the brothers dragged the roll out of the supply wagon and hauled it into the Parowan General Store across the dusty clay street.

The merchant accepted the canvas in trade at once. He had been apprised of Sterling's confirmation.

Sterling, somehow transformed and confident, negotiated three hundred pounds of flour, barley, milled oats, and some vegetables for it, all in the space of a few minutes. It was plain that the merchant was eager to make an equitable trade. The canvas was worth much; all manufactured goods were worth much, so far from their place of origin. Soon his clerks, as well as Skye, Bright, and the Jones brothers, were carrying sacks of oats, barley, and wheat flour to the supply wagon.

"We're done here," Sterling said. "Let us be on our way."

"It's a bloomin' miracle," Mickey the Pick whispered to Skye. "It's like he's not sick now."

Whatever it was, Sterling's whole demeanor had changed, and now more than ever Sterling seemed like his father, determined, relentless, and inspired by a vision of goodness.

Sterling approached Skye. "They told me there could be trouble ahead. They cannot quiet the Paiutes. Neither can they guarantee safe passage in a country dominated by local militias. These armed groups have escaped the control of the elders. But I have this," he said. He withdrew from a shirt pocket a certificate of baptism.

"That is good to have," Skye said.

"I have a letter, also. It's addressed to the LDS brothers in the Virgin River valley, and it urges them to help me build the sanitarium, and to render all possible assistance to us. Bishop Higbee signed it. I think that's going to see us through the winter, and keep us fed until our farm produces. It's what we need the most."

Skye marveled. Here was a pathway. From the beginning, he had worried about this thing: how could this small company sustain itself after it had reached the Virgin River? And now there was an answer.

"I can see that my task is coming to an end," he said. "We'll make sure you're settled, and then when you feel secure, my family and I will head north. My wife Victoria's eager to winter with her people, and that's what we'll do."

"I am grateful you have taken us to the desert," Sterling said.

Skye thought that the son sounded like his father, and all the more so now, after whatever he had accepted or committed himself to in Parowan. Skye found himself gazing at a determined adult; no longer anyone's son, but a sovereign man, and he marveled at the change.

But then Sterling coughed, and spat bright blood into a fresh and crimsoned rag.

They abandoned Parowan and continued along the well-worn trail south. To the east, a tall, arid, and monotonous cliff guarded the valley and hid the verdant mountains that rose beyond it. In that direction was lush green high country. West of this long valley lay harsh and bleak ridges, almost naked of life.

Skye was suddenly eager to leave this desert. He ached for the lush country that had become his home, the prairies and mountains where buffalo and elk and deer roamed, where the people of his wives wandered along tumbling creeks, and where the nights were cool, even in midsummer's heat. A man's very soul takes to some country and shies from other country, and Skye's soul had wedded itself to the Yellowstone. It was there that life was sweetest. The plains tribes were rich, he thought; richer than these white and red men who made a home where there was so little water.

In a few days he and Victoria and Mary and North Star would be on their way; another trip done; another task fulfilled.

They traveled that afternoon without incident, and camped for the night near a much-used well where they watered their stock. A mile west of the road was some good grass, and some small cedars for firewood, and they made that place their night's lodging.

No one troubled them. The next morning they broke camp early. Suddenly the whole company was charged with excitement. In a day or two they would reach the Virgin

River, the very place they had dreamed of, talked of, planned for, and crossed a continent to reach. Not far ahead was Cedar City, another great Mormon settlement, with its promise of safety and provisions if they should need anything. Whatever had transpired in Sterling Peacock's soul, his conversion had opened a pathway for this weary company.

This land looked west; to the east, the giant ridge walled off the world, somehow separating this country from everything familiar. Then, late that day, they reached Cedar City, which had sprung up only a few years earlier. Skye marveled. This was a solid city of red brick, which the industrious Saints had thrown up with amazing speed. It seemed more impressive than the somewhat older Parowan. But even as the New Bedford Company pierced town, riding down its broad artery, a man in black rode to meet them. He had the combed square beard so common among these people, and was astride a blooded horse, a glistening chestnut with wild eyes and foam collected around the bit.

He veered toward Skye, who was in the van, as usual, and settled into Jawbone's steady pace.

"You are the sick Pukes," he said. "Do not stop here. Ride straight through. Do not buy or sell. Do not talk to any person. Do not stay for any reason, for every second that you are among us, Cedar City is cursed."

It was a far cry from the friendly reception at Parowan.

Sterling Peacock, aboard his father's Morgan, trotted forward.

"Is there trouble?" he asked.

"None whatsoever," the man with the combed black beard said. "You will not pause. You will not stop. Not even for a drink of water at the well. There will be no trouble if you do as I say."

"I'm a Saint," Sterling said.

The man glared a moment, and then laughed quietly. "Aren't we all," he said. "Now be on your way."

There was no reason to stop. No reason to resist this messenger in the black broadcloth suit. They traversed the entire town in ten minutes, and soon were rolling through open country again. The desert seemed cleaner and sweeter than Cedar City, Skye thought.

thirty-four

*S*kye's company was lost in brooding silence. Nothing but the creaking of wagons and the faint clop of hooves disturbed the quiet. The wind had shifted to the northeast and was gusting cold.

He had never penetrated such a land as this, arid, towering, harsh, and yet grand. In watered places, thickets of green foliage shone brightly against red cliffs and purple shadowed canyons.

They topped a low divide and at last Skye could see far ahead, to a line of dense green brush he took for a watercourse. The two-rut trail headed relentlessly toward that bottom, miles distant. He gauged the time to that green streak as two or three hours, but the day was failing and he hesitated to travel through the night. There was no wood here, not a stick, and the light was failing because a massive gray cloud bank stretched across the northwest sky. A fall storm. The tumbling sun was lighting the underbelly of the clouds.

He steered Jawbone to Victoria, who was riding quietly along, attending their pack and travois ponies.

"We'll need wood," he said.

"I am thinking the same."

"I'll go ahead. We should try for that flat and hope there's water in it. That's the only wood in sight."

"It'll get damn dark with them clouds."

"If there's wood there, I'll build a fire."

She laughed, her tone mocking. He could read her mind: there were times when a fire was impossible.

He hated to leave his company behind, but he knew wood was critical. He had sick people who would need warmth. He had an infant of his own and only a small leather lodge that was a poor shelter against a torrent, especially when no fire lifted smoke and heat through its upper vent.

Jawbone loved to run, and snorted when Skye touched his moccasins to the flanks of the great gray warhorse. Skye tugged the hackamore. This would be a three- or four-mile run, and he would keep to a slow canter. Jawbone settled into an easy rocking-chair stride, and Skye let the horse pick his way toward that green flat. It took a long time. The wagons diminished behind him, and then were little more than gray spots, bugs crawling over a giant country.

The whole western and northern horizon grayed and blackened, and outliers began sailing overhead. A stiff cold wind picked up, lifting dust from the worn trail. Skye pulled the horse down to a walk to rest him, and then rotated into a hard trot, a gait Skye hated because Jawbone's trot was cruel, bouncing and hammering Skye until his legs and torso howled at him. He had spent most of a life in the wilds of the American West, and had suffered wounds and exposure, starvation and thirst, and all these had taken their toll. His body howled with every bounce of the horse.

He reached the sink at the exact moment when the first fat raindrop slapped his cheek. Swiftly he surveyed the brushy bottoms, which had a lot of living shrubbery and not much firewood. He jumped Jawbone across a foot-wide rivulet tumbling out of the northwest and found better pickings on the other side; juniper with all sorts of dead limbs, none of it ideal firewood but it would do.

He worked furiously, but the pile of wood only grew slowly. There wasn't much to burn here. And the rain thickened into a steady drizzle, soaking the wood as dusk settled. It would be a cold night. He saw no sign of his company as the twilight deepened, so he caught Jawbone and rode back toward the divide, uncertain what was delaying them, leaving the firewood behind him.

Sometimes the rain obscured the trail. Patchy ground fog had collected in hollows and shrouded his path. Jawbone was shivering in some unnatural way, and suddenly Skye knew why: ahead was a band of Indians, all on foot, their almost naked forms shining dully in the wetness. He sensed at once these were Paiutes, but probably not a war party. He saw bows and arrows, spears, clubs, and lances, and one wore a sheathed sword. They swarmed around him but did not seem hostile. They were plainly ready for trouble, and would answer it lethally.

Jawbone danced, sawed his head up and down, and was ready to commit mayhem. The rain had darkened Jawbone's hair, and now was dripping off Skye's top hat. Jawbone pawed restlessly, murder in his head. The horse would kill several Paiutes before they pincushioned him with arrows.

Skye held up his hand, palm out, a peace sign. They stared.

They crowded around Jawbone, but kept just out of kicking range. The Paiutes had few horses, unlike most of the plains tribes. These were hunters or warriors, probably searching for food of any sort. There never was much game in this part of the world.

Was this an advance guard, and were there scores more of the Paiutes tying up the wagons? At least Mary was there; the Paiutes spoke a Shoshonean tongue that she might understand. The rain sheeted down now, soaking through Skye's buckskins, darkening his shirt and leggins and puddling in his moccasins. This was a bloody bad fix, and he hadn't any idea how to proceed.

He tried finger-talk. Peace. Friend. We talk. I am Skye. My people are that way. He pointed.

They stared. Great Plains sign talk didn't necessarily convey meaning to these desert people.

A chieftain made signs too, and Skye couldn't fathom them, but it seemed the man wanted him to step down from Jawbone.

Skye tried ordinary English. "My people are back there. Come visit us."

"Mericats?"

Skye vaguely remembered something Mickey the Pick had said about the alliances the Saints had achieved with this band.

"Some are Saints. Mormons."

That seemed to be understood.

"Give eat, eh?"

"Eat," Skye said.

"Eat him." The chieftain pointed at Jawbone.

"Bad medicine," Skye said.

The chieftain pursed his lips. Then he nodded.

Skye edged Jawbone through the dusk toward the wagons somewhere ahead. The rain quickened. With every step Jawbone took, the Paiutes kept pace. Jawbone laid his ears flat back, his nostrils wide, his eyes on one and another Paiute. But walk they did, through a murk so thick Skye finally realized he didn't know where he was going, except it was slightly uphill.

Then suddenly there were many more Paiutes, their naked bodies wet. And just beyond, barely visible, were the wagons. The whole company was halted. Victoria and Mary hunched on their ponies. Mary had pulled a small leather hood over the cradleboard.

"Goddamn, Skye, we're in big trouble." Victoria muttered it, not wanting to sound alarmed.

Bright emerged from the gloom. "What outrage is this? I have only a fowling piece, and that's in the wagon."

Mickey the Pick slid forward too, barely visible. "Don't count on me, I don't even own a rock in a sock, lad."

Skye addressed Mary. "Have they said what they want?"

"I don't understand them, Mister Skye."

"Nothing?"

"Their words, I can't tell."

"I tried English and got somewhere." He turned to the chieftain. "Eat?"

"Eat, eat, eat."

The chieftain pointed at Jawbone, but Skye shook his head.

Then, one by one, the Morgan and the ponies came under scrutiny, but Skye said no, no, no. The Paiutes examined the mules gotten from Pete Hunsaker, and Skye said no, no. They worked back to the second wagon, and paused before the rain-soaked oxen, their bows ready.

Sterling Peacock materialized in the half-light. "What do they want?" he asked.

"Food. Meat."

"But we can't feed ourselves."

"Consider it a tribute for crossing their land. A toll. I wouldn't give them my horse, the Morgan, or the mules."

"Aren't they allies of the Mormons?"

"I tried that. You can try it."

Sterling approached the headman, who waited with a nocked arrow in his bow.

"Saint. Mormon. Friend," he said.

"Mericat?"

"No, me Latter-Day Saint."

The headman strolled to the hospital wagon, saw women within, and smiled.

"Eat," he said.

Sterling resolutely pointed to Christopher Carson Ox. "There."

The headman held up four fingers. He wanted all the oxen.

Sterling offered the lead and the off ox, pointing at both.

The headman smiled, held up four fingers, and laughed. This hunting party would have a feast this night, no matter whether it rained.

The entire hunting party arrayed itself around the company, bows at the ready. Skye saw how it would go, and nodded.

Bright slowly unhooked the lead yoke, and freed the two oxen from their wooden collar. Then he freed the other yoke.

The headman turned to Mickey the Pick's burro cart, and pointed to the caged creatures within. Several of his men snatched the cages of ducks, geese, and piglets and vanished with them. The geese and ducks flapped, and the piglets whined and grunted.

"Ow, ya bloody pirates, stealing from me, are ye?" Mickey howled.

Skye laughed. He couldn't help it.

"It's not the same, you 'arf-arsed 'umbug. That's food they're snatching. I've a mind to pick their camp clean."

The Paiutes howled happily and drove the four gaunt oxen into the darkness. Within a moment or two, they were invisible, and the Paiutes melted away also, suddenly gone into the murky night. The tongue of the supply wagon rested forlornly on the clay. And that noble ox, Christopher Carson, was gone.

thirty-five

wo mules, two burros. Some horses. And perhaps
fifty miles to go. The last stretch was going to be
hardest of all.

"There is no wind in our sails," Enoch said.

Trouble indeed. And nothing could be done this mean
night. Skye saw some of the invalids shivering in the rain.

"We'll make camp right here," Skye said. "We're on good
ground, well drained. It won't flood. And there's a little grass."

Victoria had already anticipated him, and was wrapping
four lodgepoles together, something she could manage even
in this darkness. In minutes, with this heavy cloud cover, it
would be utterly black.

Rain soaked Skye's buckskins, dripped off his hat.

"We'll make our bunks in the wagons," Bright said.

The Jones brothers had anticipated him and were shuf-
fling supplies around inside the supply wagon.

Skye unsaddled Jawbone and turned him loose, and then
freed the packhorses from their travois. The women had completed the lodge frame and were lifting the cover. Skye helped

them. It was heavy work, and the rain made the leather slippery. Mostly by feel, they slid the willow pegs through the slits that would button the cover in place. There'd be no hearthfire within this night, and only some emergency pemmican. Still, the Skye family would be dry. He lugged the damp buffalo robes into the blackness and spread them as best he could. Rain pattered on the buffalo-hide lodge cover.

"Dammit, Skye, that's for women to do," Victoria said. She was always ashamed of him when he did their work. She believed it was a sign of weakness in him.

Now there was no light at all. Still, Mary found her way in, and set her cradleboard away from the smoke vent, where rain was misting into the lodge. Skye wanted to talk to the rest, but knew the night was so thick he could easily get lost.

But then there was noise outside, and some wavering light.

"Blawdy arful night, eh, matey? You mind if Bright and me, we bunk in 'ere?"

Skye pushed aside the flap and discovered Bright and Mickey the Pick, lit by a bull's-eye lantern in Bright's hand.

"The wagons are full up with lungers. Women in one, lads in the other. We got under the wagon but the wind whips rain at us," Bright said.

"Room enough," Skye said. The men clambered through the lodge door.

"Bloomin' fur on the floor!" Mickey said. "Bloomin' Westminster Palace."

The pair settled on the other side of Skye's small lodge.

The lantern burned brightly in the middle, under the vent. This pair had brought blankets. Even without a lodge fire, the shelter was warm enough.

"Remarkable," Bright said, studying the lodge. "Chimney draws off smoke. Excellent engineering, I'd say."

Victoria pulled out the parfleche with pemmican in it. "You hungry, eh?"

She handed each a chunk of the waxy cake.

"What's this tallow, eh?"

"Pemmican," Skye replied. "Shredded meat, fat, and berries. It'll do. This time it's buffalo and chokecherry."

"Indian ship's biscuit," Bright said, sampling the fare.

"I'm glad you're here. We're in a fix," Skye said.

"Blawdy thieves."

"They were hungry; they saw meat," Skye said. "It's an old story."

"Whiles they was haggling with youse, the rest made off with me fowl and piggies. Not a porker in me poke."

Victoria started laughing, and so did Mary.

"Damned pirates!" Mickey mumbled.

"Four oxen, fifty or sixty Paiutes; how do you calculate it, Mister Skye?" Bright asked.

"Worn down and skinny oxen. One big feast for a crowd like that, and maybe some breakfast."

"And some ducks and piggies for dessert, the bloomin' blokes."

"We seem to be at the end of the rails, sir," Bright said.

Skye pondered it.

"We'll put what supplies we can into Mickey's cart, and alternate the mules and the remaining yoke of oxen on the hospital wagon," Skye said. "And that's if the Paiutes haven't made off with a few other animals."

He doubted they had, but no one would know until dawn.

"What's in the wagon, Mister Bright?"

"Not much. Spade, axe, pike, shovel, a plowshare, tools, rope, canvas, several sacks of seed, some oats, harness, some

250

nails and bolts. Things we'll need to get started. And my worthless fowling piece. I don't know why I brought it."

Bright was sliding into melancholia, Skye thought.

"We're probably only fifty miles from where we're going. It'll be the hardest fifty, but we'll get there."

"I have sick people, sir. They haven't any breath. They can't walk more than a little."

"My wives and I will gladly walk, leading our horses, and on each horse will be one or two of your sickest. We can abandon this lodge, and that frees two more ponies. Those will carry two more, maybe four more if we double up."

"You wouldn't!"

"We'll do what we have to do. It might be that we can stash the lodge down below in the river brush, and come back for it."

Victoria and Mary eyed Skye bleakly in the wavering candlelight of the bull's-eye lamp. Many moons of labor went into a lodge.

Skye didn't know how it would work out. But he knew the heavy supply wagon would go no farther. He knew also that the tools and implements and seed had to get to the Virgin River so these people could settle and build their infirmary. He knew some of those invalids could walk, such as the Jones brothers and Sterling Peacock, while others were much too sick, such as fevered little Peter Sturgeon and Ashley Tucker, who shouldn't walk at all and would perish if they faced a physical ordeal.

"Could we drag the big wagon down to the creek and hide it too? I'm thinking of selling it," Bright said.

"It'd be found almost at once."

"The Saints fill their purses scrounging from the trails," Mickey said.

"Are there settlements ahead?" Skye asked.

"I guess we'll find out, eh?" Bright said.

"I am thinking of riding ahead for help."

"Fat lot of help the Saints'll give ye."

Skye didn't argue it. If there weren't some sort of war going on, he didn't doubt he could find whatever help he needed. But just now no one in this company knew anything. Was there fighting? Were the Saints forming into a militia? Skye sighed. There was nothing he could do about any of that.

North Star stirred and began to whimper. He was lying free, covered with a small blanket. But now his tiny arms flailed and he sobbed.

"He is hungry," Mary said, and began to loosen her bodice.

"Ah, hold your horses," Bright said. He grabbed the lamp and blew out the candle. Suddenly the lodge was pitch-black. There was some soft stirring.

They sat quietly. Skye heard the faint sound of North Star's sucking. These visitors in his lodge had come from another world, which Skye understood and Victoria mocked.

A gust of air shivered the lodge.

"There's some settlements on the Virgin, mostly blokes what don't get along anywhere else," Mickey said. "I've 'eard tell they're a mean bunch, all right. They got fire in their eye. They's nothing to stop them from doing what they please. Old Brigham, he's way up at the capital city, and down 'ere, they's no saying what this bunch'll do."

"Then we'll have to find them and let them know our intent," Skye said. "It pays to make ourselves welcome and stay in sight."

"Ye bloomin' East Ender, what I'm saying is, don't stop 'ere. Forget the Virgin River. Keep on moving. Go to the Mohave. You won't make friends 'ere, not with sorts that don't want friends. There's some that want enemies, that ache for trouble, that 'unt for it. That's what I 'eard about this bunch of Saints down 'ere, far from anything called law."

But Bright had the answer to that. "We can maybe make fifty miles, but no more. Fifty miles, and no food, and cold coming, and nothing waiting for them but cold and starving, that's what's in store."

"In two days we may reach the Virgin River, and soon we'll find what we're looking for," Skye said. "I don't think we'll find trouble unless we invite it."

"I've lived most of this year for that day," Enoch said.

thirty-six

They set off on a cold clear morning. The desert had swallowed the rain and there was no sign of it, not a puddle or a dampened rock.

For a long moment, Enoch Bright looked at the forlorn supply wagon, which sat empty. For hundreds of miles he had maintained it, using his mechanic's skills to keep the axles and wheel hubs in perfect shape, keeping harness mended, the wagon sheet waterproof and trim, and the tires tight on the felloes. But now it stood mutely, its ribs poking the blue sky. The sheet had been removed and would go west.

Skye knew Bright was grieving. Never had a wagon gone so far and received such care. But it was no longer essential. The depleted stores fit into Mickey the Pick's burro-drawn cart. The ambulatory invalids would walk, or take turns resting on the tailgate of the hospital wagon. The sicker ones would ride the Skyes' horses, and Skye, Mary, and Victoria would walk, leading their animals. It was not necessary for the Skyes to abandon their lodge or lodgepoles.

But now it was a tiny company that started toward the

Virgin River; a wagon, a burro cart, and Skye's family and ponies.

The country here was grand, a canyon land of red rock, white rock, cedars, and sky.

On Jawbone, Anna Bennett sat sidesaddle. Eliza and Mary Bridge sat the ponies of Skye's wives. And Sterling Peacock, Lloyd and David Jones, and Grant Tucker were rotating a seat on the Morgan. Peter Sturgeon and Ashley Tucker continued in the hospital wagon. When any of the male invalids got too tired, they would rest on the tailgate.

It was perfect traveling weather, mild and sunny. Skye thought they might make the last lap in good order, and the problem now was finding a place to settle, getting shelters up before winter, and securing food. That latter was what troubled Skye the most. There were many mouths to feed and once again only a few days' food left. He wondered whether Mickey's cart and the little burros might be traded for food from the Saints. But even that was stopgap. He needed food and plenty of it.

Deserts can be the quietest places on earth. Now they were hiking through a deep silence, hearing nothing, not even the fall of their own feet and hooves. The silence was odd to Skye, who was so closely attuned to the endless songs of the mountains and rivers and plains that this desert hush made him uneasy.

There was no traffic on this trail, not even the hurried couriers of the Saints, busily marshaling the faithful to resist the Yankee bluecoats invading them. By now Skye's party was beyond the Mormon settlements and wending its way through desert wilderness.

"Too damn quiet," said Victoria.

They plunged into a canyon that worried Skye, but the

two-rut trail went relentlessly forward. They were following Ash Creek, which Skye believed to be a tributary of the Virgin River. They forded the creek again and again, continuing all that day in a land of vaulting yellow and red rock beauty. When last-light caught them, they camped on a choice flat above the creek, a place that lifted hearts. There was ample firewood so they made a merry camp, the wood smoke caught in layers above them.

The next day they reached the creek's confluence with what appeared to be the Virgin River.

"This is probably the Virgin," Skye said, drawing from the lore he had absorbed over a lifetime in the mountains.

The invalids who could walk stumbled down to its banks. The water tumbled west.

They were oddly quiet. They had come across a continent to this place. Whatever they had imagined, this little river wasn't it.

"We came all the way for this?" Lloyd Jones asked.

The silent cliffs offered him no comfort at all.

"It's the air, not the place. We came here for the air and the warmth," Enoch said. "We came here so you could rest, and that's what you'll be doing soon."

"But there's nothing . . ."

The little river purled by, oblivious of the dreams and disappointments of these ill people, who had somehow imagined a magical place, a place of gold and silver and pearl and ivory and rainbows.

"There's a settlement downstream," Mickey said. "A few nasties there," he added.

"What do you propose, Mickey?" Skye asked.

"Go upstream, blokes. Find a good flat, get settled, and lay low. Stay outa sight."

"Mister Bright?"

"We're going to need all the help we can get from set-tlers," he said.

Sterling, who had somehow assumed his father's author-ity, decided the matter: "We'll go upstream and find a good place to settle. I'm a Saint now; I'll go downstream later and look for help. They will welcome me."

Skye had no better idea.

They turned east, slowly working up the Virgin River as it wended its way out of the red canyons. They followed a faint bankside trail ever east and north, sometimes across boxed valleys, sometimes confined in startling narrows cut by the river. And they never met a soul.

Then, as evening approached, they entered a broad valley bisected by the Virgin River, a country so sweet that Skye marveled. Here was sparkling water, grassy flats dotted with live oak trees, and all this guarded by red rock cliffs covered with cedar and pine. A tributary creek tumbled out of the north.

The air was pure, dry, easy on the lungs, and scented with the aromatic plants of the desert. A great healing peace per-vaded the intimate flat, as if this were set aside as an Eden.

Enoch Bright joined Skye and his wives as they paused at the confluence of the creek.

"I know just as surely as I'm standing here, Mister Skye, that Hiram Peacock envisioned this very place."

"I think he did too. Here's the air that heals, water, fire-wood, shelter from wind and storm, and fields that can be cultivated and maybe irrigated. I think you're home."

The others pulled up and stared at this enclosed and warm valley.

"Now, take a good look. This is your place of healing,"

Bright said. "This is what Hiram Peacock dreamed of, and right here's why we've come across a whole continent."

"But where are the people?" Eliza asked.

"There's no one close by. That's part of it. It's a place to rest, lie abed, and let the sun and the air do their work."

"But I would like some neighbors, Mister Bright."

"I'm sure we'll find some," Bright said.

Lloyd Jones didn't like it. "We came two thousand miles for this?" He waved a hand at the meadow, the brooding red rock. "This is nothing. This is one more empty place in a west full of them. This is supposed to heal us?"

Mary Bridge didn't care for it either. "Are you sure, Sterling, this is what Mister Peacock had in mind? This?"

"Yes, this," said Sterling. "It's the air. The mild climate."

"But, Sterling . . . one can't find neighbors, oh, I don't know how to say it. There's nothing here. Are we to stare at this red rock for months on end? It will drive me mad. Did I come all this way to starve and die on a lonely meadow?"

Skye had a question. "Sterling, why the Virgin River?"

"It came to him, that's all, Mister Skye. It just came to him as he studied the maps."

"Had anyone been healed here?"

"No, sir, not to my knowledge."

"So Hiram Peacock's trip was to be an act of faith."

"Yes, sir. He believed. I do too."

Skye studied this vacant land, wondering why the Saints had not settled it, why not a soul was to be seen in a place that might be called paradise.

"Should we go on?" he asked.

"We could look for better," Bright said. "Maybe there's better. But we're heading into the cold season, and I'd hate to lose a minute."

Skye turned to Mickey the Pick. "We'll need supplies. How close is a settlement?"

"There's a few Saints around, you can count on it."

"Where can we go for supplies?"

"Beats me, matey."

"Mister Bright, what did Hiram Peacock plan to do? After he had selected a place for his infirmary?"

Bright could not answer. No one else offered an answer. Sterling Peacock didn't know. It was as if Peacock had set out for some Shangri-la, and once he found it, everything would take care of itself. And yet that was not Peacock's way. He was a sound man, with sound plans. But those plans had apparently died with him.

Skye eyed the company uneasily. They were scores of miles from a settlement. The infirmary would need to be entirely self-supporting and he doubted that it could be done with so few able to work.

"Enoch, we need a town nearby," he said. "Either that or enough credit to buy food and haul it here. Maybe we should keep on going until we're close to a settlement and able to buy or trade for what we need."

Sterling Peacock sat the Morgan, and volunteered nothing.

Skye felt the weight of decision falling upon him.

"All right. This is a good place to camp while we make some decisions. Good grass. There's firewood, fresh, cold water. We can make tents. We need a rest. We haven't paused for weeks. The sickest need do nothing at all, just blot up this sun and this good dry air and gather strength. We'll stop here, but maybe this won't be the last stop. Maybe there's a final resting place ahead.

"My wives and I need to do two things. We'll hunt, and I'm going to ride downriver to see about a settlement or a farm."

Skye lifted Eliza Bright down off Jawbone and helped the other invalids reach ground. They gazed upon sun-cured grasses waving in a soft breeze under an azure sky, with iron-red cliffs rising in most directions, occasionally stratified with white rock. A copse of waxy-leaved trees Skye couldn't identify offered ample wood for the moment.

He watched them drift through the bunch grass while Bright unharnessed the mules and set them to grazing. The Massachusetts mechanic had become a first-rate camp-tender and would make a good camp here.

There was something about this place that sung to him. This was a paradise and a sanctuary, what the Saints called Zion, and somehow it filled Skye with a sweetness he barely understood. He lifted his old top hat and let the dry air filter through his hair, feeling the need for a bath, for this clean and virgin place required a cleaned and freshened body. He wondered whether the others had the same strange stirrings, and thought they did.

Bright stood rapt, slouch hat in hand, his gaze shifting from grassy fields to stratified red rock to the laughing creek. The sick who couldn't walk simply sat, their gazes on the horizons. It was as if they were all in church, hat in hand, waiting to sing a Te Deum. This might be their home. Even Victoria and Mary were in no hurry to raise the lodge and make camp. Mary was unloosing North Star from his cradleboard to let the wiggling infant rejoice in the soft dry air and the setting sun.

thirty-seven

The next morning Skye rode downriver looking for a settlement. Not far below the place where his company had struck the Virgin, he found a rawboned farm. A diversion dam irrigated some stubble fields. A ramshackle adobe shack and some corrals were all that these people had managed to build. But that was natural: the crops were the main thing. Three rawboned men and a woman in a shapeless dress watched him come.

Skye approached warily. The three men had fanned out. The woman had disappeared into the rawboned adobe and wood structure that served for a house. These men were hardworking farmers, their weathered faces seamed, their hands gnarled, their bodies half crippled from toil.

Skye removed his top hat.

"I'm Mister Skye," he said.

"We know," said the oldest of them.

"I'm looking for some advice."

"We know all about you. Keep on moving."

"Who are you, sir?"

"I'm Elder Lee." He did not introduce the others.

"You've put a lot of work into this place, and I can see it's bearing fruit."

"The word is, you are not a Saint and you have come to spread sickness among us. You're the rider of the Pale Horse, and that rider is Death."

Skye scarcely knew how to respond to that. "Sickness, I suppose. We have some young people, men and women who have consumption. They're looking to be healed in the desert. They've come a long way, and some have died along the way, to come here. Like you, they're seeking their Zion."

"We were warned you'd make soft talk. No, sir, be on your way."

Skye took a gamble. "They'll be your neighbors, Mister Lee."

"Neighbors! You'll not pause here, not now, not ever."

Skye chose his words carefully. "They've claimed unsettled land up the river for their infirmary. They'll be building it this fall. The sick can go no farther. This is a beautiful land."

"Where?"

"Six or seven miles up."

"That's reserved land. You can't stay there."

"It's not been claimed, I believe."

"It's reserved for Saints."

"Has anyone title? Has it been surveyed?"

"The church preempts it."

"Has it been filed on? Registered with the government?"

"That matters not."

"If it's not owned, we will settle. These people are American citizens just like yourself, and entitled to settle there. We were hoping to trade you for food. I see you've brought in a grain crop. And your corn patch is ready. We have some horses that might prove useful. A fine Morgan mare, some ponies, a cart we might trade."

The men glanced at each other and lowered their weapons until the black bores aimed casually toward Skye and Jawbone.

"We'll not hear another word. Go or face the consequences."

"Are there other settlers nearby?"

"Pass through, do not stop."

Lee's unblinking stare, followed by a slight twitch of his fowling piece, a tiny gesture telling Skye to leave at once, was ample warning.

"Don't do anything you'll regret," he said. "Not to me. Not to these sick young people."

Lee smiled slowly. "I wouldn't regret a thing," he said, the smile widening into a leer.

Skye settled his hat. "Good day," he said, and rode off, his back itching knowing the bores of two rifles and a scattergun were following him. At the trail he hesitated, thought about heading downriver a way to look for more settlers, and finally turned back to his company upriver.

It wasn't an auspicious beginning. There was war in the air, suspicion of outsiders, fear, madness, maybe hallucination, and obviously very good communications among the Mormons. This isolated family had been well informed about who was on the road. All those couriers who cantered by in the night served the Saints' purposes.

Skye turned to look behind him. The three stood like statues, watching his every move, distrustful to the last. He steered Jawbone upriver through an achingly beautiful afternoon, desolated by all this. It was going to be very hard to feed his company until crops came in.

He reached the serene meadow late in the day and found

that Bright had moved them up the creek, well back from the Virgin River. The ponies and mules and burros were grazing greedily. Skye's lodge rose near a grove of live oak. Acorns littered the earth. A nearby slope was dotted with piñon pine and juniper, all offering abundant firewood.

He found Bright.

"There's a farm a few miles west, but they're as hostile as the rest. Their view is biblical. We are the Apocalypse descending on their people. I confess, I don't know how to deal with that."

"Let them be! We're here! We feel as if we've come home. Something's stirring us. It's as if this is what they've waited for, struggled for."

"We'll stay, then. But I should warn you, this is reserved land, or that's what I was told. The Church's holding it for more of the Saints as they come."

"But it's not patented land! It's free for the taking. Preempt it and when the surveying is done and it can be legally described, then file on it."

Skye pondered it. "You know that the Mormons may fight you for it, even if they don't claim it."

"When they see our infirmary, Mister Skye, they'll have a change of heart."

Skye looked at this meadow, nestling so serenely in the red rock, and knew it was as good a place as any. The air was soft and dry. Maybe things would work out. Courage and quietness and industry might yet win the day.

"All right, Enoch. I'm going to start hunting while you start building and preparing your fields. Maybe you could plant some winter wheat. Food's the thing. We've got to lay in food or starve."

Maybe he could make meat. It had been a while since

anyone in the company had tasted meat. He climbed up on Jawbone, who was snapping at horseflies, nodded to Victoria and Mary, and rode slowly up the creek, looking for deer scat. This ought to be mule deer country. He rode quietly, his senses aware of the wildlife around him. But one thing he did not see was evidence of any deer. He thought he would find something: this was the afternoon feeding hour, the drinking hour, the time when deer were moving from place to place. And yet he met only silence. A faint game trail took him slowly uphill, where the tributary tumbled over rapids. He continued slowly, carefully, studying surrounding hills and ridges and red rock cliffs, and saw nothing. He let Jawbone work his way up a steep slope, and then they reached a high plateau that the creek drained. Still no wildlife. But here, at least, in the fading light, he found some evidence of bedding. Deer had rested here, hollowing the grass.

There had to be game. This was fairly good game country, grass and water and shelter and brush. And yet he found none. Had the deer been shot away by settlers? Had the newly armed Paiutes killed off the deer? He couldn't say. But this was not the Great Plains, teeming with animals. He would not find great bears, many elk, or many deer or antelope. He doubted that he would see a buffalo.

At twilight, he knew he had done what he could this time. He turned Jawbone back to camp, filled with a deepening desperation.

He could not feed this group by supplying meat. He and his family could not even stay; they would need to head for the Great Plains soon, make meat and tan buffalo robes, which was their only real source of income when guiding didn't pay. He felt bad because he knew he would have to tell them what their chances were.

Tomorrow he might make meat. But what of the next day, and the day after that? December, January, February? How did one keep a large company alive until the crops came in next summer—if they came in at all? How could he supply them with a deer a day for two hundred days?

Heavy-hearted, he and Jawbone slowly worked down the creek to the soft-lit meadow where the camp rested comfortably in the gloaming.

They had eaten oatmeal. Skye released Jawbone from the saddle and hackamore, and turned his young medicine horse loose to graze. Jawbone trotted off to the creek to stick his ugly snout in the cool water.

Victoria and Mary appraised him and his empty saddle, and knew he had failed. Wordlessly he spooned some oat gruel, the only food that this company had left, into a wooden bowl and ate it. They were all staring at him, expecting this highly touted and famous guide to bring them abundant meat.

"Enoch, we should have a word," he said, inviting the leader of this group to his family's fire.

"We're in more of a dilemma than you may know," he said. "There's deer, but the population is thin. We can't count on my hunting to keep all of us fed until crops come in. It comes down to this. We need to find people who can sell or trade for food. There's no escaping it. These people have food stored in their granaries, but it's not for us to have. If we stay here, we'll swiftly starve. We're on the brink of it right now."

"Move, then, sir?"

"Not right away. One swift hunt doesn't prove anything. But over the next days if I make no meat, then we're going to need to move along until we find some people who can help us."

"I'm no diplomat," Bright said.

"I'm not either. I'd rather wrestle a grizzly bear than try to bargain with these people."

"What do we do?" Bright asked.

"Sterling's a Saint, more or less. They won't listen to me; they might listen to him. I think it's going to be up to him to bargain for food. He has the Morgan horse. We can give him a spare horse to trade for grain. I don't have any other idea."

Bright sighed. "It's the sick I'm feeling for," he said. "They made it clear across a continent, hoping to heal, not starve to death."

thirty-eight

No one wanted to leave this Eden. All the doubts had dissolved. It was as if these people had crossed a continent to come to this very spot. The horses and mules grazed peacefully on cured grass, while the invalids soaked up the gentle breezes and warm sun. They washed their travel-worn clothing, washed blankets, and slept. The red rock cliffs formed an amphitheater open on the south that nurtured and protected them and would keep winter at bay. A laughing creek running crystal cold water succored them.

"Don't ask me how I know it, but I do," Sterling Peacock said. "This was what my father looked for. He had an image in his mind, and he gave that image to me even though he was describing a place he'd never seen. He told me what the air would be like; warm and dry, like velvet in the lungs. I have a strange sense of recognition, sir. I've never before seen this corner of the world, and yet I knew it, I welcomed it, as soon as I saw it."

"Then we'll find a way to stay," Skye said.

Mary of the Shoshones, aware of things that the rest knew little of, walked quietly up a game trail and into the piñon pine forest and harvested cones, which she brought to camp and roasted until the cones opened and discharged their pine nuts. She gathered these in amazing quantities, and soon she and Victoria were taking ponies up the creek to the pine forests and loading them with piñon pinecones from above.

The big long nuts, filled with white meat, astonished everyone. This was delicious food, and nourishing too. Then Enoch Bright, armed with his fowling piece, began his own hunting and surprised a flock of wild turkeys, shot half a dozen, and returned laden with meat. The rich turkey meat seemed every bit as delicious as the meat of the domesticated turkeys these New Englanders had known.

Off a way, on the trail along the Virgin, an occasional mounted traveler passed by, but none ever paused at the isolated camp of the New Bedford Infirmary Company. Skye suspected that the company was being monitored; there was nothing in all the territory of Utah that did not escape the Saints.

He rode Jawbone high into the canyon country, looking for larger game, but the deer or elk or mountain sheep eluded him and he returned empty-handed each trip. After that, he helped his women harvest pine nuts. The piñon forests were endless, stretching as far as the eye could see, and there might be months of food for anyone who made the effort to collect the cones and roast the nuts out of them.

The ponies and mules fattened; the invalids inhaled the velvet air, and seemed less gaunt and desperate. The Jones brothers, aware that this company needed to prepare for cold, took time to build pole-frame structures and enclose them with wagon sheets and the spare canvas. They began to collect firewood against the chilly months to come.

Enoch shot more turkeys after the first were eaten, and Skye marveled that nature here was offering her riches in her own way. Skye thought he had lived too long in the northern Rockies to grasp what might be edible here. More and more, he struck out on foot, carrying his Sharps but not expecting to use it, looking for whatever nature provided. It was a learning time for him. Different foods, different meat.

But the sweetest pleasure of all was simply the change in mood among these desperate young people. Where there had been pinched faces, now he saw smiles; where there had been fever and fear, now he saw peace and quietness taking hold in their bosoms. They were not entirely quiet. Often they would rest an hour or two, then do some simple task such as washing their clothes, and return to their blankets.

The nights were chill, but the canvas-walled housing was protection enough for the time being. This was September; by November, their needs would be different. Skye began to survey the surrounding country for firewood. There was not a lot of deadwood close by, but plenty upslope, and he would need to drag a lot of it down to the meadow. The mesas and slopes above were loaded with dead pine. The sweet scent of piñon smoke was remarkable, almost like the healing sweetgrass smoke some tribes used as a form of catharsis. And the pinecones that had yielded their nuts would make a good fuel too.

He allowed himself to believe that these people could manage here after all, in spite of his dour instinct that nature was too niggardly to yield food and heat and shelter in this place. There was more to all this than he had ever dreamed.

Mickey the Pick was the only restless soul. He often wandered down to the Virgin River and scanned it, as if looking for a passing traveler—or danger. He took it upon himself to become the eyes and ears of the company, sometimes patrolling up and down the river, keeping an eye out for trouble.

One night, at Skye's campfire, he spilled his worries.

"You may think it's all jist fine, bloke, but I think we're in blawdy trouble, and the Saints, they'll put a stake through our 'earts."

"Why do you say that?" Skye asked.

"Because this is Zion. You know what Zion is? Sanctuary. We're in the middle of their bloomin' sanctuary. We're camping on the altar."

"But there aren't many Saints anywhere near here, Mister Pick."

"Mister Pick, Mister Pick! When'll youse get over your bad 'abits, eh? The Saints are 'ere, and you'll see them soon enough and you won't enjoy it when they come."

"Are they at war?"

"I picked up a bit of news, I did, talkin' to a rider jist today. That federal column, it's knocking at the gates. Colonel Albert Sidney Johnston, that's what they say. He's not far from that post up there, Bridger's Fort, zat the name? The Saints, they're going to burn it down before the federals get there. That's the talk, anyway."

"Yes, that's the name I heard. We passed through there. The Saints had squeezed the owners out. That's where we first ran into trouble."

"Well, the blawdy feds, they're going to snatch it if it's not arsh first. That Yank colonel, he's in no hurry, just plodding along like he knows all the quail's going to scatter once he marches into Great Salt Lake. But the Saints, they've got twenty-five hundred armed men, just waiting, and a mess of Indians too."

271

"Who told you this, Mister Pick?"

"You got bad habits, matey. Mister Pick! I stop the horse-men, tell 'em I'm a Saint and I want the news, and they sure give it to me."

"A lot of horsemen?"

"Blawdy parade of 'em down the river a piece. Something big's stirring, that's for sure."

"Where are they coming from? Where are they going?"

"It's coming out of Cedar City. The 'orsemen, they go back and forth from there."

"Do they know we're here?"

"Saints know every yard of the whole country, they do. If it's not us being bothered, it's because they got bigger fish to fry. A big wagon company rolled through Cedar City few days ago, Pukes, it's said. Them from Missouri or Illinois that persecuted the Saints. That's what's stirring up the 'ornets."

"Maybe they'll leave us alone, then."

"Saints don't leave nobody who's Gentile alone, let me tell youse."

"What would they do to us?"

"Right now, everyone all 'eated up, matey, they'd do what-ever they damned please."

"We're entirely at their mercy."

"You can count on it."

Mickey ate a bowl of oat gruel mixed with pine nuts, pro-nounced himself well fed, and drifted off into the purple twi-light. Skye tried to process what he knew. This was their Zion. Settling here would be, in their eyes, taking land from them. War brought extreme feelings and extreme measures.

He didn't like it a bit. He knew how to deal with wilder-ness, with wild animals, with surviving, but this time of pas-sion, of mobs, of militia, was something he knew little about.

"Some time, some night, these damned Saints, they'll come and kill us all," Victoria said, out of the blue.

Mary stared somberly. Skye looked at her, at their son, lying on a robe, his brown eyes focused on his mother. He felt Victoria's love and her worries. Maybe, somehow, they could slip away from here, hide in the canyon lands while this war lasted and then quietly return. The federal army would keep the peace.

It was a good thought, and he wondered what sort of hidden valley lay straight up this creek. He knew now that the land could support them, at least awhile. From high points he had seen vast piñon forests stretching in all directions across the high country, forests laden with pine nuts.

"No damned hiding from them people," she said. "They got the big eye."

He knew she was right. These Saints were gifted, tenacious, courageous people, and they had swiftly become masters of a sprawling desert empire. He could not hide a dozen sick people from them for long. Their only safety lay in friendship.

Skye thought about it and came to a reluctant conclusion.

"I'll ride up there to Cedar City and talk with those people a bit. I want to talk to the leaders, not the ones who take orders. The ones who make the decisions. The elders. The bishop. I think maybe I can make some headway, even if they're all primed for a war."

"What did they do to Jim Bridger, eh?" she asked.

He and Victoria already knew the answer. They had trumped up some charges about selling weapons to Indians, gotten a warrant, and came after him with a posse. Skye didn't doubt they could do the same to him. He was simply another minor obstacle in their path.

"I have to go," he said.

"Talk! Ha! They ain't talking."

She rose softly, settled beside him, and touched his face. It was an old, old gesture whose meaning was well known to both of them. She was saying that if he rode alone up there, tried to persuade them to do something they wouldn't consider, she would send her love along with him, whatever his fate.

But he had to go. These invalids might be camping in paradise, but at any moment heaven could turn into hell.

thirty-nine

kye was reluctant to leave the peaceful camp on the meadow, but knew he must. In any case, nothing he could do would make the camp any safer. Whether or not he was present, the encampment would be vulnerable. The thing to do was settle the matter with the Saints and that meant a long trip to Cedar City.

Mickey the Pick joined him, riding the Morgan horse. Maybe they'd listen to a pair of Londoners. Skye headed up the creek toward the high country, aware that he could trap himself in box canyons and mesas, but he thought he could get through to Cedar City. Little did he realize that Mickey could scarcely ride, and bounced along helplessly behind Skye. It was too late to worry about that. The little East End pickpocket would learn how to ride before the end of the trip or live with a bruised butt and chapped legs for weeks.

They saw no one. This land was so vast it could swallow armies. There was only sun and wind, silences, red rock and yellow rock, cedar and pine. The usual route, Skye knew, involved a dogleg west and then north up Ash Creek, valley travel all the way; but he was cutting the corner to save time, and working through high country that looked as if no man had ever ridden through.

It took an entire hard day of travel before they reached Cedar City, which was set in a desert bowl. It was not yet dusk. The city rested somnolently, its work done for the day. Here were civilized sights. Mercantiles, whitewashed frame houses with lilac bushes and roses. Picket fences. Wide avenues. The soft and sleepy air of the desert. Sometimes there were three or four identical dwellings in a row, but each had been rendered unique with curtains or plantings. This was a dusty place, and the town looked parched.

And song. Skye heard it clearly, and Mickey did too.

On a rise stood the whitewashed temple, its windows open, the evening breezes carrying song upon them through the small town. Skye steered Jawbone up a gentle grade toward the church, and in its ample yard he and Mickey paused, listening.

Up, awake, ye defenders of Zion,
The foe's at the door of your homes.
Let each heart be the heart of a lion
Unyielding and proud as he roams,
Remember the wrongs of Missouri
Forget not the fate of Nauvoo
When the God-hating foe is before you
Stand firm and be faithful and true.

That proved to be the closing anthem of this evensong. Skye dismounted and waited. He hadn't the faintest idea whom to contact, or what to say, or whether it would be best to wait for the morrow.

"They're serious, mate," Mickey said.

"They've been persecuted."

"Don't give the blokes an excuse. They're 'ell-bent to fight. Matey, they're itching for a fight. They'll damned well pick one."

"You know them; I don't," Skye said. "Who'll I ask for?"

"The bishop."

"Not the marshal?"

Mickey glared. "Ye 'aven't got it yet, eh? This is a church war."

Skye wasn't chastened. "Claiming land is not church business. This is territorial business."

"Ye damned Englishman, go home then."

There was a final blessing echoing from the open windows, and then the doors swung open and a few people, mostly women in gray or brown dresses, eddied into the softening light of evening.

More tumbled out, white-haired men, a crippled man on crutches, and still more women. Skye thought the congregation must be almost entirely women.

"The militia took the young men," Mickey said.

That answered Skye's question. The able-bodied men were off to war. That in itself was worrisome.

The crowd eyed Skye and Mickey speculatively but no one approached, and some of the women drifted down the slope to the town, along with children.

Then men appeared at the church doors, a slender gray-haired one, his hair brushed straight back, wearing a white collarless shirt and a shirtwaist. To either side of him stood burly younger men. These were the only young men Skye could see, and both looked to be bodyguards. But who could say?

This contingent started straight for Skye and Pick, who waited beside their horses. As the gray-haired man approached, Skye discovered muscle and determination in the man's gait; an imperial force propelling the man toward Skye. The man's flinty stare seemed the drilling probe of a Cyclops.

Then the three reached Skye. Skye lifted his top hat in polite salute and settled it.

"I'm Barnaby Skye, sir, and this is Mister Pick. To whom do I speak?"

The question went unanswered. "We know who you are, Englishman," the man said. "What are you doing here?"

"Hoping for some friendship. I'm guiding a company of invalids that plans to settle nearby, and we are seeing how it might be done."

"It won't be done."

"They have come a long way seeking healing, and have found a desert place that suits them. We've come to notify your county officials and register their claim."

"You have, in your dubious wisdom, come to the right person, and you are too late."

"I didn't catch your name, sir."

"That is because I chose not to supply it. To my flock I am Bishop Simon Wellborn. To you, who I am makes not the slightest difference."

"Mister Wellborn, the people I represent have a right under the laws of your country to take up land. They are doing it. They will exercise their right. I'll add that they pose no threat to you."

"Londoners, both of you, I have it." He turned to Mickey. "And one in bad grace with us."

"You 'ave it, mate."

Wellborn's voice escalated, almost into fevered pitch. "The

word from our elders is clear," he began, his words crackling in the hushed evening. "The Apocalypse is upon us. Zion must be purged of every Gentile, every enemy. Zion is ours. Even now, while you waste my time, a militia is enforcing the edict. You are too late. Good afternoon. It is only because you are Englishmen that you are free to go. It is a mistake; you are accomplices. But I am bound by the council."

"Who are these gentlemen?" Skye asked.

"They are deputy marshals."

"Where are the territorial officials? Where may I plead the case?"

"You have already pleaded, and I have already dismissed you. This is *Zion*."

"What may they do to appeal this, sir?"

"You seem to be slow, Skye. Have you no wits about you? What is set in motion I cannot stop, and will never stop, because I favor and bless its every act." He paused. "Flee for your safety. If you linger here, I won't care what country you come from. You will be subject to whatever fate I choose for you."

Sky nodded and boarded Jawbone. Mickey climbed onto the Morgan mare.

"They'll claim that land. And I'll defend them," Skye said.

The bishop smiled.

Skye was tired of being smiled at.

"Thanks for the warning," he said. He doffed his topper and smiled back. He kept on smiling until the bishop looked away.

They slipped out of town, each wrapped in deep quiet.

There could be no more attempts at reconciliation.

Skye chose the dogleg valley route back to the camp, fearful of getting caught in a box canyon or trapped on a mesa at night. It had been a feckless journey. All of southern Utah seemed to be caught in a hellish cauldron of bitterness. It was something new to him. In all his years in London and then the Royal Navy, he had never seen or felt such seething passion. Among the mountain men, there might be private hatreds, but not this obsessive madness that gripped so many people.

"I'd be better off lifting a man's purse in East End, I would," Mickey said. "I don't like this thing 'ere. They're sending out skull-and-bones men, is what they're doing, regular murders all whipped up. There was nawt a thing like it in London."

They could not fight, so they must hide. Skye knew he must speed back to camp, waken them, hasten them out of their tents, urge them to pack up and leave that place. He would take them up that creek, cover their tracks, dip into a canyon, find a hidden valley or a remote canyon, and hide them all from that murderous militia roaming like a hydrophobic wolf across the empty lands. Someday, this would be over and they could return to their meadow on the creek.

The September night was chill and peaceful, and the trail easy to follow by the pale emanation of a quarter moon. The valley was flanked by a single brooding cliff to the east, and that only made passage easier by orienting them at all times.

They were alone. No Saint horsemen clattered through the night, no couriers trotted by, carrying commands from the elders in Great Salt Lake, or intelligence from the outlying provinces, including all this area.

They rounded a bend, and found themselves in the valley of the Virgin, and now they hastened toward the meadow where his friends and family slumbered in soft silence.

Even in the dim light, the valley could be limned, and

Skye turned Jawbone up the side creek. The horse snorted softly and laid its ears back, so Skye slid his Sharps from its sheath, fearing trouble.

"Where's the camp, eh?" Mickey asked.

A good question. There was no camp. No wagon, no mules, no burros, no ponies, no cart, no lodge, no tents.

"The light's playing tricks. The camp must be up higher," Skye said, not really believing his own words.

But there was no camp anywhere. There was an extinguished fire. A ring of stones where Skye's lodge had stood. Disturbed grasses where the tents had stood. Wagon tracks leading down toward the trail by the Virgin River.

There was nothing at all but the sad breezes eddying over empty fields and the whisper of ghosts.

forty

Where were they? Had they fled? Were they in trouble? Anguish gnawed at Skye.

"I'd rawther be in London," Mickey said.

Skye held Jawbone quiet to listen closely, but he heard nothing. No voice calling, no snort of a horse. He eased Jawbone's rein. Let him point. But the horse just stood. Skye started to do what he always did when trying to read a story from what lay on the moonlit ground. He began a slow spiral that would take him farther and farther from the camp, until he knew where people went, and possibly knew why.

He turned Jawbone around a widening circle. And then the moon quit him. The only cloud he had seen all night slid overhead and blanked the moon. Suddenly it was pitch-dark. It was a large cloud too, one that would not quickly pass.

Why was nature so perverse? Why extinguish the lantern? He raged a moment. Half of his life he had spent raging at nature, which froze him or soaked him or starved him or thirsted him or clawed him or tormented him at the worst possible moments. But it was black now.

"Mickey?"

"Ya'ar," came a voice.

"I'm talking to guide you here. Join me."

Skye actually began humming a sea chanty, and soon enough he heard the soft rustle of the Morgan.

"What'll ye do, bloke?"

"If the cloud lets up, find the creek and head up it."

"They're well gone."

"I think trouble came and Victoria took them to safety."

But he sensed the wrongness of that even as he said it.

"I got me some dandy eyes and ears, old bloke. Leave it to this East Ender for prowling the night, eh?"

"All right," Skye said. If ever there was a nocturnal male, it would be an East London pickpocket.

"Now, follow me, matey," Mickey said.

Skye did, and soon they heard the babble of the tributary creek. Mickey turned up the creek, and Skye followed, marveling that the man and horse could go anywhere at all.

Not that the Morgan didn't stumble now and then. It was too dark for movement, and Mickey's only compass was the purring of the brook on the left.

Skye thought of discharging his rifle, and perhaps Enoch Bright would respond with a shot from his fowling piece. But that was too dangerous. A militia could be prowling this country.

But then Mickey cursed some brush that had whipped his face, and quit.

"Now, in London, every alley, it's in me head, but this isn't in me head," he said.

Patience. That's what Skye needed and what he didn't have. He dismounted and prowled restlessly, looking for edges in the black cloud mass working its way across the heaven. But he saw nothing. Just blackness.

"Limey, do ye want a fire, eh?"

"It's worth the risk. Signal fire. But there's no wood."

"Old Skye, you haven't learned about me, 'ave you? In London town, I could pick a pocket in fog, in dark so thick I couldn't tell the shape of the bloke I was crocking. Mate, I could cut a purse loose on the blackest night of the year, from a man wearing a black coat and black boots and a black hat. I got me the night sense. I know what something is without seeing it, you bet I do."

Skye felt something vague stirring, and the faintest whisper of movement.

"There, ye fool, I've got yer powder horn."

Skye roared, "Give that back."

But Mickey the Pick was laughing. "Now just sit tight. I got senses you never knew a man had, and they didn't call me Mick the Pick for nawthing."

Skye felt but did not see the little pickpocket stirring about, but there was nothing he could do but sit tight on the dew-damp grass and wait.

"Hurry it up or I'll put Jawbone on you," he grumbled.

But Mick the Pick just laughed softly.

"And now, bloke, a pinch of powder and we'll 'ave a bon-fire."

Skye saw a shower of sparks as flint struck steel, and then a flare of light a few feet in front of him, and then some flames tentatively licking a heap of twigs and sticks and dried reeds and bark. It caught, somehow, and there was Mick, a mean little smirk across his mug. Mick handed Skye his powder horn. The leather suspension cord had been neatly sliced.

"All right, get away from that flame, get into darkness,

face the darkness, and see what's out there. I know something about fires in the night, and the danger of fires, and I didn't learn it in London," Skye growled.

Both men crept well apart from the tentative flame and studied the silent valley.

There was nothing to be seen. They had, apparently, moved a quarter of a mile or so up the creek from where the camp had been.

Skye gathered the horses and drew them into darkness. "All right, we'll see what the fire does, but we're staying well away from it," he muttered.

The Pick added a few more pieces of tinder he had collected, just how Skye would never fathom, and then retreated from the flame. Skye tied the sliced cord together and hung his powder horn from his neck once again, and then the pair of them sat out the minutes and hours until a slow, glum dawn finally broke in the east. As the light thickened, and Skye could see farther and farther up and down the valley, and onto the eastern slopes of hills, he saw not a soul.

Where were the invalids? Bright? His family?

They sat quietly until dawn, when he could read the story of the meadow. He caught Jawbone and rode quietly back to the campground. There was a moil of disturbed grass, iron tire tracks, and it seemed to Skye that a lot of people had been at this place. Mickey, on the Morgan, studied the campsite too.

"They got took," he said.

Skye was coming to the same conclusion. But he hadn't yet ascertained whether the visitors were Indians or white men. The meadow yielded no secrets. He spiraled Jawbone out farther and farther until it became clear that nearly all the traffic had come from the Virgin River, had turned up this side valley with the creek, and had come to his company's camp. And there was now absolutely nothing left in camp.

But there was more. Clear travois furrows plowed up the creek toward the mesa country. And here, where there were fewer marks of passage, he thought he discerned the prints of his ponies, but he couldn't be sure.

"These are travois marks, and these tracks look like my family," Skye said.

They followed the creek toward the canyon and mesa country above, where the travois trail took them. Soon they were in cedar thickets, and climbing steadily. Then Skye halted. Ahead was an arrow protruding from a thick, twisted juniper tree. He knew in a glance whose arrow that was. It had been driven there by Victoria's bow. The arrow had Crow fletching and dyes. And it meant big trouble, watch out, be ready, and come slowly ahead.

He had double feelings, relief that his family, as far as he could tell, was safe, and worry about the rest, and what sort of mysterious trouble might lie ahead. But he unsheathed his Sharps, checked the load, and found the rifle was ready.

"I'd still rawther be in London, mate," Mickey said quietly.

"There's trouble. Study the ridges and let me know if there's anything unusual. We may be observed," Skye said.

He worked the arrow loose and dropped it into his rifle sheath. Victoria's arrows were well wrought and valuable.

He thanked her silently for the warning.

They continued up the creek, plunging into a red rock canyon, and then Victoria stood there in the trail, bow nocked with an arrow.

Skye dropped from Jawbone, raced to her, and hugged her fiercely, so glad was he to see her.

"Come," she said, and led them across naked rock and finally into a pocket hollow in a red cliff, where red walls vaulted upward, leaving only a patch of blue high above. There was Mary, and there was the boy, and there were the ponies, and lying on the clay were the lodge, lodgepoles, and his family possessions.

This hidden place held all his treasure. He gave Mary a hug, studied his boy, who stared up at him from bare ground, and then the women pressed Skye to sit. There would be much telling, and Skye dreaded what he was about to hear.

"The men came, many, many, hundred maybe, riding horses, carrying rifles and revolvers. Men with beards. They don't ride so good, but they come. It was late in the afternoon, and they come up to the camp, and then they spread out, rifles ready, and the man we know, square-bearded man, he's the boss, and he walks up when he sees no one's gonna fight.

"He's damn cheerful, they all are laughing, pleased with themselves. Bright, he feels their good cheer, introduces himself, and I don't like this so I nod to Mary, and we slowly pack up, but nobody notices some old squaws. Except the square-beard, he looks around for you, and asks, and I say you're gone somewhere.

"So the men, they say, they're taking the invalids away for protection, lots of Paiute Indians making trouble for travelers, and these men, they come to protect white people and get us to safety. So Enoch Bright, he's smiling. The sick ones are happy, they pack up, and the square-beard, he's the boss, he says the women and sick go in one wagon, the men walk. Off they go, and that square-beard, he tips his hat, winks at me, and says nothing."

"When they got to the Virgin River, which way did they go?" Skye asked.

"They all go down the river," she said.

To safety.

forty-one

Maybe it was true, Skye thought. Maybe the Paiutes were raiding travelers. Attacks on travelers were common enough on every trail heading across the continent. But it didn't make sense. Why were the Paiutes stirred up, and why were the Saints suddenly protecting travelers?

"I don't trust the sonsofbitches," Victoria said.

She was usually right.

Maybe the Mormon militia was simply rounding up the invalids to expel them from Utah, send them west once again. That did make sense. Bright's company would be told to head west and keep on going. Surely that's what all this was about. But that didn't feel right, either.

Skye ached for some sort of clue, if only to figure out what to do. But he didn't know what had happened or what to do. It was all guesswork.

"We'll look for them and come back here when we can," Skye said. "This is a good place to cache our stuff."

Victoria glared at him, her way of saying she was seeing things that he didn't grasp.

It was a perfect place to hide things, a tiny walled alcove in the red cliff. Victoria and Mary had already drawn the lodge cover and lodgepoles into the alcove, so there was little to do but pull everything under an overhang.

He realized suddenly that Mickey the Pick hadn't been informed. "We're going after our people before we lose them," he said. "That means speed. We'll try to catch up with that militia and find out where they're going. We won't be dragging the lodge. We'll take all the ponies; might have to put Peter Sturgeon on one when we catch up. If that militia's big and if it knows what it's doing, this won't be easy. The first step is to find them. Then we'll know what is happening."

Mickey beamed. "I can cut a purse from a bloke at midnight in fog; just let me cut a few invalids from the bunch."

"Mickey the Pick, you are going to be an asset," Skye said.

"They called me Lord Cutpurse, they did, long ago."

"From now on, you're Lord Cutpurse," Skye said. "Ladies, meet Lord Cutpurse."

But the name meant nothing to them. They stared.

Swiftly, Skye collected and saddled his wives' ponies. Mary slipped North Star into the cradleboard. The child had almost outgrown the board, and would soon be riding in a shawl wrapped around Mary's shoulder and back.

They left in a hurry. Skye knew that food was going to be a problem. All those pine nuts so painfully harvested had gone with the wagon. But what was more important, at that moment, was catching up. The Saint militia had almost a day's head start.

They made good time, and would have done even better if Lord Cutpurse had known more about riding a horse. The militia was not visible, but the wheel tracks were plain, and Skye knew that it would not take more than a day or so to catch up with slow-moving Mormons. Just what he would do when he spotted the armed force ahead he wasn't sure; whatever he did, it would require the cloak of night.

He let Jawbone set the pace, and the ugly brute chose a bone-jarring trot out of sheer perversity. Trotting never wearied a nag, even if the trot pounded the tailbone of any rider. Victoria's eyes became slits, but she didn't complain. Only Lord Cutpurse complained. He howled and growled, and cursed Skye and his whole tribe.

They met no one. Perhaps because the militia was roaming, no travelers were out this day. They followed the Virgin River as it flowed toward the mighty Colorado. The road was well worn and smooth, and had swiftly dried after the rain. There wasn't much to say so they rode silently, locked in their own thoughts. The long, wearisome ride took them clear to a little settlement calling itself St. George at dusk, and there the wheel tracks melded with dozens of others, and the hoofprints in the dust became indistinguishable from all the rest. The militia and its prisoners had vanished behind the closed doors of humble houses in the dusty hamlet. Skye thought to look for the mules and burros, but they, too, were hidden.

There were few people visible, and these seemed to be hurrying. An odd tension caught the settlement. Skye could hear nothing; no coughing, no talk, no barking of a dog, no whistle, no singing. He had the sense that eyes were peering at him from dark windows. He saw only one lamp, in a tiny store that had stayed open.

"Matey, it's dangerous for you here. Now this is a job for Lord Cutpurse. Let it get a little blacker and I'll have me a good look."

Skye agreed. In fact, he was worried that an armed band of men would loom out of the twilight and capture them all, his son, wives, horses, and the East Ender.

"We'll be on the river, above town," he said.

Mickey grinned.

Skye turned Jawbone, and his family softly retreated from the desert town but not before a barking dog investigated them. Nothing came of it, and Skye steered off the road and found the river purling slowly. Night settled. Skye dismounted, let Jawbone lap up water. Mary slipped off her pony and began nursing the boy. Victoria grumbled through the chores, but in time the ponies were all cared for and there was nothing to do but wait for a gifted pickpocket to slip into their camp, with news—or no news.

Skye thought of Enoch Bright, trapped somewhere in that dusty hamlet, fuming at his captors. He tried to imagine what the mechanic would do or say to Saints who wanted to purge their Zion of unbelievers. Bright would probably light a pipe and tell them their cogwheels were missing teeth. He thought of Anna Bennett, proud and aloof. Of the Bridge sisters, bravely coming west to be healed. He thought of the Jones brothers, both of them the walking sick. He thought of Sterling Peacock, probably lying somewhere, and angry at these people he had made his own. And Peter Sturgeon, sick, twelve, and bewildered.

The stars emerged, bright pricks in a clear sky, and soon it was as black a night as Skye had known. He slipped close to Victoria, who sat stolidly on the ground. Without speaking, she welcomed him, a single touch of her brown hand enough to convey her thoughts. The Dipper rotated through the night, and still they sat, awaiting word from the king of pickpockets.

Mary materialized and sat beside them, and she handed

the boy, North Star, to Skye, who hefted the chunky child and was gladdened. This little bundle of life was all he would leave behind him. For now, the boy was well. But he would have a hard life. Skye did not live in safe cities where there would be food and warmth and medicine and help. He lifted the boy to his lap.

"Ah, Dirk, it is a quiet night here. When you're older you'll know that men's beliefs get in the way of good sense," he said. "May you be wiser and stronger than your old father."

The child's smooth flesh seemed silky to the touch, not a wrinkle in this one. Dirk clamped his little hand around Skye's fat thumb and hung on, and Skye was content.

It was a slow night but not an uncomfortable one.

"Ye blawdy Londoner, where be ye?" Mickey's voice carried softly from perhaps fifty yards.

"Here, mate."

In a moment, a wraith of a man slipped into the resting place and dropped to his knees.

"There's not a one of 'em in there. They gave us the slip."

"How do you know?"

"I got eyes, they got windows and shutters."

"Are you sure?"

"It's not a big burg, mate. There's not six 'ouses."

"What do you think?"

"I don't think. They're not 'ere. Not a woman, not a man. There's not a consumptive 'ere. Not Bright, either."

"How do you know?"

"I can damned well see a ring on a pinky finger at ten paces when the fog's thick as soup."

"But these are homes."

"I can see anything anywhere."

"Closed shutters?"

"I got me a pair of ears good as my eyes. I tell you, there's no bunch of consumptives, neither are they spread out in a few houses, and there's not a shed or a loft where they might be guarded. And I 'iked along the river, below town, looking for a camp too."

"Any chance you're wrong?"

"Why do they call me Lord Cutpurse, may I ask?"

"Did we miss something on the trail?"

"That's for you, mate. Me, I'm a pickpocket. The night's my game."

"They are dead," said Victoria.

"Naw!"

She shrugged. "It is a big land."

"But why?" Mickey asked.

"Goddamn white men, why should I know?"

Skye had that bad feeling again, a sense that Victoria had discerned truth without quite knowing how or why. It was her medicine. Sometimes she saw things that turned out to be true. Still, he rebelled.

"They wouldn't," he said.

Victoria refused to answer him, always a danger sign. She saw what she saw.

"I get itchy here. We must go."

"Now?"

"Yes! Now!" she cried.

He helped her up. With nothing but starlight to help them, they collected their ponies, and Mickey the Pick found the Morgan, and they rode softly along the Virgin, not knowing where they would go or stop. Skye didn't even know whether he was employed, or whether his task was done. He had brought them to the place where they intended to heal themselves. What next?

forty-two

A rising moon broke the night open just about where the trail for Cedar City parted company with the Virgin River. Skye took it for an omen. Mostly, nature mocked a man's dreams and plans, but sometimes nature whispered her wisdom to any ear willing to listen. And Skye was listening that bitter night.

Good God, his entire company had vanished. Gone were Bright and every invalid that Bright and the Skyes had brought to the very place they felt would give them the sun, the dry air, the serenity they needed for their bodies to rebuild.

He reined Jawbone to a halt and let the cutpurse catch up. "Mickey, you know these people. I don't. Where did the militia take our company?"

"A mystery, it is. These blokes aren't like Londoners; they're like 'ottentots to old Mick."

"Then we'll look for them," Skye said to the cutpurse.

"That militia came from somewhere; that's where we'll go," Mickey the Pick said. "Let's rattle their boudoir."

Mickey had prowled down the Virgin and found nothing. That left Cedar City or Parowan.

Skye reined in Jawbone.

"Let's think about this," he said. "If there's trouble with
the Paiutes, and the militia really wants to keep our people
from harm, that's one thing. If the militia simply wanted to
rid Utah of settlers who aren't Saints, that's another thing."

"I don't suppose the blokes would put the lungers into
their 'omes, mate."

"No, they wouldn't. So our people are being guarded
somewhere safe but not in town."

"You damned blind," Victoria snapped.

"Maybe they were sent along the California Trail. Told to
get out. If that's true, they're probably all right. Enoch's a
hardened trail captain by now, and Sterling can do it. They've
some pine nuts and rested livestock. They could be miles
west of St. George now."

Victoria glared at him as if he were the dumbest man
alive.

And it was true that nothing made sense.

"Back to the meadow and wait, I suppose," Skye said.

It made more sense than chasing around southern Utah
at night. If the consumptives were released by the militia,
they would either return or send word of their whereabouts
to Skye's family on the flat.

Wordlessly, they rode their weary mounts up the Virgin
River once again, through a deep dark that made travel hard.
Each of them was immersed in the mystery. Utah is a big
place; the New Bedford Infirmary Company could be hidden
anywhere, in many hundreds of square miles of mountain,
desert, and canyon.

They reached the silent meadow in the small hours. An

open heaven lit the way. They paused where the canvas shelters had been erected, and absorbed the quietness.

An owl hooted softly. Another, from some great distance, responded.

"I'm not staying here!" Victoria snapped.

Skye knew what the owls meant to her. And to Mary also.

"There are bad spirits here," he said to Mickey.

"I'll drink to that."

"We'll go up the creek a way."

"Them's owls, but what's 'owling?"

Mickey was bravely making fun of the women. But Victoria sank deep into her saddle and steered her mare up the nameless creek, wanting no part of a place with bad spirits.

They paused at the high end of the meadow, where the red canyon walls bolted upward to the stars, and there the silence was not broken by owls.

Wordlessly, Victoria dropped to the grass, knelt beside the purling creek, and washed her face carefully. No one said anything. Skye unsaddled and picketed the horses. Then they rolled into their blankets on the hard ground. Skye didn't sleep, and he knew none of the others were sleeping either. They were all waiting, waiting, waiting for something to happen.

But all that happened was a pale creamy coloration of the sky as dawn approached all too soon. None of them slept, and not because they were worried about the Paiutes. They did not sleep because of things unfathomed, things so deep and dark that they kept sleep at bay.

Victoria arose angry, and stalked about, glaring at this beautiful canyon head as if it were hell. Mary quietly looked after North Star, and would not look Skye in the eye. This was a delightful place. The sun threw golden light on the red bluffs high above, making the whole world peach-colored. The horses grazed bunch grass peacefully.

But there was no sign of the missing company.

The women prepared two travois ponies and headed up the creek, and Skye knew they were retrieving the lodge and family possessions.

Skye and Mickey the Pick drifted across the meadow to the Virgin River. There was no sign of Indians; only the trace of iron tires rolling downstream, and the prints of a lot of shod horses. There was no sign of traffic going upstream, into the maze of red canyons where the Virgin rose. The grass around the campsite was crushed. The Saint militia had been a large force, more than needed to collect a few hapless sick people and carry them to safety.

The women returned with the lodge and gear, and silently erected the lodge exactly in the place where the hospital camp had once risen. Then they took two ponies and hiked up the creek and vanished in the canyon country. Skye knew they would return with piñon pinecones, food that would sustain them all for as long as they chose to wait for the New Bedford Infirmary Company to return. Skye knew he must hunt, but not just yet.

He waited quietly in the shade of a live oak for the missing to return and tell him where they had been taken, and why.

Mickey dropped down beside Skye.

"How long are we going to stay 'ere?"

"I don't know, Mickey."

"You think they're off to California?"

"I'd like to think it."

"You done guiding them?"

"I don't know."

"You think Enoch Bright, he'd slip a note to us? Send a messenger?"

"Yes, if he could, he would. That's what's troubling me. There was no note left here. No signal. Nothing I'd recognize. The militia didn't let him leave a note behind for us."

"How'd your old lady know it was militia?"

"A lot of armed white men on horses came in the night. Men dressed the way Saints dress, lot of beards, plain clothing. Farmers, getting a living from the earth and the rivers."

"She told you that?"

"Victoria knows white men better than I do."

"Ain't she some smart."

The day stretched slowly, and then the women returned laden with pinecones. There would be roasted pine nuts this evening. It took a while to roast the cones and extract the nuts, and the whole day's gathering scarcely allayed their hunger.

Victoria wouldn't look at Skye or Mickey, but toiled angrily at her task, but Mary's gaze fell upon them both. Mary's gaze was troubled, as if she didn't like the sight of white men and yearned only for her own bronzed neighbors and tribe and friends.

Neither woman said a word.

Skye looked across the meadow toward the Virgin River once again, just as he had a thousand times that slow day, and saw nothing. He watched a hawk circle undisturbed, and knew nothing lurked just beyond his field of vision. Time had slowed. The sun had tracked west, and now the eastern walls of the canyon were lit. This was a paradise inhabited only by owls.

He knew Victoria and Mary would have a bad time this night if the owls returned, but he wanted to stay through the night. Tomorrow they would leave.

When the western walls of the canyon blocked the sun, Skye saddled Jawbone, checked his Sharps, and nodded to Victoria, who averted her gaze. She knew he was hunting. He wanted to go by himself.

"Mickey, keep an eye on the Virgin River," he said. "I'll be back at dusk."

"Put me in a madhouse, that's where I belong," Mickey said.

Jawbone took him up the creek, and then he topped a steep grade and found himself on the cedar-dotted mesa. He paused, out of ancient habit, absorbing the land. He studied the maze of canyons, looking for a telltale column of raptors, and then felt ashamed of himself. Why would he do that? There was only transparent sky and twilight. He dropped into a hidden valley, discovered a green streak through it, and soon spotted deer pellets. A spike mule deer buck bolted. Skye whipped his Sharps up, but the deer vanished. The chance was lost. He sat Jawbone quietly. One running deer often triggered others. But he saw nothing.

He retreated at dusk, knowing he could get lost if he tarried, and made his way back to camp empty-handed. One cross glance from Victoria told him all he needed to know.

He unsaddled Jawbone and turned him loose. The horse sawed his head up and down, bared yellow teeth, bit Skye on the arm, and snapped up bunch grass.

"Avast," Skye growled.

"I'm leaving in the morning," she said. "You stay if you want. Dammit, Skye. This place got bad spirits."

"We'll go," he said.

forty-three

When dawn broke, they quit camp and left. Victoria had stayed up all night, a nocked arrow in her bow. Mickey, it turned out, had taken his bedroll down to the Virgin River, ready to intercept any of the hospital company stumbling along in the dark.

Skye marveled at Mickey. The Londoner had quit his farm to join the hospital company, comforting the sick and making himself useful to them as if that were the thing he had always wanted to do. Who could explain it? Mickey showed his colors by scouting every hill and gully for miles around, looking for the missing infirmary company. He was taking it harder than anyone else, perhaps because he suspected that something terrible had happened.

Skye wondered about that too, but couldn't imagine any fate worse than a sudden expulsion of the invalids from the Saints' Zion. The New Bedford Infirmary Company was now perhaps forty miles west and heading for the California desert, having been ejected from Zion. But here were Victoria, grim and flinty and angry and filled with foreboding, and Mickey, prowling every direction in search of the lost.

But not a word was spoken that dawn; whatever subterranean currents of feeling Victoria and Mickey were feeling remained deeply buried in the quiet of the morning. They loaded the lodgepoles and the lodge cover, saddled the ponies, studied the forlorn, lovely canyon one last time, and headed downstream on the Virgin River.

How do you search for people who have vanished at the hands of a local militia? Skye knew only one way, which was to make inquiries. He would inquire of everyone, everywhere, until he found the lost and could help them settle.

For much of that quiet morning, no one spoke. Victoria rode grimly, keeping a sharp eye on the travois ponies, and kept entirely to herself. Mickey, who was swiftly becoming an accomplished horseman riding that Morgan horse, rode alone, often probing side canyons. Mary, the most serene of them, tended North Star and made not the slightest comment. Skye pushed ahead at times, wanting to know what lay around the next curve of the trail. It was as if the loss of the sick had stopped all their communion with one another.

Late in the morning they reached the great valley that formed the artery of Utah. And here they encountered traffic at once, bearded men hurrying past, their gazes dour and dismissive. No one cared about a few Indians or someone in buckskins.

Even as they stood, resting, beside the trail leading north to Cedar City, or south to St. George, four riders raced by, most of them holding their horses to a steady jog. They did not even nod in Skye's direction, and kept their gazes glued to the trail ahead. It seemed odd.

Skye watched a southbound rider draw nigh and waylaid him, stepping Jawbone out on the trail.

"Hello, friend," Skye said.

A young man of wild eye drew up impatiently. The man's horse was lathered and weary. The man surveyed Skye and nodded curtly.

"We're looking for news," Skye said. "Something about a scare? Are the Paiutes causing trouble?"

"Sir, I don't know a thing," the man said. "I must pass."

"Well, which way is safest?" Skye asked.

"There is no trouble. None at all," the man said, touching heels to the flank of the gaunt old plug he was riding. He began to work around Skye.

"We've heard otherwise," Skye said.

"Sorry," the man replied, and hastened away.

He was plainly agitated.

"I told you so," said Victoria, somewhat mysteriously.

Skye turned to her. "Told me what?"

"He was a man with bad memories."

"Such as?"

Victoria shrugged. "Let's get the hell out of here."

"Who was that?" Mickey asked.

"Some Saint in a big hurry," Skye said.

A farm wagon was working its way north, drawn by a pair of mules. Skye dismounted and waited. The driver seemed in no hurry. Like most male Saints, he wore a trimmed beard. His wagon groaned under a load of green melons and yellow squash. And contrary to the others, he reined in the mules.

"Nice morning," the man said.

"It is. You must be taking these to market."

"Cedar City, yes. It's the only place I can sell these."

"We're looking for some people. There was an Indian scare and our people were rounded up and taken to safety."

"Indian scare?" The man peered from watery eyes at Victoria and Mary. "None around here. West, some, they was actin' a little frisky."

"I'm Mister Skye, sir. We're looking for a company of invalids."

"Oh, I heard tell of them. Lungers. They got the devil in 'em. Bible itself says them that's sick is full of sin. I reckon they'll get freed up of sin, or not."

"Have you heard where they were taken?"

The seamed old man chewed a straw, and finally gazed steadily into Skye's face. "If I knew, I wouldn't say. But I don't. Reckon they'll get what's coming to them if they're sinners. That's how the Good Lord works. Me, I've never been sick a day in my life, excepting some piles. It's rectitude. And if I didn't eat a mite fast, I'd not have piles, either. You've got to chew your food slow, just as God intended. But I never quite mastered it. I got the sin of fast eating."

"Where would your militia take our people?"

"Now you've fetched me one I can't answer. I reckon I'd better get along to Cedar City."

"Would you trade those squash for anything?"

"The prophet says, says he, not a bit of food to Gentiles, long as there's war a-coming."

"I'm a Saint," said Mickey.

"Some Saint you are, trafficking with these," the farmer said.

The man cracked reins over rumps, raising dust. The mules lowered their heads, pushed into the collars, and fell into step.

"Can you help us at all? Even a rumor?" Skye asked.

"Well, they got to be somewhere."

The mules picked up speed, and the creaking wagon rumbled north. Skye watched the wagon until it grew too small to follow and finally vanished. The farmer wasn't armed. And he was traveling alone, not in company. And he seemed utterly oblivious to real or imagined dangers.

A faint pall of yellow dust hung in the air, until it slowly drifted away. There was only the oppressive silence of the desert and the building midday heat.

It came to him that he didn't have the faintest idea what to do next.

"You got any ideas?" he said to Mickey the Pick.

"There's not going to be some 'ospital, it looks like."

Skye turned to Victoria.

"We got a few pine nuts, that's all," she said.

He offered Mary a chance.

"Go home," she said.

It was a good idea. "We're done. We delivered the company to the Virgin River. We fed them while they got set up. Sterling's joined these people here, so he can bargain. I'd have liked to say good-bye, but there's no one to say it to." He gazed at them. "Have we left anything undone?"

No one said a word.

It felt odd, not knowing the fate of the company, or saying good-bye, or making sure the contract was completed. But there was only the empty valley, the glaring sun, and the silence.

He started Jawbone north along the well-worn road to Cedar City, and the rest fell in behind him. They struck Ash Creek and followed alongside it, glad to have water and grass for a while. But nothing felt right. This was unfinished business.

He wanted a conclusion. He wanted a handshake, a sense that all would be well. But he found none of that this time.

They reached Cedar City at dusk, worn-out and starving. They had nothing. The last of the pine nuts were gone. There was no pemmican or jerked meat. The stores were shuttered. The clay streets were empty. It was as if the town was asleep, though in fact it was not late. Skye had the distinct feeling that something was terribly wrong, but it was entirely intuitive. Still, it was odd that not one soul was visible on the streets, or sitting on a front porch enjoying an evening, or stirring within a house.

They drifted on through, awakening no curiosity, and finally reached the north end of town. Now it was dark. In minutes it would be utterly black.

"You blokes go up there a mile, maybe, and wait for me," Mickey said.

"What are you up to?"

"No blawdy questions."

Skye thought he knew. Maybe it would be best not to ask. He and his weary family trudged a way up the road, found a likely spot beside a creek that watered the little brick-making town, and let the horses graze on picket lines.

One of the ponies would do for a few days, he thought. He would slit its throat and butcher it. He'd had horsemeat plenty of times. Mule meat, burro meat, donkey meat, draft horse meat, foal meat, cow meat. These ponies had been used hard and wouldn't butcher well, and their meat would be stringy. But meat was meat.

Victoria, reading his mind as usual, pointed to the smaller one. "He's no good anymore," she said.

Skye studied the pony, grazing peacefully under the starry heavens.

"Ah, there you are," said the cutpurse. "Ye can't 'ide from me."

He deposited a burlap sack of something or other before them.

"They got good gardens in that town," he said. "Old Mickey remembered that it's harvesttime."

forty-four

At Nephi, halfway to Great Salt Lake, Skye tried for food. It was a bustling little town, with a whitewashed board and batten mercantile, so Skye headed for it. Here at least the Saints were busy with their daily lives, the streets were crowded, and shutters were open.

He found the bald proprietor behind a rough wooden counter.

"I'm looking for food. I have a pony to trade," he said.

The man eyed him up and down. "You're not a Saint, I take it. No, we're forbidden to sell food to Gentiles."

"My family's hungry."

The man shrugged, a frown on his forehead.

"We're not at war with you. We're going home."

"Home to Missouri or Illinois?"

"Home to my Crow wife's people."

"I'm not familiar with that tribe."

"Look, the pony's well broke, has a good mouth, hauls a travois, can be used as a saddle horse or plow horse or a dray."

"You're not a Yank."

"Londoner."

"It's a pity. I'd trade if you were a Saint."

"We're hungry. You'll get a valuable horse out of it."

The skinny merchant wiped hands on his white apron, peered out into the sunny street. "Which?" he asked.

"The one hauling the lodgepoles. You get the poles too, and the travois."

"I wouldn't really be selling food to you, would I? I'd be trading a little grain and other goods for valuable meat, right? The Church wants plenty of food on hand for the war, and horse meat is better than a barrel of flour, right?"

Skye waited.

"Ten dollars of provisions against the pony?" the merchant asked.

"That pony's worth more."

The storekeeper wiped his hands primly. "Take it or not."

Skye stared at the man, who somehow smiled and frowned simultaneously. "What does ten dollars buy?"

The man shrugged. "Prices are posted."

Skye did it, mostly because he was sick of surviving on what Mickey lifted from gardens and root cellars and chicken coops. Silently he undid the travois, freed the harness, and turned the pony over to the merchant, and then he bought flour, beans, a little tea, some barley, and some raisins. It wasn't much. The merchant was enjoying himself; Skye was raging, but this was not friendly turf and a man could get into trouble fast.

They escaped Nephi minus one travois and pony, but now they had enough to feed themselves for a few days. And they still had the valuable lodge cover riding the other travois.

There was no more trouble. They reached Great Salt Lake

City in a few days. Skye knew what he was going to do, and started hunting for anyone connected with the territorial government. Here was a blooming, busy city, with a great adobe tabernacle, a walled square, the Lion House, the Beehive House, the Council House, some of the buildings looking like transplants from the east.

But not Brigham Young. Skye sensed he would get nowhere with the prophet, if he could even gain an audience. A federal judge if possible. Some inquiries brought him to the white clapboard home of Judge Serene Peace Thorndike, an appointee of President Buchanan.

Hat in hand, he knocked, while his family and Mickey waited in the dirt street, just beyond a picket fence. A woman opened.

"Judge Thorndike please, madam. I am Barnaby Skye."

"If it's government business, he can't help. The territory's not in federal hands."

"All the more reason," Skye said.

A few moments later the judge beckoned Skye into a parlor to the left, and Skye settled gingerly on a horsehair settee with doilies on the arms. A lamp with twin chimneys occupied a cherry side table. Thorndike wore a gray cutaway coat, a certain formality about him even in his own home. He studied Skye, noting the trail-blackened buckskins and the bear-claw necklace that hung, as always, from Skye's neck. Their gazes met.

"You have business? I take it you're not a Saint?"

"No, sir; it's about missing people."

Thorndike grunted. "I should forewarn you, Mister Skye, I have no power. I'm deposed. The Saints have taken over. I have no bailiff, no clerk, no marshal or constable. I might be a federal official, but you could call this house arrest."

Swiftly Skye told his story: employment by Hiram Peacock, taking consumptives to the desert, Peacock's death from the brutal fist of a trail guide named Manville, Enoch Bright taking over, reaching the place on the Virgin River they had sought, only to have his company vanish in the hands of a local militia who said they were protecting the group from Paiute Indians.

Thorndike listened intently, his brown eyes studying Skye.

"Who are the missing?" he asked.

"Enoch Bright, sir, a mechanic. He made the wheels turn. He encouraged and comforted the sick, and taught them to dream of a better day to come. They would not have made it without him.

"And Anna Bennett, slim, eighteen, fevered and yet strong and willful, determined to get well. Lloyd Jones, a lunger like the others but sturdy Welsh stock, who teamstered all the way. Lloyd has a brother, David, just as sturdy as himself.

"And Eliza and Mary Bridge, lovely sisters, seventeen and nineteen, both of them afflicted and fevered, yet they carried on, dreaming of a place where they could breathe once again. And twins, Grant and Ashley Tucker, twelve, terribly ill, but determined. And Peter Sturgeon, the sickest, the one who had to be carried all the way . . . Sterling Peacock, Hiram's boy, actually the heir, the one who owns the wagons and equipment and stock, sometimes fevered, sometimes strong, rallying and losing ground. He's a man with his father's gifts, sir. I should add that the Peacock family lost others along the way, Samantha and Raphael. That's a terrible sickness, sir. Hiram Peacock tried to get them all out to the desert, and bad luck dogged him all the way."

Thorndike stared out the window a moment. "This town's

buzzing with certain rumors that I will not divulge. Nothing has been proven and until there is evidence I will say nothing."

Skye sensed there was a lot happening in Utah Territory that he might never know.

Thorndike finally stared directly at his visitor. "Frankly, Mister Skye, the chances are very slim."

"Chances?"

"That they live."

"The Paiutes, then?"

Thorndike shook his head, sadly. "Now, sir, are you aware that there is a territorial warrant for your arrest?"

"Warrant, for what?"

"Theft. It says you stole a Sharps rifle from a guide named Jimbo Trimble. The complaint is signed by another guide named Manville and a Saint named Rockwell, from Fort Bridger."

Skye felt a certain horror, then rage. He stood. "Then be damned," he said. "Manville's the man who murdered Hiram Peacock, and now he's guiding a wagon train to California. Trimble shot at my company, killed a prize horse, and lost the Sharps in a scuffle. I found it."

"Whoa, Mister Skye. I haven't so much as a constable at hand, and I probably would dismiss the warrant as groundless anyway if I had a court, but I don't happen to be a sitting judge, courtesy of this little war."

Skye was poised to bolt. He had no intention of getting trapped by such accusations.

"Sit." A single wave of the judge's finger sufficed.

"Manville is simply a scoundrel. I have not administered the courts of this territory with deaf ears. And Rockwell's fired by fanaticism. A fanatic, sir, is a man who will ride roughshod over every ethic, social restraint, or law, to further his cause. This territory's full of fanatics, and to such a degree that I fear for my life and stay armed."

Slowly he drew his cutaway coat open, to reveal a small revolver at his side.

"Your course of action should be plain. Do not go back the way you came. There are twenty-five hundred of the Utah militia near Fort Bridger, waiting to take on the federal column when it comes. And some Paiutes too. You would not last ten minutes. There are other ways to escape this territory. North, for one. It is not patrolled, but you would wish to be careful even so."

Skye nodded. "To the Bear River and into the mountains. I've been that way."

"Go that way."

"We have almost no food and no way to get it."

"I can't help you. But there's game up there."

"You know the country, sir."

"Mister Skye, I wasn't going to tell you rumors, but I have changed my mind. The rumors are that a large party of California-bound immigrants, called the Fancher Train, was besieged by Paiutes at a place called Mountain Meadows, near Cedar City. These Indians had been incited to attack the train by Saints. It is further rumored that the Saints offered to intercede, take the immigrants to safety." His manner grew stern. "Then when the immigrants were freed from the grasp of the Paiutes and had surrendered their arms as a token of good faith, the Saint militiamen themselves slaughtered them, save for little children. A hundred twenty men, women, and children. It seems there were a few Missouri and Illinois people among them, though most were from Arkansas."

The federal judge spoke dryly, not the slightest emotion crowding his narration.

"Of course it's all rumor," he said. "We are wanting the facts. But there are a few loyal men here, even among the Saints, who have kept me apprised. It'll be something to report to the president when I can."

Skye felt dizzy. "What militia?"

"The county militia there. The one based in Cedar City. The Saints have militia in every community. These were the ones who, I suppose, took away your people from their camp for their safety."

It was too much to endure. Skye turned his head away so Judge Thorndike could not see his face.

forty-five

*I*n the clay street, Skye told his family and Mickey what he had learned. They listened somberly.

"They are dead," Victoria said.

"It is only rumor," Skye said.

"I knew it long ago."

Skye had learned not to dispute her ways of knowing things. He nodded.

The September sun lit the broad street in this gracious city, erected out of the wilderness by a persecuted people. He tried not to grieve. They might yet live. And yet, oddly, he had already grieved. They were gone and he would not see them again. Their dreams had come to an end on a healing field, surrounded by red rock, beside a babbling creek.

He lifted his old top hat and held it in his hand, feeling the wind riffle his hair. It was loss, not grief, that he felt. He wished that Enoch Bright might be standing beside him, his mechanic's mind repairing wagons, people, animals, and dreams. He wished Hiram Peacock might be here, his dream of healing a dozen sick young people flourishing in his bosom. He had brought them on an epic journey across a continent, looking simply for a climate that would drive the disease out of their young bodies. He had put his last penny into it, gambled that he could do it, and now there was nothing left. No Peacock survived. The family was gone.

He thought of Anna Bennett, willful, devoted to the rights of women. Mary Bridge and Lloyd Jones, whose blossoming romance Skye had been slow to discover, perhaps because their healing came first and they were afraid there would be no future for them without the blessings of dry air, sun, and rest. He thought of Peter Sturgeon, so sick he was carried the whole distance, coughing, his eyes bright with pain and fear, and yet clinging to life because his elders told him he would have a chance in this new Zion where the sick might be healed.

He thought of the Tucker twins, Grant and Ashley, and how pretty the fevered Ashley looked. He thought of Eliza Bridge, her lungs hurting, struggling west, hoping to heal, see the sun rise one more day, and one more day after that, so that someday she might enjoy a family of her own.

And Sterling Peacock, sole heir of all this after Hiram had been buried, struggling to fill his father's boots even while he wheezed his way west, the sinister disease eating away his lungs and his spirits.

He thought of them all, and at last let them be dead in his mind. They were gone.

He saw Victoria stiff before him, her body unnaturally rigid, and he reached for her and drew her to him, and comforted her, or was it that she was comforting him? He held her, and then saw Mary, still sitting her pony, the infant slung in her shawl, and he reached upward and drew her hands to his face, and kissed them, and felt her fingers in the strands of his beard.

It seemed to be a chapter of his life without an ending and yet it had indeed ended. He had been hired to deliver this company of the ill to their own Zion and he had lost every single one of them. He had lost the man who had hired him, entrusted the safety of this company to him. He had lost this man's children, his neighbors, his trusted yeoman. All were gone. Never in his life had he, as a guide, lost a whole company, every soul entrusted to his care. Had he failed? Had there been some way he might have spared them? He knew he would be worrying that in his head the rest of his days. He thought he would never again guide another party.

Gradually, the present returned to him, and he was standing again on a clay street in Great Salt Lake City, on a mild late September day, in bright sunlight. He found Mickey gazing patiently at him.

"We're going to Victoria's people, and you are welcome to come with us, Mickey."

"Naw, it's no place for two East Enders, mate. One Londoner's enough for any tribe, eh? I'll stay here."

"What'll you do?"

"What I've always done. Why did they call me Lord Cutpurse, eh? I blawdy well know how to make a living."

The little fellow smiled brightly. "Don't you worry about old Mick, eh? Let me tell you something. This 'ere profession of mine, it's right 'onorable, and it beats butchering innocent people, eh? I'll tell you something. These 'ere people, they need a cutpurse or two around, they need a crime wave to teach 'em a thing or two. Maybe if they're busy with a crime wave, they'll quit picking on strangers."

Mickey thrust a nimble hand in Skye's direction, and Skye shook it heartily.

"This 'ere's been a hard time. I like you, Skye. I surely do.

Go now, get out of this 'ere place before they decide to turn you into missing people, eh?"

Mickey grinned crookedly and walked swiftly away. Skye watched him amble down the street and turn a corner, and then he, too, was gone. There was only Skye's family there beside him, Jawbone, two riding ponies, and one hauling a travois.

Skye thought Mickey's last advice was sound. This was a war capital. Yet everywhere, in the temple square, in the architecture, in the decorum of its people, this city spoke of passionate faith.

It was time to leave. Skye climbed aboard Jawbone and his small family worked north, hemmed by the mountains to the east and the great salty lake to the west. No one stopped them. This road would take them to the Bear River and into the towering mountains beyond, and with luck they would make their way across them before the snows closed them.

This way would avoid the militia gathered near Bridger's Fort to resist the federal column. They made good time, and found abundant ducks and geese in the marshes and bays of the great lake, which Victoria gathered with her arrows. There would be food enough; more food than they had eaten or collected during their entire journey in Utah Territory. That evening Victoria and Mary industriously plucked the fowl, disemboweled them, and roasted them. Skye ate heartily. He ate as if he had never eaten before, as if he had been starved for months.

There was constant traffic en route to Ogden, but the Saints kept to themselves, and Skye's family did not interest them. Ogden was a small, bright stair-step town rising into the mountains. The Saints had made a paradise of it, putting its ample water to good use in gardens and lawns. It was a good place, but Skye and his wives hurried past. Someday, sometime, it would welcome strangers.

They rode north, the days hurrying by, but they didn't escape settlement. The industrious Saints had built homes and farms and ranches in country that only a few years earlier had been wilderness. It made Skye uneasy. He turned away from the great basin and headed toward Bear Lake, in a mountain valley to the east, a place all trappers knew and loved. It had seen many a frolic during the beaver days. But here too settlement had pushed in, so that Skye wondered whether this amazing growth would soon overwhelm the Rocky Mountains forever.

Every time they rounded a bend and found some new ranch or farm, Victoria muttered to herself. This, plainly, was uprooting her whole life, her very nature. They finally reached Bear Lake, and found the Saints busy there, turning it into an agricultural valley. Was there no end to it? Who were these people, who turned thousands of square miles of wilderness into settled country in the space of one decade?

But a few days later they ran out of Saints, and headed toward Davy Jackson's Hole on the Snake River. Now, at last, they slid into the eternal wilds. Snow laced the Tetons, but the valley was still verdant. Bear and wolves and elk roamed the bottoms. Skye had no trouble making meat.

His women cut lodgepoles and put up the lodge on a sunny meadow beside the river. This would be a good place for a while, and later they could follow a water-level route taken by the Astorians long before, and find themselves in Crow and Eastern Shoshone country on the other side of the mountains.

It had been a trip steeped in silence. They hadn't talked

about the missing, but their thoughts never strayed from those consumptives seeking their own Zion. Indian summer bloomed there, in the valley, while the aspen on the slopes turned to gold and the Snake River sparkled by.

The women scraped elk hides, made fresh moccasins, and looked after the ponies. They jerked elk meat, made pemmican, gathered nuts, and sewed new skirts for themselves. Jawbone guarded the camp, chased coyotes, and fattened on the dried grasses. Skye at last did nothing. It was enough to let the wind sing through his hair, let the October sun warm his neck and shoulders, let the deer drift by unmolested, and turn his back to the settled world to the south. Some would call it civilized. He did not.

But the thing he loved most was to see his infant son lying peacefully on a thick, brown buffalo robe before the lodge, on a sunny afternoon, sometimes sleeping, sometimes writhing, making his little muscles work. Sometimes the infant stared at Skye, recognizing him. Other times the child seemed lost in his own small world. Mary smiled at the sight of Skye and their son, stretched out side by side on the warm brown hair of the robe, getting to know each other. The boy was one year old this day, if the women had reckoned it right.

In this boy was Skye's own blood, the part of himself that he would pass along to the future. Here was a son: North Star or Dirk.

Skye counted himself lucky. Lines ceased. The Peacock family had vanished forever from the face of the earth, leaving no trace behind except Hiram Peacock's great dream and courage.

But here was a son who would grow up in a risky and changing world, one that would be unrecognizable to Skye. The boy would probably live in towns as yet not founded, or in imperial cities. He would live in comfort unknown to Skye, whose adult life had spun out in places like this.

This boy, too, might die young, might even die of consumption, or any of the white men's diseases that were decimating his mother's people. But Skye was glad the child had come into the world.

Mary, sitting beside him, lifted the boy and lowered him onto Skye's chest, where Skye's great brown hand held him in place. And she smiled.